Ashes of the Elements

He was dressed in the rough clothing of a peasant. The hose were coarse and ill-fitting, and the tunic had been patched and darned. Neatly; someone had taken care with those tiny stitches. He must have had a wife, Helewise thought, or maybe a loving mother. Some poor woman will be grieving, when she hears of this. If she was his wife, it will mean the loss of husband and bread-winner. A bad day for her, whoever she was.

As the initial shock receded, it occurred to Helewise to wonder what the man had been doing on the fringes of the forest. And had he been lying there long? Had she and her nuns been going about their business for some days, while, all the time, this poor wretch lay dead not half a mile from the Abbey?

Also by Alys Clare

Fortune Like the Moon

Ashes of the Elements

Alys Clare

NEW ENGLISH LIBRARY
Hodder & Stoughton

First published in Great Britain in 2000
by Hodder and Stoughton
First published in paperback in 2000
by Hodder and Stoughton
A division of Hodder Headline
A NEL Paperback

10 9 8 7 6 5 4 3 2

A CIP catalogue record for this title is available
from the British Library.

ISBN 0 340 73934 7

Typeset by Avocet Typeset, Brill, Aylesbury, Bucks
Printed and bound in Great Britain by
Clays Ltd, St Ives plc

Hodder and Stoughton
A division of Hodder Headline
338 Euston Road
London NW1 3BH

for Richard and Lindie Hillier,
present-day lord and lady of Acquin

Estuans interius
ira vehementi
in amaritudine
loquor mee menti:
factus de materia,
cinis elementi,
similis sum folio,
de quo ludunt venti.

A violent fury burns inside me as,
With bitterness, I speak to my heart;
Made from the fabric of
The ashes of the elements;
Like a leaf, I am tossed on the wind.

Carmina Burana:
cantiones profanae

Author's translation

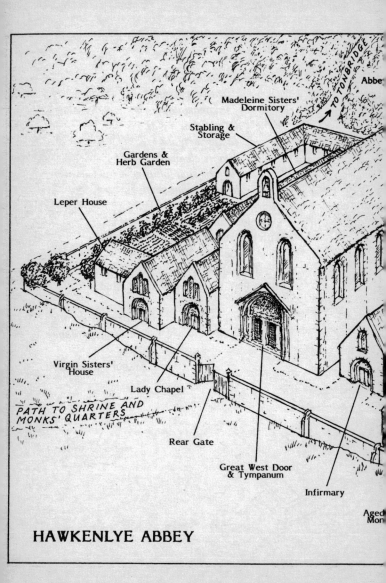

Abbe

TO TONBRIDGE

Madeleine Sisters' Dormitory

Stabling & Storage

Gardens & Herb Garden

Leper House

Virgin Sisters' House

Lady Chapel

PATH TO SHRINE AND MONKS' QUARTERS

Rear Gate

Great West Door & Tympanum

Infirmary

Aged Mon

HAWKENLYE ABBEY

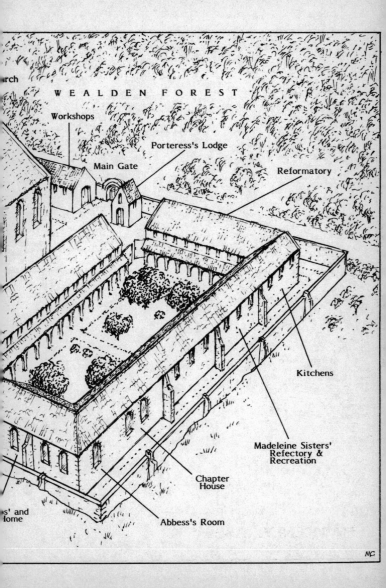

WEALDEN FOREST

rch

Workshops

Porteress's Lodge

Main Gate

Reformatory

Kitchens

Madeleine Sisters'
Refectory &
Recreation

Chapter
House

Abbess's Room

s' and
lome

NC

Into the profound silence of the forest at midnight came a sound that should not have been there.

The man raised his head. Still panting from his recent exertions, he tried to quieten his rasping breath, the better to hear.

He waited.

Nothing.

Spitting on his hands and preparing to go back to work, he tried to summon a wry smile. It must have been his imagination. Or perhaps some night creature, innocently abroad. And his own nerves, plus the great forest's reputation, had done the rest.

Shaking his head at his own foolishness, he renewed his efforts. The sack was already getting nice and heavy; a little bit longer and he would—

The sound came again.

And this time it went on.

He stood up, the sweat of toil on his forehead and his back suddenly icy cold, his damp skin breaking out in goosepimples. In a flash of intuition, he thought, I should not be here. As if some dark and ancient memory were stirring, he realised, with sick dread, that the midnight forest was a forbidden place. For very good reason did people fear to venture into it . . .

Ruthlessly he stopped that terrifying train of thought before it could undermine him. Carefully putting aside the axe with which he had been hacking at the fallen oak's thick roots and lower trunk, he clambered out of the hollow he had dug under the majestic old tree. Then, using the thick ground cover of early summer to conceal himself, he gathered his courage and began to creep towards the source of the sound.

Because, if this were someone having him on, enjoying themselves at his expense, then he was going to make sure they knew he wasn't amused. If it were Seth and Ewen, God damn their eyes, sneaking out and spying on him – on him! the

brains behind the whole thing! – then he'd get
even. He'd . . .

But the sound was louder now, increasing in
insistence so that the man could no longer block
it out. Could no longer try to tell himself that it
was Seth and Ewen, playing tricks.

Seth and Ewen couldn't make that sound. It
was doubtful, really, that any human could.

The man ceased his furtive crawling. Ceased all
movement and all thought, as the strange, eerie
humming seemed to sweep over him and absorb
him into itself.

He felt himself begin to smile. Ah, but it was a
lovely bit of singing! Well, it was more like chanting, really, like the very sweetest sounds of some
abbey choir, only better. As if it didn't come from
men or women, but from the cold, distant stars
themselves.

Hardly aware of what he was doing, he began to
move forward again. He was no longer creeping
stealthily through the undergrowth; enchanted, he
was obeying a summons he barely recognised.
Straight-backed, head held high, he strode through
the ancient trees and the new green growth
towards the open space that he could see ahead.

And stopped dead in his tracks.

Eyes round, mouth gone dry, he stared at the incredible sight. Lit by the full moon directly above the clearing, so that its bright rays bathed the scene as if intentionally, he watched in total amazement.

He'd never believed those old tales! He'd dismissed them as the ramblings of daft old women. Women like his own mother. And, latterly, his wife, who'd tried to stop him disappearing into the great Wealden Forest, especially by night, nagging on and on at him, over and over again till he'd had to hit her. But, even when he'd done so – broken her nose, that last time – she'd still persisted. Gone on telling him it wasn't safe, wasn't right.

Hah! He'd show her! Her, and the rest! They wouldn't nag at him when they knew what he'd found!

And, anyway, even if there were some element of truth in their old legends, then it wasn't quite the way they said it was. Wasn't he here, now, witnessing with his own eyes the very proof that, for all that they still muttered about those dread things, they'd got it wrong?

4

He'd show them, all right! Just see if he didn't! He'd—

He felt the gaze upon him as if it were a physical assault. His braggart thoughts came to an abrupt end as, screaming through his numbed mind, bursting from his mouth like a wail of agony, came the one word: *'NO!'*

Turning, bounding over brambles and tufts of tough grass, he raced away from the clearing. Running, panting, gasping, stumbling, he heard sounds of pursuit. He sneaked a quick look over his shoulder.

Nothing.

Nothing? But he could *hear* them!

Forcing his legs to work, he raced on. Oh, God, but it – they? – was all around him now, quietly, stealthily, menacingly, surrounding him with such a sense of threat that his sobbing breath came out as a terrified howl.

For still he could see nothing.

Heart hammering, legs and lungs in agony, he spurred himself on. Half a mile, a mile? He could not tell. The trees were thinning now, surely they were! A little further – not much, oh, not much further! – and he'd be in the open. Out on the grassy fringes of this ghastly forest, out in the clean, cool moon light . . .

There was brightness ahead. As he ran on, stumbling in his desperate exhaustion, he could see the calm, sleeping land out there. As he passed the last few giant trees, he could even see the cross on the top of Hawkenlye Abbey's church.

'God help me, God help me, God help me,' he chanted, repeating the words until they lost all meaning. Then, suddenly, he was out in the open, and, after the darkness beneath the thickly growing trees, the moon made the night as bright as day.

Ah, thank God. *Thank God!*

Safe now, and—

But what was that? A whistling noise, close by, speeding closer, closer.

The agonising pain as the spear drilled through the man's body was intense but brief. For the spear's point was sharp, and, thrown with deadly accuracy, it pierced his heart.

He was dead before he hit the ground.

PART ONE

DEATH IN THE GRASS

Chapter One

In the small room which was Abbess Helewise of Hawkenlye's own sanctum, the Abbess leaned forward to refill her visitor's mug.

'May I pour you some more?' she asked. 'It is a good restorative, and I am aware that you—'

She broke off. It was hardly diplomatic, to remind her guest that she needed restoring.

'You are aware that I have a tedious journey ahead of me and that I am far from being in the first flush of youth? Ah, Abbess, how right you are, on both counts!' With a gutsy laugh, the woman held up her cup. 'Yes, pour more for me. It is quite delicious.'

Relieved, the Abbess did as she was bid. 'A concoction of Sister Euphemia's,' she said. 'My infirmarer. She is skilled in the use of herbs. This wine she makes from balm, thyme and honey. It is popular with her patients.'

'I have no doubt.' The older woman glanced at the Abbess. 'Some of whom, I dare say, are not above prolonging their sickness so as to go on receiving of Sister Euphemia's bounty.'

'Probably,' Helewise agreed. 'Although, in truth, our precious holy water remains our most popular medicine.'

'Ah, yes, the holy water.' The visitor sighed. 'I had intended, as you know, to pray this morning at the Blessed Virgin Mother's shrine, down in the vale. But I fear I will not have time.'

Abbess Helewise, reluctant to appear pushy and impertinent, nevertheless knew how her visitor felt about the community at Hawkenlye. In particular, about the miraculous spring that was the reason for the Abbey's existence. It was, after all, at her insistence that there was such a grand Abbey there in the first place. And it was even more due to her that the Abbey was presided over by a woman. 'Could you not spare even half an hour?' Helewise said gently. 'Could the world not wait for you, my lady, just this once, while you do something purely for your own pleasure?'

The Abbess's guest gave her a rueful glance. And, with a short laugh, Queen Eleanor said, 'No, Abbess. The world, I fear, is far too impatient for that.'

There was a brief and, Helewise thought, companionable silence in the little room. Risking a glance at the Queen, she observed that Eleanor had her eyes closed. Leaning back in her great throne-like wooden chair – Helewise's chair, in fact, although Helewise was willingly perched on a wooden stool so as to give her guest the most comfort that the Abbey could offer – the Queen's still-beautiful face was, Helewise thought, a little pale.

Even if she has not the time to visit the shrine, Helewise decided, then we shall at the very least feed her before she departs. Silently rising and moving to the door, she opened it and crooked a finger at the nun standing in attendance outside.

'Yes, Abbess?' Sister Anne asked eagerly. Like all the nuns, she was aware what honour a visit from the King's mother bestowed on the Abbey. Such was the community's love for Eleanor that Sister Anne – also like all of them – would have

11

walked barefoot over hot coals if the Queen had demanded it.

Helewise laid a warning finger across her lips. 'Hush. The Queen is resting,' she whispered. 'Sister, please will you go the refectory and ask Sister Basilia to prepare a light meal? The Queen looks so weary,' she added, half to herself.

'That I will, and gladly!' Sister Anne hissed back. 'Poor lady, it's no surprise, why, all that travelling, and at her age, too! Why, she should be—'

'The food, Sister?' Helewise prompted gently.

'Yes, Abbess, sorry, Abbess.' Sister Anne blushed and hurried away.

Helewise went back inside the little room, quietly closing the door behind her. She did most things quietly, with a serene grace of which she was unaware. Even the large bunch of heavy keys that always hung at her belt were quiet, kept from jingling and rattling together by the Abbess's hand laid on them whenever she moved.

Queen Eleanor opened her eyes and looked at the Abbess as Helewise resumed her seat. 'You are too big for that stool,' she observed.

'I am quite comfortable,' Helewise lied. 'My

lady, I have taken the liberty of ordering food for you. Even if you must rush off after but one night with us, will you at least take a moment to eat before you go on your way?'

Eleanor smiled. 'You are too kind,' she murmured. 'And, yes, indeed I will.' She shifted in her chair, with a quick wince of pain. 'Your sister out there was quite right. I am far too old for all this charging about.'

'I am sorry,' Helewise said quickly. 'She shouldn't have spoken with such disrespect.'

'Disrespect? No, Abbess, I heard only kindness.'

Sensing a mild reproof, Helewise said, 'I meant only that it is not appropriate for us to gossip about how Your Majesty sees fit to conduct her life.'

Even to Helewise, it sounded a pompous and fawning little speech, so she was hardly surprised when Eleanor gave a sudden shout of laughter. With a glance up at the Queen, Helewise grinned briefly and said, 'Sorry.'

'So I should think,' Eleanor murmured. 'My very favourite retreat, so conveniently placed between London and the coast, and its Abbess' –

she met Helewise's eyes – 'also my favourite, incidentally, starts speaking like any other ingratiating subject wishing a boon of me.' Leaning forward suddenly, she said, 'Helewise, please, *never* become like everyone else.'

Not entirely sure what the Queen meant, nevertheless Helewise said, 'No, my lady. Very well.'

There was a timid tap on the door, and, in answer to Helewise's 'Come in,' a novice from the refectory sidled into the room, bearing on one arm a wide pewter dish. 'Her Holiness's meal,' the girl whispered.

'Majesty will do,' Eleanor remarked mildly. 'I am not a pope, merely a queen.' She frowned briefly. 'A queen mother, indeed, now,' she added under her breath.

Helewise had been longing to ask the Queen a hundred questions about that very matter for the past twenty-four hours, but, lacking anything that could possibly be regarded as an opening, had managed to learn little more than the barest details. Now, watching the Queen swiftly demolish the appetising and prettily presented meal – Sister Basilia had put a posy of dog roses on the edge of the dish – Helewise waited until the last piece of bread had wiped up the last drop of gravy. Then she said, 'The marriage will be a success, do you think, my lady?'

Eleanor leaned back in her chair, patting at the corners of her mouth with a linen square. 'A success?' She gave a faint shrug. 'It depends, Abbess Helewise, what you mean by success. If you mean, will the union prove fruitful, then I can only say that I pray day and night that it will do so. If you mean will my dear son and his bride find joy in one another's company, then my answer is that I very much doubt it.'

Helewise said softly, 'Ah.' There was, she reflected, little else she could say.

'It had to be done!' Eleanor exclaimed. 'I knew, as soon as I saw Berengaria, that she was not the ideal bride for him. But what was I to do?' She spread her long hands, palms up, the fingers heavy with rings, towards Helewise. 'Richard has been King of England for almost two years, and, but for four months, he has been out of the country.' Eleanor clenched one of her hands into a fist and, with some vehemence, thumped it down on to the long table which, desk-like, stood in front of Helewise's chair.

'Crusading, always crusading!' she cried. 'First, he alienates his new subjects by that brazen sale of offices, then he dashes off to France to receive his pilgrim's scrip and staff! A brief pause while he supervises the mustering of his enormous fleet, and then off he goes to Outremer!' Eleanor's wide, dark eyes held passionate anger. 'Not a thought, Helewise, for what he has left behind him for others to sort out! Not a care that, even before he left, already there was talk that he did not intend to return! That, far from applying himself to the great duty of reigning over England, he had ambitions to become the next King of Jerusalem!'

'Surely not!' Helewise exclaimed. The rumours were not, in fact, new to her; she had heard them before, many times. Heard worse, too; some said darkly that King Richard's conduct since ascending the throne was so ill-considered that surely he must be unbalanced. That he suffered from some secret sickness which affected him in both body and mind, and which would probably kill him before the Crusade was out. But those rumours, Helewise decided, she certainly wouldn't pass on to Richard's mother.

Certainly not while those remarkable eyes still looked so furious.

'*Why* must he insist on this course!' Eleanor was saying. 'What, really, does it matter to the average Englishman *who* rules over the Holy City?'

'But surely—' Helewise began.

Eleanor's eyes fixed on to hers. 'Helewise, do not try to tell me that you give a jot either way,' she said. 'Whilst it is all very laudable to express the opinion that Our Lord's city must be occupied and governed solely by Christians, I cannot believe that you truly feel that the aim of recapturing it is worth all the effort. The expense of it, Abbess! Not to mention the pain, the losses, the anguish. The deaths.' Her face fell, as if, speaking of such things, she was imagining them happening to her beloved son.

Helewise leaned towards her. 'Your son is a great man, my lady,' she said gently. 'A superbly brave and capable fighter, even if—' She broke off.

'Even if that is all he is?' Eleanor said.

'But what a man!' Helewise, desperate to make up for her gaffe, put all the sincerity she could muster into her voice.

'You see, Helewise,' Eleanor went on, as if she had barely noted the interruption, 'he is a man's man. A fighting man, as you say, a man who belongs in an army. At the head of an army, leading it to victory!'

'Amen,' Helewise intoned.

'Of course, I've been crusading,' Eleanor said dismissively. 'When I was married to that fussy old woman, Louis of France.'

'Indeed,' Helewise murmured. Should she really be hearing this? Was it not virtually treason, to hear one monarch decry another, even if he *were* dead?

'Back in 1147, it was,' Eleanor said, a reminiscent smile on her face. 'I had a wonderful time. Louis didn't want me to go, but what he did or did not want was never of great relevance.' She laughed aloud. 'Do you know, Helewise, a rich young Saracen emir wanted to marry me? I might have accepted, too, had I not had Louis tagging along.' She sighed. 'What was I saying? Ah, yes! The crusading fervour. You see, my dear' – she reached out to tap Helewise quite sharply on the shoulder, as if to make quite sure she was attending – 'the way I see it, there are far more important things that Richard should be doing. Rescuing the Holy Land pales into insignificance when compared to the crucial matter of securing the accession.'

'But King Richard now has a wife,' Helewise said, 'thanks to Your Majesty's efforts.'

'Yes, yes, indeed,' Eleanor acknowledged. 'What a journey it was!' Then, as if one train of thought had led to another, she said, 'Naturally, he couldn't marry Alais of France, no matter how hard King Philip pressed his sister's case. Betrothed they might be, but Richard couldn't go through with it. Even if it did create all that unpleasantness, when Richard and Philip were setting out for Outremer.'

'Indeed,' Helewise said. There was no need for the Queen to upset herself recounting the reason why Richard could not marry Alais; Helewise already knew.

But, 'She was damaged goods, that Alais,' Eleanor said. 'My husband, the late King Henry, seduced her and impregnated her, although the little bastard that resulted had the discretion not to live.' Furious indignation and hurt pride were very apparent in the old face. Oh, my lady,

Helewise thought, do not distress yourself over matters so far in the past!

'Not a fit bride for my son,' Eleanor said, bringing herself under control with an obvious effort. 'Despite the fact that a union between Alais and Richard would, I was told, have been permitted by the Church, nevertheless, for a man to marry his own father's discarded mistress smacks, to me, of incest.'

'I see what you mean,' Helewise said. Diplomatically trying to change the subject, she said, 'But what of Berengaria of Navarre, my lady? Is she as beautiful as they say?'

'Beautiful?' The Queen considered. 'No. She is rather pale and wishy-washy. When I arrived at her father's court in Pamplona and first set eyes on her, I admit I was a little disappointed. But, then, what do looks matter? Besides, there was so little choice – Richard is related to most of the other royal young women of Europe, Berengaria is one of the few who were eligible. Anyway, he did actually express a favourable opinion of her, you know – he saw her at some tournament of King Sancho's that he attended a few years ago, and he wrote her some pretty verses. And, even if she isn't beautiful, she's virtuous and learned.'

There was a small silence. As if both women were thinking the same thing – that virtue and learning were hardly qualities to make a woman appeal to Richard the Lionheart – their eyes met in a brief glance.

Eleanor spoke, too softly for Helewise to be sure of what she said. What it sounded like was, 'I don't care for passive women.'

'Then you took her right across southern Europe to meet her bridegroom,' Helewise said hurriedly into the awkward pause. 'My goodness, what a journey! And you crossed the Alps in the depths of winter, I believe it is said?'

'I did,' Eleanor said, not without a certain pride. 'And I'll give Berengaria her due, not a word of complaint from her, even when the going got really bad. Snow, bitterly cold lodgings, bedding alive with lice, inadequately salted meat, all the dangers of the open road, she took them all with her head held high and her mouth buttoned up. Unlike most of our attendants, I might add, who, to a man, moaned like a group of sickly dowagers.'

'And, when you finally met up with the King's

party in Sicily, it was Lent, and so the marriage could not take place,' Helewise said, recounting what the Queen had already told her.

'I handed Berengaria over into my daughter Joanna's care, and told her to get the girl wedded to Richard at the next stop, which was Cyprus,' Eleanor continued. 'I am reliably informed that they were married in the spring.'

'I wish them luck,' Helewise said.

'So do I,' Eleanor agreed fervently. 'So do I.'

'And now you go back to France, Your Majesty?' It seemed wise, Helewise thought, to turn Eleanor away from contemplation of the apparently slim chances of her son's marriage being a successful one.

'I do. But not until the morrow. This night I stay with my dear friend Petronilla de Severy. Petronilla Durand, I must now call her, for she has a new husband.' The Queen paused. 'A new *young* husband. And, Helewise, I have to admit, although it pains me equally much to do so, that there is as little chance of this being a good marriage as there is of my son's.'

Helewise's surprise and discomfort at receiving the Queen's confidences had disappeared.

Now, she felt honoured. Deeply honoured. Hadn't Eleanor said earlier that Hawkenlye was one of her favourite places? If she felt that way because it was only here in the privacy of the Abbey that she was able to speak of private concerns, then Helewise could do no better than offer a discreet and sympathetic ear. 'You emphasise the youth of your friend's new husband,' she said. 'Is that a factor in the marriage's chances of success?'

'Oh, yes,' Eleanor said. 'Petronilla is a rich woman – her father left her extremely well provided for – but even those of us who love her couldn't call her beautiful. She is tall, thin, with an indifferent complexion and those narrow lips which, when a woman grows old, appear to fold in on themselves. And dear Petronilla *is* old.'

'What is the age difference?' Helewise asked.

'Petronilla is, I think, forty-two. Possibly more. Tobias Durand cannot be much over thirty, and I believe I have heard that he is even younger.'

Involuntarily Helewise said, 'Oh, dear.'

'Oh, dear, indeed,' Eleanor agreed. 'And he is a handsome man, by all accounts, of good height, well-built.'

'But impoverished,' Helewise guessed. There seemed no other reason for such a man to have married a plain woman so much older than himself.

'Again, you guess right.' The Queen sighed. 'I doubt she will keep him. She is probably too old to bear him a son, which alone might have ensured the continuance of his attentions. As it is, once he has access to her wealth . . .' She did not finish the sentence. There was, Helewise thought, no need.

What sorrow can be ushered into people's lives by marriage to the wrong partner, she reflected. And, at the opposite end of the scale, what joy when the choice is good. Briefly she pictured her own late husband. Ivo had been a good-looking man, too, tall and broad in the shoulder like this opportunist Tobias. And what a sense of humour he'd had.

Out of nowhere a memory flashed into her head. She and Ivo, enduring an apparently interminable visit from one of Ivo's distant cousins, had crept out of their own house and, packing up food and drink, gone to spend a few blessedly private hours in a secluded spot by a stream. Ivo had stripped off and waded into the water, and, drying off on the bank, been stung on the left buttock by a bee.

'What is amusing you, Abbess?' The Queen's chilly tones brought her abruptly back to the present.

Recalling what she and Eleanor had been talking about, Helewise hastened to explain her laughter. Fortunately, the image of a dignified knight of the realm lying face down while his wife extracted a bee sting from his bottom appealed to Eleanor's sense of humour, too.

'I recall that you mentioned your marriage at the time I appointed you as Abbess here,' Eleanor said. 'It was clearly a happy union.'

'It was.'

'And you had children, I seem to remember?'

'Yes.'

'Daughters?'

'Sons. Two.'

'Ah.' The Queen fell silent.

The two of them, Queen and Abbess, sat for some time without breaking the silence. Helewise wondered if, as she was, Eleanor also was thinking about her sons.

After some minutes, there was another tap on the door. Getting up to open it, Helewise was greeted by the sight of the porteress. Craning round Helewise to catch a glimpse of Queen Eleanor, Sister Ursel said, 'Abbess, a party has arrived for the Queen. A man who says he's Tobias Durand, and he's come with a retinue to escort Her Majesty to his house.'

'A retinue,' the Queen murmured. 'Does he not realise I already have one? *Two* retinues will only serve to double the dust.'

'Perhaps the lady Petronilla has sent him,' Helewise remarked shrewdly, 'eager to impress Your Majesty with the sight of her handsome young husband in all his finery, at the head of a band of his own men.'

Eleanor glanced at her. 'How right you are,' she observed.

Sister Ursel was watching them from the doorway. 'Go and tell Tobias Durand that we shall join him directly,' the Abbess ordered.

'Yes, Abbess.' With one last look, Sister Ursel hurried away.

Helewise went to stand beside the Queen, trying to be ready to help her up if necessary, but without making it too obvious.

But Eleanor said, without any apparent attempt to conceal her need, 'Give me your arm, Helewise, I've become stiff from sitting too long.'

As they made their slow way out of the room and across the cloister to where Tobias and his party could be seen, mingling with Eleanor's own escort despite their best efforts not to, Eleanor leaned her head close to Helewise's and said softly, 'Thank you, Abbess.'

There was no need to ask, for what? Instead Helewise replied, 'The thanks are mine, my lady.'

'I shall come back,' Eleanor said, 'and, if my arrangements permit, I shall stay with you for rather longer than a day and a night.'

'The Abbey is at your disposal,' Helewise replied. 'Nothing could give us more delight, than to have Your Majesty as our guest.'

'Nothing could give *me* more delight,' Eleanor muttered. 'But it is not yet time for me to do what pleases me.'

As the two of them approached the waiting ladies, men and horses, Helewise was quite sure she felt the Queen give her arm an affectionate squeeze.

Chapter Two

Helewise stood for some time, watching the Queen's party disappear down the road. As Eleanor had predicted, all those mounted men had indeed made an almost intolerable amount of dust. Thinking that a breath of clean air would be pleasant, Helewise delayed her return within the Abbey walls, and set out instead for a brisk walk along the track that led off towards the forest.

The warm air of early June was bringing the wild flowers into bloom, and a soft, sweet perfume seemed to fill the air. Somewhere nearby, a blackbird sang. Ah, it was good to be alive! Straightening her shoulders and swinging her arms, Helewise increased her pace and marched towards the first of the trees. She would not go far into the forest, she decided, because it was always dark in there; even in June, the sun did not seem to penetrate, so that the atmosphere always struck chill. She would just take a brief turn around the perimeter of the woodland, a mile or so, no further, then—

She almost trod on him.

Hastily stepping back, twitching the full skirt of her habit away from the blood pooled on the fresh green grass, she pressed her hand to her mouth to stifle the horrified reaction.

He was dead. He *had* to be. He was lying face down, and the long shaft of a spear protruded from his back; from the angle, it appeared that the point, buried deep in the torso, must have penetrated the heart.

He was dressed in the rough clothing of a peasant. The hose were coarse and ill-fitting, and the tunic had been patched and darned. Neatly; someone had taken care with those tiny stitches. He must have had a wife, Helewise thought, or maybe a loving mother. Some poor woman will be grieving, when she learns of this. If she were his wife, it will mean loss of husband and loss of breadwinner. A bad day for her, whoever she is.

As the initial shock receded, it occurred to

Helewise to wonder what the man had been doing on the fringes of the forest. And had he been lying there long? Had she and her nuns been going about their business for some days, while, all the time, this poor wretch lay dead not half a mile from the Abbey?

She bent down and touched the back of the man's neck; it was, she couldn't help but notice, filthy dirty. There were lice active in his greasy hair; would they not have left the corpse, had the man been dead for any length of time? Surely such little blood-suckers only supped on fresh, uncongealed blood . . . The flesh retained some semblance of warmth, although, Helewise realised, that could be because he was lying at least partly in the sun. Tentatively she picked up one of the man's outflung arms: the limb was getting stiff. The rigor that came to the dead was beginning.

Had he died, then, during the past night?

Helewise stood over the corpse, a frown deepening across her brows. Then, abruptly, she turned away. Hurrying back towards the Abbey, she thought, I must get help. I must send word to the sheriff. This is a matter for him.

Breaking into a trot – not a dignified mode of locomotion for an Abbess, but she didn't notice – she reflected that it was just as well this death – this murder – hadn't come to light during Queen Eleanor's visit. Had it done so, then everyone would have been far too preoccupied for the Queen and the Abbess to have had their calm and private little tête-à-tête.

Hard on that thought came another: that it was scarcely appropriate to be pleased about such a thing when a man lay dead, brutally murdered. Her shame at her own musings adding haste to her progress, Helewise gathered up her skirts and sprinted down the track to the Abbey gates.

Sheriff Harry Pelham of Tonbridge was an odious man.

Helewise, sitting listening to his pronouncements on the murder, had to bite down her irritation. At having to listen to his opinions – grandly stated, as if he alone could be right, as if she, a mere woman, could not possibly have any valid contribution – and at having to tolerate his very presence in her room.

He was a big fellow. Solid, squat, a chest like a

barrel, and short legs which seemed barely up to the job of supporting the rest of him. He was dressed in a well-worn leather overtunic, and, when he performed his frequently repeated mannerism of flinging out his chest, it was as if his intention were to draw attention to the battle scars which criss-crossed the tough leather. As if he were saying, look! See what perils my duties take me into! See what cudgel blows and broadsword thrusts I have fended off!

It had apparently been quite a job to make him leave his own sword and knife at the gates. Sister Ursel, so Helewise had been informed, had stood her ground like an aggravated hen with her feathers ruffled out, and told Harry Pelham that, sheriff or not, *nobody* bore arms into God's holy place.

The same observant nun – it was Sister Beata, who, as a nurse, was always observant – also reported to the Abbess that Harry Pelham's sword was stained, and his knife looked as if he'd recently used it to carve his meat.

And it is this careless man, Helewise now thought, listening to his booming voice, who is our sole protector of law and order. Efficient he might be – he *must* be, she corrected herself, for he was appointed by the Clares of Tonbridge, and they surely did not tolerate slackness in their officers – but, oh, what an oaf he is!

'Of course,' Harry was saying, leaning back on the little wooden stool so that its rear legs squeaked a protest, 'of course, Hamm Robinson was a well-known felon. Me, I'm not in the least surprised someone's done him in, no, no, not at all, ha, ha, ha!'

Unable, for the life of her, to see why that was funny, Helewise said in a cool tone, 'Felon, Sheriff? What was the nature of his crime?'

Harry Pelham leaned towards her, as if about to confide a secret. His fleshy nose had semi-circles of little blackheads in the creases where the nostrils met the cheeks, and there were oily-looking creamy flakes in his eyebrows and at his hairline. 'Why, Sister, he was a poacher!'

'A poacher,' she repeated. 'My word, Sheriff, a dangerous man.'

Entirely missing the mild irony, Harry Pelham nodded. 'Aye, Sister, dangerous, desperate, all of that.' He hesitated, and she had the strong conviction he was wondering how far he dare exaggerate the details of what he was about to say. Leaning close again – she wished he wouldn't, he didn't smell any too fresh – he said, 'Come near to apprehending him, I have, on several occasions. Tracked him, see, through those old woods.' He jerked a thumb over his shoulder in the vague direction of the forest. 'Ah, but he was a sly one! Wormed his way through that undergrowth like some wild animal, he did, all silent and swift, like. Reckon he knew the lie of the land like the back of his hand.' Harry Pelham shook his head. 'Never could quite lay my fists on him.'

'Perhaps he heard you coming,' Helewise remarked neutrally.

The sheriff shot her a quick glance. 'Aye, that's as maybe. And it's also maybe my good fortune that I never did catch him, desperate man like him! Why, *maybe* I wouldn't be sitting here now talking to you, Sister, if I had of!'

'Yes,' Helewise murmured, 'he'd have put up a rare fight, of that I'm quite sure.' Deliberately she stared at Harry Pelham's broad shoulders. 'Was he a big man, would you say, Sheriff?' she asked, raising innocent eyes to his. 'I only saw him dead, and it was hard to tell.'

The sheriff went, 'Humph,' and 'Ha!' a few times, then grunted something barely audible.

'What did you say, Sheriff? I didn't quite catch it.'

'I said, he was big enough,' Harry Pelham growled.

'Ah.' Helewise bent her head to hide her smile. Then, straightening her face, she said, 'He was killed by the spear thrust, and, when hit, he was running from the forest. Yes?'

Another grunt. Then, grudgingly, as if he resented her awareness of even such bare facts, 'Yes. That's how it was.'

'And from that, you hazard the guess that he was killed by – what did you call them, Sheriff? The Forest People?'

'Aye. Forest People, Wild People, folks refer to them by both names.'

'And you know for sure that these Wild People were in the forest the night before last?'

'Aye. It's June, see. They come here in June.' He frowned. 'Leastways, they sometimes do. They have done in the past, anyhow.'

'I see.' It seemed, Helewise thought, slim evidence on which to convict this unknown, hitherto unsuspected group of people who, apparently, were wont to camp at certain times of the year, almost on the Abbey's doorstep. 'And – forgive me, Sheriff, if I seem to be questioning your actions, only what with the murder being so close, and—'

'And what with you finding him, Sister,' the sheriff interrupted her. 'Aye, I understand.' A patronising smile stretched the moist lips. 'You go on and ask me,' he said earnestly, 'anything I can tell you, to set your mind at rest so you and the good sisters can lie easy in your beds at night, I will!'

'How kind,' Helewise murmured. 'As I was saying, Sheriff, you've been up into the forest, I take it? You've found evidence that these Wild People have been there recently?'

'Well, I . . .' Again, the frown. More like a scowl, really, Helewise thought, deciding that, frown or scowl, it probably meant that Harry Pelham was about to tell her a lie. Or, at least, try to get away with a fudging of the truth. 'There's not much point in looking for signs of the Wild People, see, Sister. They're cunning and canny, and they don't go about cutting down trees or hacking off branches to make shelters. They're more, like, open-air folk. They live under the trees, under the sky. They've been there forever, they have, carrying on in their strange ways. Old even when the Romans came, some say.' Remembering the point he was making, he repeated, 'No use looking for evidence. None at all. Although, of course, I sent some of my men up there anyway.'

'Of course.' A likely story! 'And they found nothing.' It was a statement, not a question.

Harry Pelham grinned. 'No. Like I said.'

Helewise carefully put her hands together, resting her chin on the tips of her fingers. 'What we have, then, Sheriff, is a dead poacher, whom, despite any evidence, you are quite sure was killed by these Wild People. Who, since you have not managed to locate them, cannot be questioned.' She shot him a direct look, and felt a totally unworthy pleasure in seeing him flinch slightly. 'Therefore you have no proof of their guilt, other than your own conviction.'

Harry Pelham rallied quickly. Giving her his most threatening scowl, he said, 'My conviction's quite enough for me!' As if even he realised the flimsiness of that, he added, 'Anyway, you tell me who else could have done it! Go on, tell me!'

'Not knowing anything of the man or his background, naturally, I can't,' Helewise said mildly. 'But, surely, that is your job, Sheriff? To discover how and where the man lived, if he had any enemies, if anyone would be likely to gain from his death?'

'Ha!' the sheriff cried, punching the air as if to say, got you there! 'I *know* who he was. He was Hamm Robinson, like I said. He has a wife – poor meagre little woman she is, Hamm bullied and beat her within an inch of her life, the good Lord alone knows why she didn't make off in the night – and, as for what he did, he was a poacher.' He pointed a grubby finger at the Abbess. 'Told you that, too.' He exhaled a big sigh, and said, 'If you ask me, the world's well rid of him.'

'Perhaps so!' Helewise cried. 'But he was a man, Sheriff! A living, breathing man, until someone threw a spear at him and killed him. Is he not as entitled to justice as any other man?'

Harry Pelham, she was certain, almost said, 'No.' That, she thought, would have been the truth. Instead, the fleshy, greasy face took on its patronising look once more. 'Like I keep telling you, Sister,' he said, 'I'd do what you want and go and accuse the Wild People if I could. Arrest them, bring them to trial, hang a few, if it was in my power! But how can I if they've gone?' He chuckled. 'Even I can't arrest a man if he's not there, now can I, Sister?'

There was, Helewise thought, little point in pursuing it any more. She couldn't make the sheriff do anything he didn't want to; clearly, he was far beyond being shamed into action by anything she said.

She let the tense silence continue a little longer. Then, rising to her feet, said, 'Very well, Sheriff. But, please, do let me know if your enquiries arrive at any sort of satisfactory conclusion.'

Realising he was being dismissed – which, judging from his expression, he didn't much like – Sheriff Pelham stood up. The Abbess opened the door, and he trudged out.

'You may reclaim your weapons at the gate,' Helewise told him. 'Sister Ursel will have taken good care of them. I wish you good day, Sheriff.'

He muttered something in reply. It could have

been 'Good day', but it could equally well have been something far less polite.

When she was quite certain he had gone, Helewise left her room and crossed the courtyard to the infirmary, where she begged Sister Euphemia to part with some of her precious lavender-scented incense. Despite her efforts to think charitably of the sheriff, still Helewise felt a very strong desire to fumigate her room of his presence.

Later that day, she went back up the track to the forest.

It was, she had discovered, very difficult to leave the matter there. A man had been brutally murdered right by the Abbey, and she had all but stepped on his body. It appeared there was no chance of his killer ever being brought to justice, and Helewise could see no way to alter that.

I must, she thought, striding up towards the trees, have one more try myself. Take one more look. See if I can find some clue that the sheriff and his men overlooked, and, the dear Lord knows, surely *that* wouldn't be hard.

She found the place where the body had lain. There were still bloodstains on the grass. She walked a few paces on into the forest, and thought she could detect trodden-down under-growth where the dead man's running feet had passed. But what of the killer? Had he run in the dead man's tracks? He must have stood still to throw the spear . . . She wandered on under the deep shade of the trees, not really knowing what she was looking for.

Some time later, she gave up the search. It was, she realised, quite hopeless.

She went back to the place where the man had fallen. There was some flattened grass a few paces off; she went to look.

There, amid the brilliant green, lay the spear.

Someone – Sheriff Pelham? – must have wrested it out of the dead man's back and thrown it away. Its head and the first few inches of its shaft were still sticky with blood.

Helewise bent down and picked it up.

Carefully she wiped it on the fresh young grass, feeling, as she did so, an illogical but very strong urge to apologise for this act of desecration.

Then, when it was as clean as she could make it, she had a good look. The tip of the spear was made of flint.

Flint?

Helewise had lived for most of her life close to the South Downs, and she knew all about flint. One of her brothers had amused himself on a wet afternoon by making a flint knife, and had discovered that knapping wasn't as easy as one might think.

But whoever had made this spearhead was a master in the craft. The point was exactly symmetrical, and shaped most beautifully. Like an elegant leaf. The knapped edges were perfect.

And the point was as sharp as any knife.

Helewise – who had learned her lesson over testing the sharpness of worked edges – tried the spearpoint on a patch of dandelions. It seared through the leaves and stems as if they hadn't been there.

A flint spearhead, she mused. Why flint, in this age of fine metalwork? Did it mean that wretched sheriff was right, and this murder *was* the work of some band of primitive forest-dwelling people, who lived not in the present day but in the manner of their distant stone-working ancestors?

The idea sent an atavistic shiver of dread down Helewise's spine. And here I am, she thought, not ten paces from the forest.

She turned and hurried back towards the Abbey.

But, disconcerted or not, still she took the spear with her. Even if this did appear to be the end of the matter, it seemed a good idea not to throw away evidence.

Back in her room, she found that the lavender incense had failed to burn properly, and the air still stank of the sheriff. In addition, the various tensions of the day had produced the beginnings of a headache.

And, to cap it all, it was Friday. Which meant it was carp for supper.

With quiet vehemence, Helewise muttered, 'I *hate* carp.'

Chapter Three

Josse d'Acquin put his strong hands under his small nephew's arms and, glancing back towards the house to make sure his sister-in-law wasn't watching, hoisted the boy up on to the broad back of his horse.

'Gee-up!' cried the boy, his voice shrill with excitement. 'Gee-up, horsey!'

Josse quickly stilled the sharp little heels digging into the horse's flanks; Horace was a good, strong mount, normally even tempered, but you never knew how even the calmest animal might react to such unexpected provocation.

'Hush, Auguste my lad,' Josse said. 'I've told you before, gee-up isn't the thing to say.'

'What *is* the thing to say, Uncle Josse?' piped the boy. 'I keep forgetting.'

'Well, you can go *hup*! if you must,' Josse allowed. 'But horses, as I've explained, respond to your legs, your hands and your voice, so you don't use any of them without thinking about it.'

'And your bum, Uncle Josse! You said you had to use your bum, for sitting down hard with!' The child was squirming with mirth, loving the unaccustomed freedom of being with his lenient uncle. Being allowed to say 'bum' twice and get away with it.

'Indeed I did.' Josse grinned. 'Sit down hard in the saddle, I said, let old Horace here know you're on board.'

'I want to go without you holding on!' Auguste cried. '*Please*, Uncle Josse!'

'Certainly not!' Josse took an even firmer grip on the rein. 'Your dear mother would flay me alive if she knew I'd so much as put you on the horse,' he muttered.

'What's *flay*, Uncle Josse?' Auguste had sharper ears than Josse had realised.

'Oh – er – nothing. Now, Auguste, laddie, once round the courtyard, then—'

'*Josse!*' shrieked a woman's voice. 'Josse, what do you think you're doing! Oh, careful! Be *careful*!'

Running out of the house and across the yard as she spoke, Theophania d'Acquin, wife of Josse's youngest brother, Acelin, looked furious. Mother not only to the six-year-old Auguste, but to his younger sister and his baby brother, Theophania's protective maternal urges were easily aroused. Particularly by Josse, and virtually any contact he had with her children.

'The lad's fine!' Josse protested, trying to control Horace; largely untroubled by having a small boy on his back, even if the child were kicking and yelling, the horse was reacting to the shrieking woman. 'Shut up, Theophania!' Josse shouted, hanging on the reins in an effort to keep Horace's heavy head down. 'Can't you see you're unsettling him?'

'*Well!*' cried Theophania. 'How dare you speak to me like that?'

Josse, preoccupied with supporting Auguste's weight – the child had evidently decided that on the back of Uncle Josse's horse was no place to be, not with *Maman* racing across the courtyard in full battle cry – and, at the same time, holding Horace, muttered under his breath.

Again, he had underestimated a six-year-old's

acuteness of hearing. Just as Theophania, bristling with righteous anger, swept her child from Josse's shoulder, Auguste asked innocently, 'Uncle Josse, what's *salope*?'

There was, quite naturally, music to face.

That evening, when Theophania had gone grumbling upstairs to see to the baby, Josse sat down with his brothers and his other sisters-in-law, aware that the assembled company was not entirely pleased with him.

Hell and damnation, he thought, reaching for more wine, whose house is this? I'm the eldest brother, I can do what I like in my own home!

But that, of course, was the problem. And Josse was fair-minded enough to appreciate it. Acquin, both the large fortified manor house itself and the wide estates, belonged legally to Josse: he was the heir, he had inherited both property and title on the death of his father, Geoffroi d'Acquin, fifteen years ago.

But Josse had always known he was not destined to be a country landowner. He had no skills with the land, nor with animals, other than horses; no interest in organising his tenants and his peasantry into working for the good of all who depended on Acquin. His brothers, Yves, Patrice, Honoré and Acelin, were the ones who loved and understood the land.

Josse, anyway, had left home as soon as he could after coming into his inheritance. He'd been away before, apprenticed as page, as were so many eldest sons, to another knight's household, to learn a very different profession from agriculture. He'd even spent a couple of years living in England with his mother's kin, where his maternal grandfather, Herbert of Lewes, had given him a hearty welcome, apparently having got over the shock of his beloved Ida having left home to marry a Frenchman. When he was old enough, Josse had become a squire. And, in time, won his spurs.

When he was but a youth, he'd ridden with King Richard himself, not that he'd been King then. But he was now.

Through the generosity of the new King Richard, Josse had a manor house in England. Or he would have, when the builders finished. And God alone knew when *that* would be.

In the meantime, while Josse tried to be patient

with delay after delay, he was back living at home. In what was legally his home, but in which, as he was all too well aware, he was now more of a guest.

And, at times like this, not a very welcome one.

He flung himself down on a stout wooden bench, feeling both angry and embarrassed.

'I was doing the lad no harm!' he protested, drinking down a huge mouthful of wine.

'Maybe you weren't,' said his sister-in-law Marie, Yves's wife. 'But that isn't the point. Theophania asked you not to let Auguste ride your horse, and you took no notice.'

'The lad's too mollycoddled!' Josse cried. 'He only gets to ride that tiddly pony of his, which is no challenge whatsoever to a red-blooded lad! And there are too many women here – he needs a bit of masculine company.'

'He has that, in plenty!' Acelin said, clearly affronted. 'He has me, and he has his uncles Yves, Patrice and Honoré. In addition, there are Yves's boys, Luke, Jean-Yves and Robert, and, when he has grown bigger and stronger, soon Honoré's little boy will be a playmate too. Enough male company there, surely, Josse, even for you.'

'That's as maybe.' Josse had the unpleasant feeling that he was not only outnumbered, but also being out-argued. 'All the same, he'd be well used to riding a big horse by now if he'd had the upbringing *I* had, let me tell you!'

'You were still here when *you* were six, galloping about on a pony not much larger than Auguste's, and making a thorough nuisance of yourself,' Yves said pedantically. 'You didn't go off to be Sir Guy's page until you were seven.'

'Yes I did!'

'Didn't!'

'*Did!*'

'Oh, stop it!' Marie shouted. 'Really, Josse, what is it about you, that you make sensible grown men act like small boys again?'

'They're my brothers,' Josse muttered.

'Oh, that explains it.' There was a definite note of sarcasm in Marie's voice. But she did, nevertheless, give Josse a smile; she had always been fond of him.

'Josse should not have called Theophania a— called her what he did,' his brother Honoré said piously. 'It was *very* rude. And *very* inaccurate.'

Acelin, furious all over again at the insult to

his wife, made a choking sound.

'Sorry,' Josse said quickly, before Acelin could get going on a renewed bout of self-righteous indignation. 'It just slipped out.'

'What *did* you call her, Josse?' Marie whispered, while the two youngest brothers were nodding and agreeing about Josse's lack of respect. 'Acelin wouldn't tell me, and Theophania threatened to go into hysterics when I asked her.'

'I'm afraid I called her a bitch,' Josse admitted. 'I'm very ashamed of myself, Marie. I'm thinking of going to market and buying her a pretty fairing – some ribbons, a bolt of fine cloth – to make amends.'

'She'd probably much rather you just left her son alone,' Marie remarked shrewdly. 'Although, me, I tend to agree with you. There's a little too much petticoat government round here, when you're away.'

'You're the senior wife,' Josse said. 'And surely Agnès would support you, even if Pascale didn't.' Agnès was married to Patrice, and Pascale was wife to Honoré; mother of a sickly child, Pascale was usually too preoccupied with caring for him to enter into family arguments.

'Can't you improve things?'

'Hmm.' Marie looked thoughtful. 'Possibly. Only you know what Theophania's like. When she's crossed, she gets one of her sick heads.' She paused to bite off a thread; round and placid with advancing pregnancy – a state that suited her well, Josse reflected – Marie was sewing some small garment made of fine linen. 'And when Theophania has a sick head, we all suffer,' she concluded. 'The whole household.'

'Quite.' No wonder I don't fit in here, Josse thought sadly. My four brothers and this sensible woman, the eldest of my sisters-in-law, all let themselves be led by the nose by the least sound person in the house. All for the sake of a quiet life!

'Where's Theophania now?' he asked presently.

'Feeding the baby,' Marie said.

'But I thought she'd have engaged—' He broke off. It was Theophania's business, after all.

'You thought she would have engaged a wet nurse?' Marie looked at him. 'Ah, no peasant woman's milk is good enough, not for the child of Theophania.'

'Oh,' said Josse.

Marie bent her head over her sewing; tactfully,

Josse did not pursue the matter.

I'll buy Theophania a gift, he resolved, and repeat my apologies. I was unforgivably rude, and to a woman to whom, even if I don't actually like her, I owe respect.

But, when I've been forgiven, I shall go.

Even if the refurbishments to his new manor house were still incomplete, even if the rain came in and he had to sleep in a barn, it would be better than life at Acquin.

For the time being, anyway.

King Richard Plantagenet had given Josse his English manor house in the winter of 1189, in gratitude for a certain service which Josse had been able to do for the King.

Richard, in that cold January season, had been preoccupied with planning his great Crusade; Josse often thought that it was only because Richard's mother, the good Queen Eleanor, had reminded her son of his obligation, that the manor had come Josse's way at all.

The manor had formed part – quite a large part – of the rich estates of the late Alard of Winnowlands. Josse's gift was a stoutly built but dilapidated house, which, so he was informed, had been constructed a good seventy years ago, some distance from the main hall, to accommodate a particularly sour-tempered mother-in-law. The house had a small walled garden, an orchard, and several acres of pasture, some of which gave on to a swift flowing river bordered by willow trees.

It was a splendid gift. Josse was thrilled with his new property, and thought it a more than fair exchange for swearing fealty to the new King; Josse was already a King's man anyway. He had inspected the house with a builder, who came highly recommended by Josse's neighbour, Brice of Rotherbridge. The builder, after sucking his teeth for most of the morning and gloomily shaking his head in the general manner of builders, finally announced that there was a great deal of work to be done, but that, yes, he agreed with Josse that the house was fundamentally sound. And that it would, in the fullness of time, make a fine dwelling.

Back then, almost eighteen months ago, Josse hadn't quite realised just how full that time was going to be.

Over the months that the builder and his men had worked on the house and its outbuildings, Josse had made several visits to check on progress. It had been interesting to note how the character of the house had slowly changed; in the beginning, when there were gaping holes in the roof and spiteful draughts under ill-fitting – or totally missing – doors, the spirit of the miserable and moaning old woman for whom the house had been built seemed still to be hovering around. The very house had an air of dejection, as if it stood with slumped shoulders feeling sorry for itself. The place had been, Josse had to admit, quite depressing.

But, as the repairs and renovations progressed, it appeared to Josse that the house began to stand up tall. To hold its head up with a new pride, to say, as its original beauty was slowly – very slowly – restored, See! See what a fine place I am, fit for the knight who is to live here!

Those were not, however, the sort of thoughts a man mentioned to his builder. And, indeed, when Josse remarked to Brice of Rotherbridge that the house was beginning to welcome its new master when he visited, Brice had shouted with laughter and told Josse not to bring those weird and fanciful foreign ideas over *here*, thank you very much!

As well as taking over a part of the late Alard of Winnowlands's estates, Josse also found himself taking over the man's servant. Will, who had served and, latterly, nursed Sir Alard with quiet and efficient devotion as the old man slowly and painfully succumbed to the lung rot, had presented himself at the new house one morning when Josse was arguing with the builder about whether or not to turn the western tower into a small solar (an argument which, even though Josse wasn't entirely sure what he would do with a solar, he won).

Waiting patiently until the matter was settled, Will then stepped forward, swept off his hood and said, 'Sir Josse d'Acquin? You won't remember me, sir, but—'

'I do remember you, Will.' Josse hurried forward to greet him. 'How are you?'

Will gave a faint shrug. He looked thinner than Josse remembered. 'I do all right.'

Josse doubted that. The man's master was dead, after all. With Sir Alard had gone Will's livelihood. 'I see.'

Without preamble, Will said, 'You'll likely be needing serving folk for this here house, sir. I know the area, I know the people. I'd take care of you, *and* your property, if you'll have me. Watch over your interests, like, when you were from home.'

Josse stared into the deep eyes for some moments. It was not that he did not trust Will; quite the opposite. What held him back from instantly engaging the man was a certain concern about Will's temperament. Josse, in the main a light-hearted, optimistic soul, was not sure he could cope with someone as dour of mien as Will.

'I—' Josse began. Then, after an awkward pause, 'Will, I – er – I mean, are you over your grieving for Sir Alard? I know that his death hit you hard, and—'

To Josse's surprise, Will smiled. The smile broadened, quite altering the severe expression, and Will began to laugh.

'Why not come right out with it, Sir Josse?' Will said. 'A cheerful fellow such as yourself doesn't welcome the idea of having a miserable bugger like me tending to his needs. Isn't that it?'

'No! Not at all! I—' But Josse, too, was laughing. 'Very well. Yes, that's it. Exactly.'

Will's face straightened. 'Sir, I'll tell you straight, I thought a deal of Sir Alard, God rest his soul.'

'Amen,' Josse muttered.

'But he's gone. I did my best for him, and I've nothing on my conscience regarding his death. No nor his life, come to that – we had our ups and downs, did Sir Alard and me, but we understood each other. He knew I was his loyal man. Reckon that's why he left me a tidy bit, when at last he left us what remains on this earth.'

'Ah.'

'But all that's in the past,' Will resumed, 'and life must go on, like. So, Sir Josse, will you take me on?'

'I will,' Josse said, 'right gladly.'

'Hah!' Will looked pleased. 'Oh, and there's my woman, sir, my Ella. Would you have need of her, too? She's a good, clean soul, hard-working, can turn her hand to most work of a domestic nature, whether it's making the butter come quick, turning out a room, milking a cow, sewing a fine seam or cooking a tasty stew.'

Josse grinned, slapping Will on the back. 'Such a paragon of talents shouldn't be allowed to sit idle, don't you agree, Will?'

'No, indeed, sir.'

'We'd better have her, too, then. Your Ella.' He paused. 'But where will you live?' He looked around. 'I don't think there's anything suitable, I'd better—'

'There is, sir,' Will interrupted, looking slightly sheepish. 'I've taken the liberty of having a look, and there's a tidy little cottage tacked on the end of that row there.' He pointed to a barn and several lean-tos, on the far side of the courtyard; Josse, who hadn't had a close inspection, had imagined most of the row would have to be pulled down.

'There's a cottage? In that lot?' he asked incredulously.

'Aye. Run down right now, but it's dry. The timbers are sound, it just needs a bit of work. Me and Ella'll soon put it to rights. Given your permission, sir, naturally.'

Again, Josse started to laugh. In the space of a quarter of an hour, he had found himself a manservant and a first-rate domestic woman, and agreed to their refurbishment of a cottage he hadn't known he had.

All in all, not bad going.

Now, riding towards New Winnowlands – he was quite pleased with the name – on a warm June afternoon, Josse felt for the first time a sense of coming home.

The house stood on its slight rise, walled courtyard in front, walled garden stretching out to the rear. All of those walls looked strong, and the manor itself was soundly roofed, with a whisper of smoke from some cooking fire floating up on the gentle breeze.

It looked, at last, as if the house was almost finished.

Josse rode into the courtyard. As if he had been waiting, Will appeared from the barn, and came to stand at Josse's horse's head.

'Shall I take him for you, sir?' he asked. 'Ella's been baking, she can have food ready for you in a trice.'

'Yes, thanks, Will.' Josse dismounted, handing over Horace's reins. 'Oh, just let me get my pack. I'll have to see to—'

'Ella'll see to your kit. If you'll let her, sir, that is. Fine washerwoman, my Ella, and nimble-fingered with a needle, should any mending be called for.'

'I had an idea she might be,' Josse murmured. Then, out loud: 'Please ask her, then, Will.' He grinned at his manservant. 'I must say, it's quite a novelty, to be so well-received.'

'This is your home, sir!' Will said, clearly surprised. 'Should not a man be welcomed, in his own home?'

My home, thought Josse. Ah, how good it sounded!

He spent a lazy evening, and, replete after an excellent supper, retired early to bed. His chamber had been swept so clean that he could have eaten his food off the floor, and his bed had been made up with bedding that smelt faintly of lavender. The straw-filled mattress lay, he noticed, on a layer of dried tansy leaves; Ella had made sure he wasn't going to be troubled by any small biting creatures.

He slept long and deeply, and awoke from a vivid dream in which he had been waving a hay fork violently above his head, to stop strange, black, winged creatures from alighting on a steep church roof.

Not very surprising, he reflected as he got up, that he should dream of a church. Because, as he'd been drifting off to sleep, he'd been thinking about his friend Abbess Helewise of Hawkenlye, whom he had not seen for almost two years.

And he had decided that, now he was installed as master of New Winnowlands, it was time to pay her a visit.

Ella served him a very substantial breakfast, and, when he had finished, rather shyly brought for his inspection his favourite tunic, whose hem had been coming down where he'd caught a spur in it. Not only had she carefully stitched up the hem, she had also brushed off quite a lot of mud and sponged away a gravy stain.

Rested after his good night, well-fed, dressed in his best, Josse set out in the sunshine for Hawkenlye, feeling in such good spirits that, presently, he began to sing.

Chapter Four

In the few days since the murder of Hamm Robinson, and Sheriff Harry Pelham's dismissal of it, Abbess Helewise had found scant moments in which to dwell on the matter.

Life as Abbess to a community of nigh on a hundred nuns, plus the fifteen monks and the lay brothers who tended the holy spring down in the Vale and cared for the pilgrims who came to visit it, was demanding at the best of times. Helewise's everyday duties, on top of the hours spent each day in the Abbey's round of devotions, meant that there was little, if any, time to spare. So that when, as now, a problem seemed to be looming, it was no easy matter for Helewise to find the occasion to give it due thought.

It was her custom, when there was something

important demanding her attention, to slip into the awe-inspiring Abbey church on her own. And that – having the church to oneself – was not easily achieved, either.

Today, she was in luck; re-entering the church after the noon office, she found there was nobody else there.

She made her way towards the altar, then, moving into the shadow of one of the great pillars, fell to her knees. Praying quietly for some moments, soon she found she was sufficiently calm to put her troubled thoughts in order.

But the words, when they came, were not to do with poor dead Hamm Robinson and the problem of finding out who killed him. Another matter, perhaps less dramatic but, certainly, closer to Helewise's heart, had taken precedence.

'Dear Lord,' she said softly out loud, 'what am I to do about Caliste?'

Caliste, now a member of the Abbey community, had spent the first fourteen years of her life answering to another name. As a tiny infant, no more than a few days old, she had been found on the doorstep of a small and already overcrowded household, in the little hamlet of Hawkenlye. Wrapped in a piece of fine wool which had been dyed the dark purply-black of sloes, the baby was naked but for a beautifully worked wooden pendant, tied around her neck on a slim leather thong. On three sides of the wood – a long, narrow sliver of ash – there were strange, carefully incised marks. If they had a meaning and were not mere random patterning, then nobody in the Hawkenlye community either knew or could guess at what that meaning was.

Whoever had deposited the baby on that particular doorstep had known what he, or she, was doing. For the family who lived within, although equally as poor as their neighbours, equally as ignorant and equally as dirty, were loving people. Matt Hurst and his sons kept pigs, his wife Alison and her daughters tended their hens. Between them, the family also worked their strips of land, more diligently than did many of their neighbours, so that, although there was never an abundance of food on the table, the Hursts rarely went hungry.

The Hursts were God-fearing people. When, one summer's night, a mysterious female infant was left at their door, they accepted that this was a duty put on them by the Almighty. Not only did they take the child in, they cared for her as if she were one of their own. They named her Peg.

If there had ever been any idea in Matt and Alison's minds of keeping Peg's strange provenance from her, then they had to abandon it, because Peg herself seemed to know. Knew, at least, that she was not their child, although, in truth, that would not have taken any particular psychic powers. The Hursts, both the women and the men, were short and dumpy, with reddish or light brown hair, pinkish, freckled skin, and pale eyes fringed with almost colourless lashes. Peg was slim and willowy, with a smooth, cream complexion, dark hair, and eyes like the midsummer sky at dusk.

Peg was, in short, quite exceptionally beautiful.

But, despite her awareness of all that separated her from her adoptive family, she was an obedient and hard-working child, doing what was asked of her without complaint, ever grateful to the kind-hearted people who had taken her in. Throughout her early childhood she fed chickens, mucked out their smelly runs, collected their eggs and went to market to sell what the family would not use. She also learned to cook and clean. But it was only when Alison Hurst began to teach her garden lore that Peg seemed to come alive; from that time on, from the exciting spring when the Hursts discovered that Peg had a green thumb, she was excused all other duties and put solely to cultivation.

But even that was not enough.

When Peg was fourteen, she presented herself at Hawkenlye Abbey and asked to be admitted as a postulant.

Helewise, who made it her policy to try not to turn anyone away, had grave misgivings about Peg. For one thing, the girl was very young. For another, she had seen nothing of life outside the small confines of Hawkenlye: how could the child be sure that convent life was for her?

The Abbess's most important doubt, however, was that she could detect little of a religious vocation in Peg.

She did her best to discover it – sometimes, she had found, a woman kept her love for God very close to her heart, so that it was not readily apparent to an outsider – and she spent many an afternoon walking and talking with Peg. She also visited Alison Hurst, who, when asked a direct question, replied, after considerable thought, 'The lassie's what you might call *spiritual*, and no mistake, Abbess. That I'll swear to right willingly. But as to whether she worships the same Holy Spirit as you and me . . .'

She had left the sentence unfinished.

Helewise, after much thought, had decided that it would do no harm to accept Peg for a trial period, but with the condition that her postulancy should continue for a year instead of the usual six months. She gave as her reason Peg's youth.

But Helewise had accepted postulants of fourteen before, many of whom had grown up to be good nuns. The true reason for her decision regarding Peg was that a full year would give Helewise more time to assess this strange spirituality of the girl's. To decide either that it was truly Christian in inspiration – or Christianity in some other similar guise – or whether it was something else.

That something else Helewise did not define, even to herself.

Thus, right from the start, there was a difference about Peg.

Within a few weeks of being in the convent, Peg's talents in the garden were being put to work. She was apprenticed to the elderly Sister Tiphaine, who grew the herbs which Sister Euphemia used in her tonics, medicines and ointments. Sister Tiphaine took a shine to the girl, and reported favourably on her to the Abbess; but Helewise took Sister Tiphaine's enthusiasm with a pinch of salt, since the old woman herself had always verged on unorthodoxy.

Then, one morning in late autumn, when there was little to occupy her outdoors, Peg knocked on the Abbess's door and asked to be taught to read.

Amazed – for few of the sisters either read or had the least desire to – Helewise demurred. Thought about it for a couple of days, saw no earthly reason to refuse. Finally agreed, and took on the task herself.

Peg was an apt pupil, and was reading simple words within a few months; she would have reached that milestone earlier, had her Abbess had more time to spare for lessons. By the following spring, Peg was begging to be allowed to read the precious manuscripts kept in the Abbey's scriptorium; despite the vehement objections of the young, aesthetic and highly intellectual Sister Bernadine, who had the care of the valuable books, Helewise gave permission.

From then on, Peg could be found most mornings, seated on a bench in a corner of the Chapter House, poring over one of Sister Bernadine's manuscripts, with Sister Bernadine tutting and sighing close by. Peg would, Helewise thought, have read all day, had she been allowed to; but, both for Sister Bernadine's peace of mind and because no nun, especially a postulant, could be permitted such a luxury, Helewise limited Peg's study time to the short period between Sext and the midday meal.

One morning, curiosity overcoming her, Helewise stopped by Peg's bench and looked down over the girl's shoulder to see what she was reading. It was an ancient and, to Helewise, almost incomprehensible manuscript on tree lore.

When Peg's year as a postulant was up, she renewed her request to take her vows and be admitted to the community. Helewise, still dubious, could find no valid reason to refuse; in the midsummer, when Peg was fifteen, the girl took the veil and became the youngest novice that Hawkenlye Abbey had ever had.

When Helewise was preparing her for her first vows, Peg had said, 'Abbess, may I be known by another name?'

Initially surprised, Helewise quickly understood. Or thought she did. 'Yes, Peg. Sister Peg, I do see, is not the most harmonious of epithets, is it?'

Peg smiled. 'No. But it's not that. My foster parents chose according to their own lights, and I have never complained. It's—' She stopped. Then asked, 'Need I give a reason, Abbess?'

Helewise, who reflected that she was usually prepared to accept unquestioningly what every other new nun chose to call herself, saw no justice in making an exception now. 'No, Peg. I suppose not. What name do you wish us to call you?'

Peg said, 'Caliste.'

Sister Caliste had spent the past year as a willing and obedient novice. In much the same way,

Helewise thought, as she had probably spent her early years as a dutiful chicken-tending peasant child. What troubled the Abbess was that, just as the life of a peasant could have utilised only a fraction of Caliste's potential – only a fraction, apparently, of her soul – the same could be said of her life as a novice nun.

There is no complaint I can make against her! Helewise repeatedly told herself. She is always punctual, always diligent, always does her best to please. Never complains – which was more than could be said for many of the sisters – even when the most arduous tasks are laid on those straight young shoulders.

Why, then, did the Abbess feel so uneasy about Caliste?

Helewise rose from her knees, suppressing a groan of pain; she had been praying for an hour, foregoing the midday meal in the hope that offering her hunger to God might please Him, as a fair return for beseeching His help.

Quietly closing the great west door behind her, Helewise left the church.

Oh, but I do not feel any easier! she thought

miserably as she crossed the cloister and made for the privacy of her room. I *still* cannot decide what to do, although that indecision itself makes me feel that the girl's final vows must be postponed, at least until this present and deeply unsettling business has been—

'Abbess?' called a voice.

Helewise turned. Sister Ursel was hurrying towards her, a broad smile on her face.

Helewise, crushing the thought that a long conversation with the porteress was the last thing she wanted just then, arranged her own features into a corresponding smile and said, 'Sister Ursel. What can I do for you?'

'Abbess, you've got a visitor!' Sister Ursel said. 'Sister Martha's just seeing to his horse, and he's having a bit of a natter with her, but then he says he'd like to come to see you, if that's all right? Only I said I thought it would be.'

Helewise waited patiently for her to finish. Then said, 'And who, Sister Ursel, is "he"?'

'Oh, didn't I say?' Sister Ursel chuckled. 'No, I didn't, did I? It's just that I was so pleased to see him again, looking exactly the same, for all it must be two years since he came to see us, and . . .'

'Sister Ursel?' Helewise interrupted gently.

'That Josse, Abbess!' Sister Ursel exclaimed. 'That Sir Josse d'Acquin, I should say. Come over from his grand new house, he has, to pay his respects!'

As she sat in her room waiting for Josse to finish his gossiping with Sister Martha and come to join her, Helewise reflected on what a wonderful piece of chance it was, for Josse to turn up just now. Why, it might be heaven sent, it was so perfect! An outsider, but a friend nevertheless, whom she knew to be sensible and trustworthy, arriving at the very moment that she had need of a wise and sympathetic ear!

As she heard Josse's heavy tread outside, she saw, in a flash of insight, that heaven sent was precisely what he was; her hour-long, desperate prayers had been heard after all.

The Abbess Helewise looked well, Josse thought, sitting down on the same insubstantial stool he remembered from two years ago; had nobody suggested to her, in all that time, that the larger of her male visitors might be easier in a chair? She had the same calm expression, same clear grey eyes, same wide mouth.

But, knowing her as he did, for all that – for all that she might appear well – there was something on her mind. There had to be! Because, as he rambled on and on about his new house, about this plan and that, about Will and Ella and their respective skills in looking after him, he suspected quite soon that she wasn't really listening.

'Oh, really?' she said, and, 'Lovely!' and, 'How very pleasant.' When he said, feeling slightly mean, 'There's a terrible smell in the main hall, I think it's probably been used by wild boar,' and she answered, 'Oh, how nice,' then he knew she wasn't listening.

He leaned forward, noticing, from a closer vantage point, the fine lines of anxiety between her brows. 'Abbess Helewise,' he said gently, 'that wasn't the right answer.' Briefly he confessed to what he had just done, and, her pale cheeks flushing slightly, the Abbess apologised. Waving away her discomfiture, he said, 'Why don't you tell me what's wrong?'

Her eyes flew to his. 'Nothing! I'm worrying

about nothing, I'm quite sure. And, anyway, I shouldn't be unburdening my concern on to you, why, you've only just arrived!'

'Ah.' He bided his time.

After several moments, she said, 'It's Sister Caliste. A young novice.'

'Ah,' he said again.

She sighed. He perceived in her the struggle between her natural reticence and her need for the relief of talking. Eventually – as he had hoped it would – the need to talk won.

'Yes.' Another sigh. 'You see, my strong instinct is to put off the first of her final vows, and I can give no good reason for it.'

'Must you explain your decision?' he asked.

'Officially, perhaps not.' She smiled briefly. 'But Caliste is a sensitive and intelligent girl, and I feel I owe her an explanation.'

There was a reflective silence in the little room. Then Josse said, 'You and I, Abbess Helewise, have shared our worries before, to both our own and others' benefit.' He hesitated. Should he go on, even bearing in mind all that they had endured together in the past?

Yes, he decided. He should.

He said gently, 'Why don't you tell me about her?'

After a slight pause, Helewise did so.

Listening, Josse thought, I think she's quite right, for what it's worth. Another year as a novice will give both girl and the Abbey some much needed extra time.

'. . . you see, Sir Josse,' the Abbess was saying, 'and, what with her odd behaviour since the time of the murder, well, it's just the final straw.'

Realising he had missed something – something rather important – Josse said sharply, 'Murder, Abbess?'

She murmured something; it sounded like, '*Now* who's not listening,' then proceeded to tell him the few slim facts about the death of Hamm Robinson all over again.

'I bring you bad luck,' Josse observed when she had finished. 'The last time I was here, it was because of a murder. Now here I am again, and, heralding my return, someone else is slain.'

'People have been killed in the intervening years,' the Abbess said. 'Much as it pains me to say so, we live in violent times, Sir Josse. When men are hungry, when they act recklessly and fear retribution, such things lead all too easily to the swift blow, delivered too hard.'

Sobered by her words, yet at the same time relieved that he was not actually some dread harbinger of death, Josse nodded. 'But the murder of Hamm Robinson was unusual?' he prompted. 'Killed with a spear, you say?'

'Yes,' she agreed. 'A spear with a flint head. Which, according to our friend the sheriff, implicates the people of the forest, but, as I told you, since they've left the area, he has abandoned any faint hope of bringing them to justice.'

'It could equally be some devious soul making it *look* as if the forest dwellers are responsible,' Josse said.

'Exactly what I thought,' the Abbess said.

'Hmm.' Josse frowned in concentration. The concept of these Wild People, as the Abbess had called them, was new to him. He knew the old legends, everyone did, but to have figures from the ancient tales apparently take on flesh and blood and kill a man, well, that took a bit of swallowing. 'Abbess, about these forest folk who—'

'Sir Josse, there is no point in pursuing this!'

she interrupted. 'We must follow the sheriff's example, and accept that the matter is closed.'

'Hm,' he said again. Then, remembering something, 'Abbess, you were saying that your young novice began acting up – how did you describe it? Behaving oddly? – when this Hamm Robinson was killed? Surely, then, you can't forget about it, since it affects one of your nuns?'

'It was not the death that made her behave oddly,' the Abbess said firmly. 'I must make that plain, because there is no question of her being involved, in any way.'

'Ah.' Why, Josse wondered, are you denying it so strenuously, unless you really fear the opposite?

'No, indeed,' the Abbess went on. 'It was merely that – oh, it sounds silly and insubstantial, now that I try to put it into words.'

'But, please, Abbess, do so.'

'Very well. You see, Sir Josse, a couple of nights before Hamm Robinson was slain, I heard Sister Caliste get up out of her bed. I think she was walking in her sleep – certainly, she gave no sign that she was aware of me, following her.'

'I see. And what did she do?'

'She walked to the door, quietly opened it, and stood on the top of the steps outside.'

'Innocent enough,' Josse said. 'Perhaps she merely needed a breath of air.'

'In her sleep?' Abbess Helewise spoke with faint irony. 'And that's not all. Standing there, straight as a reed, she was gazing out over the wall.'

'Over the wall,' Josse repeated.

'Yes. Her eyes were wide open, and she was humming softly under her breath, some weird succession of notes, so very different from anything I've ever heard before that . . .' The Abbess gave a faint shudder. 'Well, never mind.'

Josse, trying to remember the layout of the Abbey, was picturing the scene. 'Top of the steps leading to the dormitory, you said, and looking out over the wall?' The Abbess nodded.

He sighed. He was beginning to understand the Abbess's unease.

'Then, Abbess,' he said heavily, 'your young Sister Caliste, whether knowingly or not, was staring out over the forest.'

And the Abbess, her eyes full of anxiety, said, 'Exactly.'

Chapter Five

Seeing Josse on his way, Helewise felt much calmer than she had done earlier. It was not so much that he had resolved the problem of what to do about Caliste, more that it had been such a luxury to speak frankly with someone of Josse's sound common sense.

'You must certainly postpone the girl's admission into the ranks of the fully professed,' he had agreed. 'It wouldn't be fair, Abbess, either on the girl or on the community, to promote her to a life of dedication and maturity for which, from what you tell me, she isn't yet ready.'

As well as endorsing Helewise's own view, he had, however, also ventured a suggestion of his own. A typically practical one, and one which the Abbess herself should have thought of. And I might have done, she had reflected, listening to him, had my mind not been fixed on the abstract things of the spirit, at the expense of the more tangible matters of the day to day.

'Why not put the girl to working with one of your nuns with a particularly strong but, if I may use the word, simple faith?' Josse had said tentatively. 'If you have such a sister.'

'Indeed I have!' Helewise said, lighting on the idea. 'Sister Beata, whom you have met – a nurse in the infirmary. She is *just* such a one, and the perfect mentor for a novice who needs to be coaxed more firmly into our spiritual fold!'

But, dampening her enthusiasm, another thought struck her.

'What's the matter?' Josse must have read the sudden doubt in her face.

'Oh – merely that, at present, I have another young woman working in the infirmary. She has been with us for a couple of months while we and others search for a permanent post for her. Her name is Esyllt, and she arrived with her late mistress, a very old and crippled woman who died while she was with us, taking the holy waters. Esyllt was left with nowhere to go, and we thought it better to keep her here than to let her roam the countryside alone.'

'Ah, it's a big world out there, fraught with perils for an innocent young girl,' Josse agreed.

'Well, it wasn't exactly—' Helewise made herself stop. No need to gossip about Esyllt, and why Helewise was quite sure she wasn't a suitable companion for the novice Caliste. Anyway, for sure, Josse would see what she meant, if and when he ever met the girl. 'I shall move Esyllt to the aged monks' and nuns' home,' the Abbess said decisively. 'The Good Lord knows,' she added in a murmur, 'her vivacious spirit should have an excellent effect there. And Esyllt has gentle hands, and is used to caring kindly for the very old. Her late mistress spoke highly of her,' she explained to Josse, 'and it is partly at her earnest behest that we are at such pains to secure the right place for Esyllt.'

Esyllt transferred from infirmary to old people's home, she had mused, Caliste moved from her pupillage under the wise but controversial Sister Tiphaine, to work under the watchful eye of Sister Beata, whose childlike faith might just work the necessary miracle.

Yes, I have much to thank you for, Sir Josse, Helewise thought now, as she watched him mount up. It occurred to her, not for the first time, that, at some point in his life, Josse d'Acquin must have become very used to the command of men . . .

'Oh, Abbess, I almost forgot!' He stilled the circling horse and gave Helewise a rueful grin. 'I encountered a friend of yours on the road, a man named Tobias Durand. He asked to be remembered to you.'

'Tobias Durand?' She frowned, then recalled. But she would scarcely have called him a friend, having barely met him. 'Indeed? And was there a message for me?' Perhaps he had sent word regarding the Queen, who must surely have left for France by now.

'No message,' Josse replied. 'Merely to send the Abbess Helewise of Hawkenlye his respects.'

'Charming,' Helewise murmured. Then, aloud, 'Where did you say you met him?'

'I didn't. In fact it was on the track leading from the forest, some five miles off to the north-east.' Josse waved a hand behind him. 'The fellow was hawking. Said it was good land there, where the trees give way to fields and hedgerows. Plenty of small game, for the training of a new bird.'

'Oh!' Helewise was faintly surprised, since she had understood from Queen Eleanor that Tobias and Petronilla lived quite close to the coast. It seemed unnecessary, to come all the way to this particular stretch of the Wealden Forest, when there must surely be good hawking to be had nearer to home.

Still, it was none of her business.

'Perhaps Tobias will pay us a call,' she said.

'Not today, he won't.' Josse turned his horse. 'Said he was off home when I saw him.'

'But I thought you said you met him this morning?'

'Aye, I did.' He steadied the horse, who was impatient to be away. 'Wait, Horace! We'll be off directly!'

Then Tobias must have left his home very early, Helewise thought, still puzzled. Unless he had been staying with friends hereabouts? Yes! That must be it!

'Was he alone? Tobias, I mean?' she asked Josse. 'Or with a company?'

'What?' Josse, clearly, wasn't really interested.

'Oh, quite alone. Now, Abbess, I must be on my way. Good day to you!'

'Good day, Sir Josse. Come to see us again.'

'I will.' Josse grinned. 'Apart from the pleasure of your company, Abbess, I'm intrigued by this poor dead body you trod on.'

'I didn't—' she began. But, with a wave of his hand, he was gone.

Yes, she thought, walking back towards the cloister and her room. I might have known. Mention the words 'suspicious death' to Josse d'Acquin, and you ensure yourself of the pleasure of *his* company. At least, until the murder is solved.

The new arrangements were put into effect straight away and, as far as Helewise could tell, seemed to work well. Esyllt, who had a strong and melodious singing voice, which she liked to use as she worked, quickly became a favourite with the old monks and nuns living out their retirement at Hawkenlye Abbey. True, one or two of the more straight-laced old people expressed shock, that a young woman who wasn't of the community should be allowed to tend them, and one old monk in particular took exception to Esyllt's song about the young lad and his lass, and what they got up to on a moonlit harvest night. But the dissenters were overruled by the majority, who grew to cherish Esyllt for her brimming happiness and her loving touch on ancient, painful bodies.

Quite what it was that made Esyllt so cheerful, nobody knew or thought to enquire. Everybody worked hard at Hawkenlye Abbey; to have someone among them who had a pleasant word for all, who sang as she went about even the most crude of tasks, seemed like a gift from a thoughtful God, to brighten the long days.

Sister Caliste settled down too, in the infirmary. Sister Beata had at first confessed to Helewise that she was afraid the remarks of the infirmary patients might affect Caliste; most of those cared for by the nuns were from the outside world, and many didn't know about convent etiquette, that forbade the making of personal remarks. Caliste, whose beauty shone like a beacon, was, in Sister Beata's opinion, the recipient of far too many compliments.

But even Sister Beata had to admit that the girl

hardly seemed to hear. 'In fact, Abbess,' Sister Beata went on, 'sometimes it's quite hard to make her hear anything! It's as if—' Sister Beata's face crumpled into an uncharacteristic frown as she sought the words. 'As if she's listening to inner voices. Or music, perhaps, since, quite often, she starts to hum softly, as if she's joining in.'

'I see.' Helewise did see, all too clearly; it was that strange humming of Caliste's that had so disturbed the Abbess, the night she had found the girl sleepwalking.

Caliste might appear settled in her new work. But Helewise was very afraid that there were currents moving beneath the smooth surface. Currents that would, she feared, bring trouble.

Josse had discovered, in the first few days of his homecoming, that his impression of work on New Winnowlands being all but finished had been an illusion.

The builders were still busy on the kitchen, and there was a problem with the solar, which, apparently, only the master builder himself could put right. It was entirely Josse's fault, was the implication, for being so daft as to want a solar in the first place.

Josse tried to help, making suggestions, rolling up his sleeves and offering his strong arms and back.

But it was made quite obvious that he was not wanted; the builders, who never actually *said* so, managed to imply that, by hanging around where they were working, Josse was offending against some unwritten but unbreakable rule.

So he retired to his hall.

But there was nothing to do!

The long summer days drew him outside, yet, once there, he had to keep dodging workmen. In desperation, he remembered the Hawkenlye murder.

And thought, damnation and hellfire, I'll see if I can do better than that sheriff fellow!

He arrived in Tonbridge, where, enquiring for Sheriff Harry Pelham – bless the Abbess, for informing Josse what the man's name was – he learned that, it being the midday hour, the sheriff would likely be taking his dinner.

Fortunately for Josse, the sheriff's preferred inn was the one where Josse had himself once put up; leading his horse into the yard, he met the innkeeper, Goody Anne, hurrying across from one of her storehouses with a side of ham under one strong arm.

'Well! Good day to you, stranger!' she cried, giving him a broad smile. 'And just where have you been all this time?'

Grinning back, Josse said, 'Here and there, Anne. How are you?'

'I'm well. We're very busy, but that's how I like it. Are you eating? I've a side of beef just broached, and this here ham's in its prime.' She gave the haunch a friendly slap.

'I'm ravenous,' Josse said. '*And* I've a thirst on me like a man lost in the desert.'

Anne batted her eyelids at him. 'You've come to the right place to see to your appetites,' she said. With a seductive swing of her ample bottom, she disappeared through the door into the kitchen. Faintly her voice reached him: '*All* your appetites!'

In the taproom, Josse ordered beer and food. Then, casting his eyes round the company, he tried to guess which man might be Sheriff Pelham.

He was in luck. A newcomer entering the room shouted out, 'Sheriff? I've a message for you!' and a stout, strongly built man in a battered leather tunic stood up and said, 'Here!'

Josse waited until the newcomer had given his message and left. Then, casually, he sauntered across to where the sheriff was tucking into his meal and said, 'May I sit beside you?'

The sheriff waved a knife on whose point was speared a leg of chicken. 'S'a free country,' he said, spitting out small pieces of pale meat which landed, like minute snow flakes, on the front of the already stained tunic.

Josse tucked into his own dinner. Observing the sheriff's progress as he did so, he waited until the man had finished, wiped his greasy mouth with an even greasier sleeve, burped, taken a draught of beer, said, 'Ah! That's better!' and relaxed, leaning back against the wall.

Only then did Josse say, 'I was visiting Hawkenlye Abbey recently. They tell me a man was killed, and that you, Sheriff, went to investigate?'

'Aye?' the sheriff said warily. Josse could almost hear the silent, *and what's it to you, stranger?*

'I'm known to the good people of the Hawkenlye community,' Josse went on. 'I hear there's a suggestion of some weird forest tribe being involved in this death? They say that someone cleverly put two and two together, and virtually solved the crime there and then.'

His vanity thus appealed to, the sheriff became voluble. 'Well, stands to reason,' he said, leaning confidingly towards Josse. 'See, the dead man was a poacher, a no-good fellow, I've had my problems with him before. Anyway, how I see it is that he goes into the forest after game, he comes across this group of Forest People, they don't like him trespassing into what they see as their preserve, so they chuck a spear at him. Kill him stone dead.'

'Very likely, very likely,' Josse agreed. 'Clever deduction, Sheriff! The only solution, really, isn't it? Especially when you knew these Forest People were in the vicinity that night.'

'Well . . .' the sheriff began. Then, more aggressively, 'That uppity Abbess woman, she didn't believe me! Me, who's lived round here man and boy, who's known about the comings and goings of those wild folk all my life! Why, my old father used to talk of them, and his father before that!' He picked a piece of meat out of a back tooth, spat it on the floor and said, 'Women! Eh? Think they know it all!'

'I am actually rather impressed with the Abbess Helewise,' Josse remarked.

It was a mistake. The sheriff, anger darkening his face, said suspiciously, 'She sent you here, didn't she? Sent you to talk to me, try to trip me up!' He put his face right against Josse's. 'Well, let me tell you, Sir Knight, whoever you are, that Harry Pelham doesn't take kindly to folk making a fool of him!'

'I'm not trying to do that, Sheriff Pelham.' Josse got to his feet. 'There's no need,' he added, 'for anyone to *make* a fool of you.'

Harry Pelham, who seemed to be working out whether or not that last remark came to a compliment, sat with his mouth open as Josse shouldered his way out of the room.

Riding up the ridge towards Hawkenlye, Josse thought about the death of Hamm Robinson.

Not that it took him long; the facts were brief enough to be summed up in a single sentence. And, as Abbess Helewise had said, nobody seemed to have investigated the matter. Not at all.

I shall, Josse thought. I shall visit his family, his friends, if he had any. Visit the spot where he was found.

I shall *think* about this strange slaying. And, only when I have done so, shall I know if to accept this all-too-obvious, all-too-convenient conclusion.

Arriving at the Abbey, he was informed that the Abbess was in the infirmary, speaking with a man dying of the wasting sickness, whose last hours were being made even more agonising by his fear over what would become of his wife and his many children.

Josse went over to the infirmary. Standing just inside the door, left slightly ajar to let in the sweet-smelling air, he looked around him.

Yes. There was the Abbess, kneeling beside a poor, feeble-looking man who was clutching her hands tightly in his. So the man had a large family? Yes. Josse had observed before how often men suffering from the terrible blood-spitting were yet potent enough to father a whole tribe of offspring. Josse studied the Abbess's intent face. She was speaking earnestly to the man, nodding as if in emphasis, every part of her clearly determined to get her message across.

Josse, unable to hear what she was saying, couldn't tell what that message was. Assurance of God's mercy? Hope for the afterlife? It occurred to him that, if he himself were dying and desperate, there was nobody he would rather have, both at his side and on it, than the Abbess Helewise.

A soft voice said, 'May I help you, sir?'

Turning, he saw a young girl in nun's black, over which she wore the white veil of the novice. She was quite tall, slimly built, and carried herself like a queen. The skin of her finely boned face was cream and smooth, and her eyes were deep blue. Despite the stark habit, despite the fact that her sacking apron was stained with something Josse didn't want to dwell on, the girl was beautiful.

He knew who she was, or was almost sure that he did. 'Sister Caliste?'

She nodded. 'And you, I think, are Sir Josse d'Acquin.'

He returned her smile. No man still able to see could have done anything else. 'Aye. I have come to speak to the Abbess, but I see she is busy.'

Caliste looked over to where Abbess Helewise was smoothing the brow of the dying man. 'She is. She gives him such comfort, sir. She is telling him what will be done for his wife and his little ones.'

'I would have thought she'd be praying with him.'

The great blue eyes turned to him. 'That too. But I think that he will not concentrate on his prayers until his anxieties are assuaged.'

Such perception, Josse thought. And the girl had a way with words that suggested some education. 'I will wait outside,' he said.

'I will keep you company, if you wish,' the girl offered politely. 'The Abbess likes our visitors to feel welcome.'

'Most kind,' Josse said. 'If you're sure I'm not keeping you from your work?'

Caliste smiled again, removing her dirty apron. 'I have just finished one of my less agreeable duties. I was about to visit Sister Tiphaine, to request some herbs for Sister Euphemia's medicines. If you would care to accompany me, sir?'

Outside, he fell into step beside the girl. Observing her covertly, he noticed that she had adopted the upright glide of a nun, that her hands, temporarily unoccupied, were automatically tucked into the opposite sleeves. Yes, she *looks* like a nun all right, he thought. But . . .

But?

He couldn't define exactly what there was about Caliste. But, as Helewise had discovered before him, in truth, there was something . . .

'It is more usual to go to Sister Tiphaine's workroom the other way, passing the front gate,' Caliste said, breaking the silence, 'but I like to go this way. For one thing, I can have a passing look at the tympanum, over the door of the church' – she withdrew a hand and pointed up at the great carving, depicting the Last Judgement – 'and, for another, this way you go through the herb garden.'

They walked on, past the door of the Lady Chapel, past the virgin sisters' house, past the windowless, doorless walls of the sinister little building which, Josse knew, was the Abbey's leper house. Sister Caliste, he noticed, crossed herself as they passed. He did the same.

Then, around the corner, sheltered against the south wall of the Abbey, they came to the herb garden.

The month was June, and many of the plants were in full leaf. Stopping, Josse took a deep breath, and the combined aromas of rosemary, sage, mint, lavender, and a dozen other plants whose names he did not know, filled his head. He breathed deeply again, and again, then, feeling dizzy, abruptly he stopped.

Beside him, Caliste giggled. 'It's not really very wise to do that, Sir Josse,' she said. 'The herbs are powerful just now. You have to treat them with respect.'

'I see what you mean,' Josse said. Gingerly, he stepped forward; the dizziness seemed to have gone.

'This way,' Caliste said, stepping out along a narrow path bordered neatly with box hedging. 'Sister Tiphaine's workroom is just ahead.'

He waited outside the little shed while Caliste went in to fetch whatever it was she had been sent for. She was not gone long, but, even so, her absence gave sufficient time for a warm exchange of words between her and the herbalist. And a soft outburst of laughter.

'You used to work with Sister Tiphaine, I believe,' he said as he and Caliste made their way back to the infirmary. 'Do you regret being moved to nursing duties?'

'I—' Caliste hesitated, shooting a quick, assessing glance at him. 'I will tell you the truth, Sir Knight,' she said, obviously deciding in his favour. 'I loved working with Sister Tiphaine, who was kind to me and generous with the sharing of her wide knowledge. When I was told of my new duties, I was sad. But I am a nun, and I must do what I am told.'

Moved to pity, he said, 'I am sorry for you, child. I know what it is to have to obey, when the dictates of one's heart say differently.'

'Do you?' She stopped, staring at him. 'Yes,' she murmured, 'I believe you do.' As if recognising in him a kindred spirit, she smiled. But this time, the expression seemed to include all of her soul.

Quite shaken, he smiled back.

After a pause, he said, 'Have you settled down in your new work? Are you happy, Sister Caliste?'

She replied, 'I have, and I am. I tell myself that, if I am to make a good nun, then I must learn not to have – what was it you said? Dictates of the heart? Yes. Not to have those. And I *am* happy.'

There seemed nothing else to say. They walked, in silence, side by side back to the infirmary.

But, as she stood back to let him go in first, Caliste said, 'Thank you for asking, Sir Knight. It was kindly done.'

In a barely audible whisper, she added, 'And I do not forget a kindness.'

Chapter Six

When Helewise finally emerged from the infirmary and spared a few moments to greet Josse, he realised without her having to tell him that she was both preoccupied and very busy. In addition to the dying man, a woman in the nuns' care had just given birth to twins, one of whom was sickly. So sickly that the Abbess was anxious to fetch the priest and arrange for immediate baptism. 'Just in case,' she added, with a sad little smile.

Also, one of the monks from the vale was being treated for a septic foot, and Brother Firmin had asked the Abbess to send down an extra pair of hands to help deal with the sudden rush of pilgrims, encouraged by the fine weather to come and take of the holy waters.

'Does Brother Firmin not appreciate how busy

you are, you and the sisters, with your own concerns?' Josse asked her mildly.

A flash of anger briefly lit the Abbess's grey eyes, there and gone in an instant. After taking a rather audible deep breath, she said, 'Brother Firmin's duty is to his pilgrims, Sir Josse. If he feels that he is short-staffed and cannot fulfil his duties properly, then he is right to ask for help.'

'Ah,' Josse said quietly. And folded his lips over what he would have liked to say next.

'I'm sorry that I can't help you in this matter of the murdered man,' the Abbess said, looking around her as she did so. 'Now, where is Brother Saul? I want him to act as my messenger, and go to find Father Gilbert . . .'

'I wouldn't dream of imposing,' Josse said. 'I shall proceed on my own, Abbess, and, in due course, report my findings. If I may?'

'Yes, yes,' she said, still looking for Brother Saul. 'Ah! I see him.' She hurried off towards the distant figure of Brother Saul, raising a hand and hailing him as she did so. Then abruptly she stopped, turned, and called back to Josse, 'He lived in a tiny hovel down by the ford. His woman is called Matty, and he has two fellow-poachers named Ewen and Seth. Seth, I believe, is Hamm's cousin.'

As Josse thanked her, he wondered how, in the midst of all she had on her mind, she had, first, discovered that information, and, second, stored it away and remembered it to pass on to him.

A remarkable woman, the Abbess of Hawkenlye.

Hovel, he reflected as he rode down the track to the ford, had been about right.

The track petered out into a muddy slipway as it neared the water. The stream issuing out of the forest was quite wide just there, fast-running over a good, firm base, the water slightly brown from the peat, and from the centuries upon centuries of fallen leaves that had gone into the making of the stream's banks and bed.

It would have been a lovely spot, had it not been for the row of dwellings straggling up the track on the far side.

Two were deserted; even the most desperate of people, surely, could not live in a house with no roof and half its walls gone. The middle three were reasonably sound, and the last in the row was no more than a lean-to built against its neighbour, now being used to house livestock. A scrawny pig and a handful of miserable-looking chickens raised their heads as Josse splashed through the water, and a dog on a short length of fraying rope dashed out, gave a token few barks, then ran back into the lean-to with its tail curving tightly over its backside, as if in anticipation of a good hard kick.

Somewhere within one of the dwellings a baby cried, until it was silenced by a woman's harsh voice.

Dismounting, Josse put his head into the doorway of the first hovel. The baby was sitting on the mud floor, naked but for a tattered shirt several sizes too big. It had its fist in its mouth, streaks of greenish snot ran from its nostrils, and the filth on its cheeks was lined by the tracks of tears. Close to its small right buttock was a turd, its end smeared from where the child had sat on it. There was no sign of the woman with the harsh voice.

He went on to the next doorway. The door was closed, and through a gap at the top, he peered inside. There was nobody there.

In the third house, a woman sat on the step, just inside the door. From the chipped pot on the floor beside her and the meagre pile of earth-covered turnips and carrots in her lap, it seemed she was meant to be preparing vegetables. In fact, she was staring listlessly in front of her, face cast down into lines of dejection. If she had heard Josse's approach, she was not sufficiently interested to peer out and see who it was come a-visiting.

Josse said, 'Are you the widow of the late Hamm Robinson?'

She looked up at him, tears welling in her eyes. At some time, she had suffered a broken nose; there was a big lump midway between the tip and the bridge. She had also lost several teeth. She said dully, 'Aye.'

Josse went to stand beside the woman. 'I am sorry for your loss,' he said.

She sniffed and wiped her nose with the back of her hand. 'Don't know what'll become of me,' she said mournfully, sliding a quick glance up at him. Her voice took on the familiar whine of the professional beggar. 'Nowhere to call me own, no man to bring in a bit of this and that,' she moaned. 'Where me next meal's a-coming from, the dear Lord above only knows.'

Josse reached into the purse at his belt and took out some coins. 'Perhaps these will tide you over.' He dropped them into her lap.

Her hand shot out and the coins disappeared. 'Thankee,' she said.

Josse hesitated. There seemed little point in asking this browbeaten, dejected woman if her husband had had any enemies. Would she know? And, if she did, would she tell Josse?

He asked instead, 'I believe your husband – er – worked with his cousin Seth? And another man – Ewen, is it?'

The dull eyes raised to his had a sudden spark of life in them. 'You're very well informed,' she said tartly. 'What's it to you?'

'Woman, it may interest you to know that I'm about the only person hereabouts who has the slightest interest in bringing your husband's murderer to justice!' he cried, suddenly angry. 'I am trying to find out all I can about him, and I shall want to talk to everyone who knew him!'

'Huh! *That* won't take you long! There's me, and I don't know nothing about what he got up to, leastways, except he used to go into the forest, for all that I tried to stop him.' She sniffed, making a thick snorting sound in her throat; had Josse not been standing in front of her, she might well, he thought, have hawked up the loose phlegm and gobbed it out on to the road. 'Right, weren't I?' she flashed, with a sudden angry spiritedness. 'Seeing as how them Forest People've gone and done for him!'

'Yes, I know. As I said, I'm sorry.' Josse brought his irritation under control. The woman was, after all, recently bereaved. 'Did these men Ewen and Seth go with Hamm into the forest?' he asked, trying to keep his tone conciliatory. 'Did they – er – hunt with him?'

She eyed him with half-closed lids. Her eyes, he noticed, were an indeterminate pale colour, and the lashes were short and sparse. 'They were poachers, the three of them,' she said baldly. 'As well you know. Everyone knows that, someone'll have told you by now.'

'Yes, I did know,' Josse acknowledged. 'The general view is that your husband was poaching the night he was killed, and that the Forest People didn't like it.'

'T'aint their game, no more'n it were his,' the

woman said bitterly. 'They've got no call to go stopping other folk helping theirselves. Not to the game, anyhow, and as to the other—' She bit off whatever she had been about to say.

'The other?' He tried to keep the excitement out of his voice.

'No,' she said firmly. 'I'll not say no more. I've been beaten by my own man long enough, I won't risk one of them others starting where Hamm left off.'

'But—'

'*No.*'

And he watched as, with a dignity he wouldn't have thought she possessed, the woman got to her feet, carefully picked up her pot and gathered her vegetables up in her fraying and filthy skirt, then stepped down inside her house and firmly closed the door.

Josse came upon Hamm Robinson's partners in crime by sheer fluke. Riding up into the outer fringes of the forest, intending to have a look at the place where Hamm was found, he heard their arguing voices.

His luck did not extend to overhearing anything useful; hearing his horse, instantly they stopped talking. Far from being cowed like the woman, though, they went on the offensive.

'Oi! What d'you think yer doing?' one man called out.

The other was brandishing a stout staff. 'State yer business!' he said grandly.

Josse rode right up to them; Horace was a tall horse, and, being mounted, Josse felt he had the upper hand. Despite the stout stick.

'Ewen and Seth, I take it?' he said. 'Friends of the late Hamm Robinson? Or should I say fellow thieves?'

It was a stab in the dark. But it got a response; the man carrying the stick began to swing it threateningly above his head, crying, 'It were his idea! Hamm found it, it were Hamm made us go in along of him! I never—'

At that point, the other man hit him. Swung his elbow violently into the man's stomach, so that he bent over into a right-angle, whooping for breath.

'Take no notice of Ewen,' Seth said over his friend's gasping. 'He's right, sir, it were Hamm who said there was good game to be had in the forest, and us what went along with him.'

'Game,' Josse repeated. The wounded man had not, he was quite sure, been speaking of game. But, whatever he *had* meant, Josse wasn't going to find out.

'We've got our bellies to fill, same as everyone else,' Seth went on self-righteously. 'When there's rabbit and deer aplenty in there,' he jerked a thumb back towards the dark forest behind him, 'then where's the harm? That's what I say, sir!'

'Quite,' Josse said. 'Only someone, apparently, didn't agree. To the extent of slaying your late cousin with a well-aimed spear.'

The man paled visibly at the reminder, but stood his ground. The wounded man – Ewen – renewed his moaning. 'I *told* you, Seth!' he said shakily. 'Told you, aye, and him too! Hamm, I says, you go in there again, and they'll—'

He was, Josse observed, not a man to learn a lesson quickly; as before, what he had been about to say was abruptly cut off. This time, the blow was severe enough to floor him; as Josse turned Horace's head and kicked him into a trot, he saw Seth aim a booted foot at his fallen friend's head.

*

All the way back to the Abbey, Josse puzzled over what a smalltime poacher and, probably, petty thief, could have discovered deep within an ancient forest. What could be valuable enough to make not only Hamm but his two colleagues go into that place of fearful legend? Superstitious, like all their kind, it must surely have been something extraordinary.

Whatever Hamm had discovered, it seemed to have led directly to his murder. It had always struck Josse as fairly unlikely, that these mysterious forest folk should have speared a man to death purely for snaring a brace of coneys; it was far more credible that, somehow, Hamm had uncovered something they preferred to keep secret.

But what?

Something, probably, that Hamm reckoned he could turn readily into cash, for nothing else, surely, would have made him risk the forest by night.

Buried treasure? A hoard of Roman coins? The rumours spoke of Roman occupation of the great Wealden Forest; they had extracted iron from it, made sound tracks through the primeval wood-land, traces of which could still be found now, a thousand years later. Had Hamm, in the course of his poaching, dug into a rabbit warren under some ancient oak and come across a bounty he didn't expect?

Speculation. It was all speculation. No matter how likely it was beginning to sound, Josse had no proof.

And, he concluded as he rode through the Abbey gates, there was only one way to change that.

Abbess Helewise was sitting in the cloister, eyes closed, the late sun on her face. Josse didn't like to disturb her, but, on the other hand, she *had* said he might report any findings to her . . .

He was still hovering, trying to decide if to wake her or not, when she said, 'I'm not asleep. And I know it's you, Sir Josse, nobody else here wears spurs that jingle when they walk.'

He went to sit beside her on the narrow stone ledge. 'I'm sorry to disturb you. I know you've had a busy day.'

She sighed. 'Indeed. But the outcome has, in

part, been satisfactory. The sick baby was bap-
tised – his brother, too – and he has, I think, taken
a turn for the better. He is suckling well, and has
a little colour.'

'Thank God,' Josse said.

'Amen.' There was a slight pause, then she
said, 'And you, I imagine, have news, too?'

'Aye.' Briefly he told her what he had discovered, and what he now thought had happened.
'I'm going to have a look,' he added, with an
attempt at nonchalance. 'Tonight, probably.
Nothing like striking while the iron's hot!' He
attempted a laugh, not very convincing, even to
himself.

The Abbess said slowly, 'You think Hamm
Robinson was killed by the Forest People because
he had found out about something they prefer to
keep to themselves, and now you propose to go
into the forest tonight, and try to find out what
this something was.'

'Aye.' Funny how, when she said it, it did
sound a little foolhardy. 'I'll be all right, Abbess, I
can take care of myself.'

'Yes, Sir Josse,' she said with heavy irony, 'you
have, I'm well aware, eyes in the back of your

head which will see the spear coming.'

It was not a good thought; he felt the muscles of his back contract in a brief involuntary spasm. 'I'll be armed,' he said defensively. 'And, unlike poor Hamm, I'll be on the look out.'

'*That's* all right, then,' said the Abbess.

'I have to do *something*!' he said with sudden fierceness.

'Hush!' she hissed swiftly, 'someone will over-hear!'

'I want to find out who killed him and why,' Josse went on, in a whisper that was almost as loud as his normal speech. 'I can't just let it go, even if you can!'

That last remark was unfair, and he knew it. Regretting the words as soon as he had spoken them, he said, 'Sorry, Abbess. I know you would find the killer if it were within your power.'

She didn't reply for some time, and he was afraid he had mortally and irredeemably offended her. But then, stretching out a hand in his general direction, she said, 'I will have a pack made up for you – some food, drink, a flint and a torch. If you are going into the forest by night, it is only sensible to take precautions.'

'But—' He didn't want to be burdened with a pack. Still, if doing what she could to help him was her way of showing that she had forgiven him – and that she, too, wanted to do her bit to catch the murderer – then it seemed he had little choice but to accept.

He valued her friendship too much to let ill-feeling remain between them.

'Thank you,' he said humbly. 'I shall be grateful.'

He ate with the sisters that evening, and, on an impulse, went with them to Compline. The last office of the day, it had, he found, a particularly calming effect on his stretched nerves. It was always that way, he reflected, listening to the heavenly sound of the choir nuns, just before going into action. Muscles and sinews taut as bowstrings, mouth dry, heartbeat unsteady. Whereas, as soon as the fight began and you—

But that didn't seem a very suitable thing to recall, in church listening to hymns of praise. Deliberately he turned his thoughts to his devotions.

*

He slipped out of the Abbey a couple of hours later. All was quiet, and, as he raised the Abbess's small and neatly prepared pack on to one shoulder, not a single light showed from any of the Abbey buildings.

He collected his sword and his knife from the corner of the wall between the porteress's lodge and the Abbey's front wall, where he had concealed them earlier in the day. Sliding his sword into its scabbard, he felt his confidence grow. He opened the gates just enough to slip out, and carefully closed them behind him.

Then he set off up the track into the forest.

The moon was waxing, and, only a day from the full, gave sufficient light for Josse to make his way without stumbling. Until, that was, he moved deep under the shadow of the trees. He stopped and waited for his eyes to adjust, fiddling idly with the strap on his pack.

His hand encountered something. An object – made of metal, to judge by its cool smoothness – fastened to the flap. Feeling all around it with his fingers – it was quite small – he thought it was a little cross.

The Abbess, he thought. She put it there, for protection.

God bless her kind heart!

His night vision had sharpened as much as it was likely to. With gratitude for such a friend giving a lift both to his spirits and to his steps, he headed on into the depths of the forest.

Chapter Seven

As he trod warily deeper and deeper into the forest, despite his best efforts Josse found his mind filling with every bad thing he had ever heard about its sinister reputation.

In the stillness beneath the thick tree canopy, he developed the odd sensation that he was within some great living thing, some dark creature of unimaginable mystery and strangeness. His careful footfalls on the forest floor could, if one did not keep tight rein on the imagination, be mistaken for a quiet, steady heartbeat. And the distant sound of the faint breeze stirring the treetops sounded very like patient, watchful breathing . . .

Deliberately Josse stopped, stood up very straight and, with his hand resting on the hilt of his sword, said aloud, 'I am not afraid.'

It helped. A little.

He made himself take in the details of the woodland all around him.

Oak, birch and beech. Ivy and lichen-covered trees, some of them huge with age. Yes. The forest was ancient, had been old even when the Romans came. It had been the haunt of mysterious men and women who understood the trees, worked with Nature, worshipped Her, sacrificed to Her. Went out under the moon to gather the mistletoe with golden sickles and perform rituals in Her honour.

Some said they were still there, the secret people from the far past. Still living deep in those vast tracts of impenetrable woodland, still emerging, briefly, to do terrible violence and then withdraw once more into their leafy strongholds . . .

Determined not to let his renewed fear overcome him, Josse's hand crept to his pack, sought for and clasped his talisman. The cross fitted into his palm, and, as his fingers closed around it, he detected a loop at its head, made of the same metal.

Stopping, he unfastened it from the pack.

Pulling out from under his tunic the length of leather cord on which he wore the crucifix given to him at baptism, he untied the cord and slung the Abbess's larger cross beside it.

Proceeding once more, holding the Abbess's cross in his hand, suddenly he felt a good deal braver.

He could tell by the stars that he was going almost due west; there were regular clearings amid the trees, wide enough for him to see quite large areas of the sky and locate the Plough and the Pole Star. Having worked out which way was north, the rest was easy.

He would be in trouble if, when he was deep in the forest, the sky clouded over. If that happened, he'd be there till morning.

Not a pleasant thought.

After about a mile of fairly easy going, he came to a wide track. Relatively wide, at any rate; the paths he had followed until then had been mere deer or badger tracks. Or perhaps boar; he had noticed the marks of scrabbling feet on the banks either side of some of the better-defined paths that were typical of wild boar. Now, the track was wide enough for two to walk abreast.

He walked along it for possibly half a mile, whereupon it branched. Left or right? He hesitated, unsure. He became aware of an urging voice in his mind: go right!

Well, he had to do something.

He set off along the right-hand track.

And, soon afterwards, came across a length of plaited braid. Tripped over it, in fact.

He picked it up. Unless he was very much mistaken, it was part of a snare. Dropped by Hamm, or one of his poacher friends?

Thoughtfully Josse wound it up and tucked it into his pack.

A little further on, he saw ahead of him a patch of bright moonlight, startling in the dim forest. Approaching, he realised what had happened: a great oak had fallen, right across the path, and its falling had left a hole in the leaf canopy above.

Josse went into the patch of light. Not one tree but two lay on the ground. One seemed to have fallen from some natural cause; its roots, torn up out of the earth, soared above Josse's head in a great semicircle, leaving a deep hole where they had been. There was water at the bottom of the hole.

The other tree, slightly smaller than its fellow, had been felled by the action of man. Not very expertly felled, at that; the furrowed trunk had been savagely hacked at in several places before the main cut had been made that had brought the tree crashing to the ground.

Why had it been felled?

Josse edged forwards, peering down into the hole beneath the bigger tree. There was a gap, a sort of earthy cave, opening off the side of the hole . . . Taking a firm handhold on one of the oak's thick roots, and swinging the Abbess's cross over his shoulder and out of the way, Josse climbed down.

What had looked like a cave was in fact the mouth of a tunnel. Not a very long one, but it must have led straight under the tree that someone had cut down.

With the tree lying on the ground, the next task had apparently been to dig out its roots. Someone had been doing that, too. Further along, the tunnel was open to the night sky.

Scrambling out again, standing up and brush-

ing earth off his knees, Josse thought he had probably found Hamm Robinson's treasure trove.
And, also, the secret of the Forest People, which
they had killed to keep.

He had been going to delve down into the
tunnel, to see if Hamm had been disturbed before
he had cleared everything out of it. But, suddenly,
that didn't seem like a very good idea. Apart from
anything else, he would need to make a light.
And a light, even a small one, could attract attention that he wouldn't welcome.

Especially not when, for all that he was trying
to master it, he kept having the distinct and
highly disturbing feeling that eyes were upon
him . . .

Looking round for his pack, he picked it up and
hurried away from the clearing and the fallen
trees. Then, trying not to break into a run, he set
out on the track that led back to the outside
world.

For what remained of the night, he slept in a
corner of the monks' shelter down in the vale.
There was a family of pilgrims also putting up
there, comprising a couple, an elderly man and a

child with a withered limb, all of whom were taking the holy water and attending the monks' services in the shrine, praying for a miracle.

Josse, knowing that they would be there, was careful not to disturb them.

Settling himself as quickly and as quietly as he could, he made himself put aside images of the deep, mysterious forest and whatever secrets it held. His breathing growing steady and even, very soon he was asleep.

Brother Saul brought him bread and water for his breakfast. The family of pilgrims had gone; with a smile, Brother Saul informed Josse that it was mid-morning.

Josse hurried to wash, dress and head up to the Abbey. He had news for the Abbess, and she might well be eager to hear how his venture had gone.

Going up towards the rear gate that led into the Abbey from the vale, he saw a figure hurrying along in front of him, coming round from the other side of the Abbey. A woman, young, not wearing the habit of a nun. Increasing his pace, he noticed with some surprise that she was not actually running. She was dancing.

And, as he heard when he was within earshot, she was also singing.

'. . . and the sweet birds do sing,' came her voice, light, happy, holding the notes purely.

She became aware of someone behind her. Surprising Josse again, she said, without turning, 'You should be gone! And don't you go trying to make me jump, now, you—'

At that instant she looked over her shoulder, saw Josse, and instantly ceased what she was saying. 'Good morning, sir.' She lowered her eyes, and, in a flash, her tone had altered. From being lush, warmly affectionate, now it was merely courteous.

'Good morning,' Josse replied. And just who, he wondered, did she think I was? 'You're bound for the Abbey?'

She gave him a mischievous smile. 'Now, where else would I be going? Why, we're almost at the gate!'

He smiled back. It was hard not to. 'You must be Esyllt,' he guessed.

'Indeed. And you, I imagine, are Sir Josse d'Acquin.'

'Aye.' He was just working out how he could phrase a question that might elicit from her where she had been when she pre-empted him.

'Staying with the monks in the vale, are you, sir? I hear tell they offer a tasty breakfast.'

'Well, I—' No. She was teasing! 'Indeed,' he said instead. 'Juicy beef fresh-carved and dripping gravy, the softest of bread, the finest of French wine.'

She threw back her head and laughed. 'Now why didn't I think to join you?' she said. 'Me, I made do with the weak porridge we give the old folks. No teeth, you see.' She bared her own, which were strong, white and even.

'It appears to be doing you good,' he observed.

She laughed again. 'Ah, it's full of nourishment, really.' She looked serious suddenly, as if she could only joke for so long about her charges. 'We do look after them, you know, sir. It's not just a matter of putting them in a corner and waiting till they die.'

'I didn't for one moment think it was,' he said gently. 'And I am reliably informed, Esyllt, that you are highly regarded in your work.'

'Are you?' She looked delighted. 'Thank

you, sir. I'm right glad to hear it.'

They were through the gate now, and she turned off to the right, towards the aged monks' and nuns' home. He went with her.

'Are you coming to see my old dearies?' she asked.

'I – no, Esyllt, not at the moment. I have to see the Abbess.'

She actually looked disappointed, as if it had mattered to her that he go with her, that she had procured a visitor to brighten up her old dears' morning. 'Oh.'

'I *will* come,' he said. 'I promise.'

She smiled again. 'I'll hold you to that,' she murmured.

And, heading off for the door of her old people's home, she left him standing on the path.

Wondering why, when her words had been so innocent, he was feeling as if a very lovely and seductive woman had just made him a not very well-veiled proposition.

Abbess Helewise had been expecting Josse for some time when he finally knocked on her door. Impatient to know what, if anything, he had discovered, she had managed to resist the temptation to send for him. For one thing, it was hardly the thing, to *send* for a man of Josse d'Acquin's standing. For another, if he had been up for much of the night, then he had earned his rest.

'Come in,' she said in reply to his tapping.

She watched him move into the room. He looked much as usual, which was a relief. 'Good morning, Sir Josse,' she said.

'Good morning, Abbess.' He smiled, pulled up the stool and sat down. Without preamble, he said, 'There *is* something in the forest. A pit, where a great oak has fallen, and signs that someone – maybe more than one person – has been excavating there.'

'Ah! And you think that Hamm Robinson discovered it, whatever was hidden there?'

He shrugged. 'I can't say, not for certain. Although poachers had been active nearby, and we know Hamm and his friends were poachers. But, Abbess, it seems something of a coincidence otherwise, wouldn't you say?'

'Indeed I would.' She frowned as a sudden thought occurred to her. 'Sir Josse, did you see – I mean, was there any sign of the Forest

People? What I'm trying to say is—'

'Was I scared?' he finished for her, with a grin. 'Abbess dear, I was terrified. At one point, I had quite convinced myself I was being watched, and I ran out of that strange grove as if all the demons in hell were at my heels.' His smile widened. 'Of course, it was all in my imagination.'

'Of course,' she echoed faintly.

He was reaching inside his tunic. 'I forgot – thank you for my talisman.' He pulled at a length of leather cord fastened around his neck, threading it through his fingers until he found what he was looking for. 'It was a thoughtful gift, Abbess. As you see, I took it from my pack and put it round my neck – it helped, to have it close by.'

She gazed at the small object he was holding out to her. 'But I didn't give you that!'

'What? But it's a cross, and I thought that . . .' He was holding it about a foot in front of his face, focusing on it. 'It's not a cross,' he said tonelessly. 'It looks more like a sword.'

She leaned forward to have a better look. 'May I?'

He lifted the thong over his head and handed it

to her. As well as the sword, there was a small gold crucifix on it. She held the sword in her right hand, staring at it. It was about the length of her palm, made of metal, exquisitely worked with a decoration of vivaciously swirling patterns all over the blade. Where the blade met the narrow hilt, there was a tiny head, bearing an expression of distinct ferocity.

'What is it?' For some reason, he spoke in a whisper.

'It is, I think, an amulet. It's not a real knife – too small. And the blade is dull. I imagine it is a protection against evil, to be worn when one is going into danger.'

'I've never seen anything like it before,' he said.

'It resembles the workmanship of old,' Helewise murmured. 'My father possessed an ancient brooch which he found in a stream-bed, and it was decorated with the same swirls and circles as this.' She was absently tracing the biggest swirl as she spoke; it was odd, but, as she reached its heart, she seemed to feel a slight tremor go through her. There and gone in an instant, but it had felt . . . Stop it, she ordered herself. This is no time for fancies!

'If you didn't give it to me,' Josse said slowly, 'then who did?'

She had been wondering that, too. 'Someone who knew you were going into the forest. Someone, moreover, who wanted you to be protected.'

She met his eyes. It was at the same time a thrilling concept and a faintly alarming one.

'Abbess, I shall have to go back,' he said. 'What I discovered last night is only the beginning. I have to see if there is anything still buried, and, although I fear to say so, I must seek out the Forest People.'

'No!' The denial was instinctive. 'Sir Josse, they have already killed to keep their secret! If they find you digging under some fallen tree, they might—' But what they might do was unthinkable.

'I don't believe they would harm me,' he said gently. 'For one thing, it will be me seeking them, not the other way round. And, for another—'

'You intend to go back into the forest, stand in that clearing and shout, here I am, forest folk! Come and find me!' she said incredulously. 'Come and *kill* me!' Absurdly, she felt a sob rise in her throat. Swiftly she controlled it.

He was looking at her in faint surprise. 'Abbess!' he said softly. But whatever he had been about to say, he must have changed his mind. Shaking his head, he muttered something.

'What was that?' she asked, with some asperity.

'Nothing.' His eyes met hers. 'Abbess Helewise, please believe me, if I felt there was peril in this venture, I would not be contemplating it.

'Oh, wouldn't you!'

He pretended not to hear that. 'I am quite sure that, if I make an open approach and appeal to these people's sense of honour, they'll respond. Perhaps it'll be a question of my assuring them that we'll do our best to stop people like Hamm Robinson meddling in their affairs, perhaps then they'll—'

But whatever nonsensical thing he had been going to go on to say, Helewise didn't hear it. At that moment, after a perfunctory knock at the door, Sister Euphemia burst in.

'Abbess, Sir Josse,' she panted, red in the face, 'forgive my interruption, but it's Sister Caliste. She's disappeared!'

Chapter Eight

Sister Caliste had, it transpired, been missing for some time.

They established this fact, over the course of the next hour, by working out who had seen her last. She had been present at Tierce, that was quite certain; a lot of the nuns remembered that. She had then gone about her morning's work in the infirmary, including a visit to Sister Tiphaine for some white horehound; Sister Euphemia needed to make more syrup for an elderly woman suffering from chest pains and a racking cough.

'I *know* she came back here with the herbs,' Sister Beata said, clearly suppressing tears of distress. 'I remember telling her to take them straight to Sister Euphemia, who was anxious to have them and who really had better things to do than twiddle her thumbs waiting for some novice to get a move on!' The threatened tears spilled down Sister Beata's cheeks. 'Oh, do you think I upset her? Do you think I made her run off?'

'Not for a moment.' Helewise briefly touched Sister Beata's hand. 'If you did issue a reprimand, then I'm perfectly certain it can have been but a mild one.' She gave the worried nun an encouraging smile. 'You are not capable of unkindness, Sister.'

Sister Beata looked a little more cheerful. Then, her face falling again, 'But Sister Caliste is still missing. Whoever's fault it was.'

'Quite,' Helewise agreed. 'However, Sir Josse and I are questioning everyone, and we'll soon know where she's gone.'

She gave Sister Beata an encouraging smile; whether its chief aim was in fact to encourage the sister or herself, she didn't stop to think.

Helewise searched out the remaining sisters who could possibly have useful information. There was, for instance, little point in talking to the Madeleine nuns who lived in the Virgin Sisters' House, since they hardly ever left it, nor to the sisters who devotedly, and in total isolation, cared for the lepers. But, these nuns apart, she consulted all the rest. Nobody had anything useful to tell her on the subject of Sister Caliste.

The afternoon was well advanced by the time she had finished. Josse, in the meantime, had been down in the vale, and had even, so she had been told, gone riding off after some pilgrim family who had left that morning, just in case they could shed light on Caliste's disappearance.

He returned looking dejected; there was no need to ask if he had met with success.

The two of them were discussing what they should do next when, again, Sister Euphemia came in search of them.

This time, she looked not so much disturbed but annoyed. 'Abbess Helewise,' she said, her face tight, 'would you please come with me? One of my patients' – she almost spat out the word – 'has something to tell you. And for the life of me I can't think why she didn't speak up earlier,' she added in a mutter as she led the way over to the infirmary, 'truly I can't!'

She marched through the door and along the length of the room, stopping at the foot of the cot occupied by the old woman with the cough.

'Hilde!' she said, in a loud voice. 'I have brought Abbess Helewise and Sir Josse d'Acquin.' If she had hoped to cower the old woman by announcing Helewise and Josse so loudly and grandly, then, Helewise observed, Euphemia was in for a disappointment.

'Oh, aye?' Hilde said hoarsely. 'Nice, it is, to have visitors! Good day, lady! Good day, Sir Knight!'

Sister Euphemia was shaking her head in annoyance. 'Never mind all that! Hilde, kindly tell the Abbess here what you just told me! Right now, if you please!'

The three of them waited while Hilde shifted first to the left, then to the right, punched the straw-filled pillow a couple of times, coughed, then settled herself comfortably. Clearly, she was intending to make the most of the brief attention. 'Well,' she began slowly, 'I heard you're looking for that sister, the pretty blue-eyed one with the white novice's veil?'

'*Yes!*' Sister Euphemia said crossly. 'Do get on with it!'

'Didn't ought to be a nun, that one,' Hilde

said. 'Too pretty, like I says. Ought to be warming some fellow's bed at night, eh, Sir Knight?' She shot a look at Josse and cackled with laughter, which brought on a violent fit of coughing.

Sister Euphemia, at once the caring nurse, sat down beside her, supporting the thin shoulders while Hilde coughed and choked. Then, when the fit began to subside, she gave her first some sips of water, and then a measure of some light-coloured syrup from a stoppered glass bottle.

'Aaagh,' Hilde said, lying back again, 'I reckon I'm not long for this world!' Having closed both eyes, she opened one again, just a slit, to take stock of how her performance was being received.

'Do you think you could stay with us long enough to impart this vital information?' Helewise said gently, smiling down at the old woman.

Hilde opened her eyes again. Grinning a gap-toothed smile in reply to Helewise's, she said, 'Aye, Abbess. Reckon I could.' Abandoning her delaying tactics, she said, with admirable brevity, 'If you want to know where Sister Caliste's gone,

I can tell you. She's gone into the forest.'

'Into the *forest*?' Helewise and Josse spoke together, with the same surprise. Although, Helewise thought, I don't know why I, at least, should be surprised. Not after I witnessed the girl emitting that weird humming. As if she were calling out to the great tract of woodland.

Or – which was even more unnerving – answering its summons to her.

'What did Sister Caliste say, exactly?' Josse was asking Hilde.

'She said she weren't going far,' Hilde said, which was reassuring. 'Said something about the other sister what was in there.'

'Another sister?' Helewise queried. 'Are you quite sure, Hilde?' She could think of no other nun who had ever expressed the least interest in entering the forest; quite the contrary, she often felt they were too in awe of it, too reluctant even to let the shade of its trees fall upon them. Superstition! Ignorant, stubborn superstition, that was what it was, and it ought to have no place in the minds of women who had given themselves into God's holy care! In Helewise's opinion, such sentiments demonstrated a distinct lack of faith in the

Heavenly Father's protective powers.

But: 'I'm quite sure, Abbess Helewise,' Hilde was saying firmly. 'Like I says, I didn't really catch the full story, but I heard the young 'un say that about the other sister.'

'Could it have been Sister Tiphaine?' Josse muttered to Helewise. 'Gone in to pick mushrooms, or fly agaric, or belladonna?'

'It's possible,' Helewise agreed. 'After all, Sister Beata did say that Caliste had been sent to Sister Tiphaine for supplies. Perhaps Caliste thought Sister Tiphaine would be in the forest.' She frowned. 'But it makes no sense! Even if that had been so, Sister Caliste wouldn't have known, surely, that Sister Tiphaine was in the woods? And, even more to the point, Sister Caliste would have been back by now!'

Josse put a hand briefly on the back of Helewise's. A swift light touch, but, she found, reassuring. 'Don't worry,' he said. 'Now that we've been given a clue as to where she was going,' he glanced down at Hilde and grinned, 'I can go after her. I'll find her, Abbess.'

Helewise and Hilde watched as he strode off down the length of the infirmary, heavy boots making a dull thump, spurs ringing out melodiously.

'Aaah,' said Hilde. 'Fine fellow that, eh, Abbess?'

'He is an honourable and courageous man,' Helewise replied somewhat stiffly.

'Wish I were a dozen years younger,' the old woman sighed. 'Well, twenty years, mebbe.' She sighed again. 'What I wouldn't have got up to with a man like that! Abbess, don't you—'

Whatever Hilde was about to say, Helewise decided it was probably better not to hear it. 'Thank you, Hilde,' she interrupted, 'you've been most helpful. Now, if you will excuse me, I have things to see to.'

'Off you go, Abbess.'

Helewise couldn't help but notice that, as she turned to go, the old woman gave her an exaggerated and very suggestive wink.

As Josse made his way back into the forest, along the same tracks and paths he had taken the previous night, he had a sudden thought. As he played with it, mentally trying it out, his conviction grew until he was tempted to return to the

Abbey and discuss it with the Abbess.

He came to a stop, thinking hard.

Hilde had said that Caliste was going into the forest after another sister. But supposing the old woman hadn't really heard properly? Had jumped to conclusions – which would have been understandable – and only *thought* that Caliste had meant another nun?

Perhaps what Caliste had really said was that one of the *others* had gone ahead into the forest, and Hilde, on the basis that the others were all nuns, had translated the remark and understood it as 'one of the sisters'?

I know one of the Hawkenlye community who goes into the forest, Josse thought. At least, I think that's where she'd been, when I met her on her way back to the Abbey. This very morning.

Had Esyllt returned there now? Was it she whom Caliste had followed?

There was only one way to find out. Deciding that there was little point in dashing back to talk it over with Abbess Helewise, instead Josse hurried on into the forest.

He realised quite soon that he was lost.

He had imagined it would be far easier finding his way in late afternoon than it had been by the moonlight of last night. But, unfortunately, a thick bank of cloud had come up from the west, so that, deep within the trees with no sun to guide him, he had no way of getting his bearings. And, as he was quickly discovering, one path looked much like another. One stand of ancient oaks was indistinguishable from the next.

It began to rain.

With no clear idea which way would lead him further into the forest and which would take him back to the world outside, he crawled into the shelter of a yew tree, pressed his back against its trunk and waited for the rain to stop and the skies to clear.

He sat under his yew tree for a long time. Its dense foliage kept out most of the rain, but sitting still meant that he grew cold. After what seemed like hours, he realised that it had become quite dark.

And that the rain had, at long last, ceased.

He stepped out from under his tree, feeling a sudden and inexplicable urge to thank it for its protection. Going back and putting a hand to the trunk, he actually found himself framing the words.

Fool! he thought, hurrying away. It's only a tree! It can't *hear*.

Back on the track, he followed it until he came to a clearing. Staring up, he saw a sight that released in him a flood of relief: a perfectly cloudless sky. The moon was full, and riding high, giving nearly as much light as day, and, over to the north, he could make out the Plough and the Pointers.

Now that he knew which way led out of the forest, he felt less inclined to take it. He hadn't actually achieved anything yet; all he had done was to get himself lost and shelter from the rain beneath a tree. He had found neither Esyllt, Sister Caliste, nor any sign of either of them.

Working out which direction he had taken the previous night, making a mental map of the forest, he stepped out under the brilliant full moon and headed on into the heart of the woods. He was still wearing the talisman, on his leather thong; he reached inside his tunic and, drawing it out, clutched on to it.

*

Nobody had told Josse that Hamm Robinson had been killed on a full moon night. Exactly one lunar month ago, Hamm had trespassed into the Great Forest, and somebody had spitted him with a spear.

Perhaps it was as well, for Josse's peace of mind, that he didn't know it.

More by luck than judgement, Josse found himself back at the grove with the fallen trees. In the midst of congratulating himself on his skill, he was suddenly overcome by an urge as strong, if not stronger, than the strange emotion he had felt underneath the yew tree. Not understanding, and with the sense that he was outside himself, a witness to his own actions, he stepped slowly across to the larger of the trees. Putting out his hands, he held them palm-downwards above the great trunk.

At first he felt nothing. Then, right in the middle of each palm, he began to feel a tingling. It grew swiftly in strength until it was almost burning him, only just tolerable. And, at the same time, he was hit with a devastating sadness, a mourning, almost, for the vast dying thing that lay at his feet.

Moving across to the smaller oak, he repeated the action. This time, as well as sorrow, there was anger.

Someone had killed this tree, deliberately.

And the forest was furious.

Josse felt that fury. Standing there, a profound, deep dread upon him, he began to shake with fear.

Summoning his courage, he stepped away from the fallen trees. Squaring his shoulders, standing up straight, he said softly, ' "Yea, though I walk through the valley of the shadow of death, I will fear no evil, for Thou art with me, Thy rod and Thy staff do comfort me . . ." '

He trailed off. No, it was not evil that he feared. He stood in awe of some vast natural power, but it was not an evil force. He was sure of that.

Comforted by the familiar words of the psalm, he took some deep breaths, then set out to explore the far side of the clearing.

Beyond the spot where, according to Josse's theory, Hamm Robinson, Seth and Ewen had been digging for treasure, there seemed to be another disturbance in the forest floor. Josse hadn't noticed it the previous night, but now, staring at it, he began to wonder. If he'd been right about the treasure being Roman in origin, then might that not suggest there were other relics of the Romans in this area of the forest?

He made his way carefully to the edge of the clearing. There were stones there, ancient, worked slabs of stone, forming the rough shape of a right-angle . . . The remains of two walls of a building?

Pushing his way into the undergrowth, Josse followed the line of the better-preserved of the walls. And came to a gap, spanned by a flat slab. A doorway?

Stepping back to have a better look, he tripped over something. Feeling with his hands, he found a circular stone, broken off at an angle.

Hurrying now, he searched first to the right, then to the left. And quickly found five more round stones.

They were, he was certain, column bases. Which, from what little he knew about Roman buildings, strongly suggested that this edifice had been a temple.

He circled the walls, finding the remains of a stone floor, and, leading away from the entrance, a paved road, badly broken up, overgrown, all but gone.

But it was evidence enough. The Romans – or someone – had built a temple here, deep in the forest. They had mined here, that Josse knew already, built their roads here. Now, if he were right, it must be concluded that they had also buried something very valuable out here.

We must come back here with a proper working party, Josse thought, bring ropes and—

He heard voices.

Muttering voices, speaking quietly as if anxious not to be heard.

Very close at hand.

Moving as silently as he could, Josse hurried back into his temple. Crouching down behind the ruined wall, he pulled down a branch of hazel to cover his head and peered out into the clearing.

Two men were approaching the fallen trees, carrying what looked like a spade and a sack. They were still muttering, and Josse thought he could detect fear in the higher pitched of the voices.

'. . . still ain't happy, all the same, not after you-know-what,' one was saying.

'Shut up and dig,' said the other.

And Ewen and Seth clambered down into the hole under the trees and began to shovel out earth.

Josse watched them for some time. Periodically one or other would emerge, put something in the sack, then disappear into the ground again.

When the noise came, it scared Josse as much as it did Seth and Ewen.

It was a humming sound, rather lovely at first. Sweet, like singing. Or chanting, perhaps.

But then, as if the strange music had slid into a scale that no human ever used, it began to chill the very soul. As it grew louder, making the night air vibrate with its sound waves, Josse, crouched down behind his walls, trying to make himself small. Trying to make himself invisible. For, illogical though it was, he was assailed by the fear that there were people out there, watching him from their hiding places, deep-set eyes penetrating the shadows, lighting on him, *knowing* him . . .

He felt a moment's pity for Seth and Ewen, out there in the middle of the clearing, exposed and vulnerable. Ewen had his hands over his ears, Seth, clutching the half-full sack to his chest, was trying to look challenging, but succeeding only in looking afraid.

'Oo's there?' Seth shouted. His words made no echo: their sound was instantly cut off, as if someone had closed a mighty door.

'I'm off!' Ewen sobbed, running and stumbling out of the clearing. Seth began to go after him, but just at that moment the humming stopped.

Seth stood quite still, looking all around him as if suspecting a trap.

But there was no further sound.

He climbed back into the ground, coming up again, grunting with effort, bearing some large object in his hands. Stuffing it into the sack – with some difficulty – he had a last look around the clearing, then, slinging the bulging sack over one shoulder and picking up his spade in the other hand, set off after Ewen.

Josse gave him a few minutes' start, then, coming out from his hiding place, moved stealthily back into the clearing. Staring first down the path which the men had taken, then around the circumference of the encircling trees, he began to suspect his eyes were playing tricks.

Either that, or—

No. The alternative didn't bear thinking about.

What Josse *thought* he saw was a figure.

Human, and, by its slenderness, female. Robed in white, a little stooped. And, in her hand, a long wand.

But it must have been his eyes, seeing imaginary sights. Because, when he rubbed them hard and looked again, she was no longer there.

Josse clutched at his talisman. He felt the point of the sword press into his hand, and the small sharp pain brought him back to himself.

It was just the effect of the forest, he told himself, of the watchful, silent trees, of the ancient workings, the ruined buildings and edifices of a long-gone people. And that humming – that dire, haunting humming – was probably no more than some weird effect of the wind in the branches.

But the night was still and calm.

There wasn't any wind.

He tried to stay calm. Telling himself that he was making a rational decision, that the dark, swooping waves of alien power he could sense emanating from the dense wood all around him had nothing whatever to do with it, he concluded that there really was no purpose in staying out any longer. That, for all the good he was doing, he might as well head back to the Abbey. He was on the point of doing just that when another, very different, sound seared through the forest.

It wasn't humming, this time. It didn't even begin as a sweet sound, and there was no suggestion in it whatsoever of music, of singing.

It was a scream.

A human scream, beginning faintly, swiftly escalating to a high-toned, vibrant pitch of sheer terror.

It ended, abruptly, in a sort of groan.

Then, as the echoes died away, the utter silence of the brooding forest closed in once more.

And Josse, at last losing what little remained of his self-control, heedless of the brambles and the tangling undergrowth that tried to hold him back, raced out of the clearing and off down the path that led to the outside world.

PART TWO

DEATH IN THE FOREST

Chapter Nine

Josse returned to the Abbey to find, for all that it was after midnight, the community still awake, with torches blazing in the courtyard and lighting the shadows of the cloisters.

After the frightening darkness deep within the trees, it was a blessed relief.

He found the Abbess in her room, with the door open; it was, he thought briefly as the impression hit him, as if, in that night of anxiety and disturbance, she wanted her nuns to feel that she was close by. Accessible.

She got up as he came into the room.

'Abbess, I haven't found her,' he began, 'but I think—'

At the same moment, she said, her face full of joy, 'She's here! Sister Caliste has come back, and she is quite safe! Quite unharmed!'

'Thank God,' he said quietly.

'Amen,' the Abbess echoed, then hurried on, 'Sir Josse, would you credit it! She's dreadfully sorry to have caused us all this worry and trouble, she says, but she went for a little walk under the trees and *forgot the time*! Dear me, did you ever hear such a silly idea?'

'She forgot the time,' Josse repeated. He didn't want to admit it to the Abbess, but, knowing the forest now rather better than she did, in fact he could see all too clearly how such a thing could happen. 'Where is she?' he asked, turning his thoughts with an effort away from the mystical spell of the forest and on to more urgent matters. 'You say she is not hurt, but has she taken a chill?'

'She's fine.' Abbess Helewise's relief was evident in her wide smile. 'She is on her knees in the Abbey church. She is full of remorse, as I said, and praying for God's forgiveness for having upset all her sisters so badly.'

Sisters. That reminded him. 'Abbess, this may sound a strange question, but do you know where Esyllt is?'

'*Esyllt?*' Clearly, it did sound a strange question. 'She sleeps in a little dormitory in the aged monks' and nuns' home,' the Abbess said, frowning. 'Often they need attention during the night, you see. I'm quite sure that's where she is.' Eyes turning to Josse, she demanded, 'Why?'

'Could you send someone to check?' he urged. 'Abbess, I wouldn't ask if it were not important!'

She seemed to recover herself. 'No, of course you wouldn't. Wait here, I'll go myself.'

He waited. Sank down on the wooden stool, leaned back against the wall and closed his eyes.

A little later, she came back. One look at her face told him he'd been right.

'Not there?' he asked.

'Not there.' The frown was back, deeper than before. 'Do you know where she is, Sir Josse?'

'Where she is now? No, not exactly. But I have an idea where she went earlier.' Briefly he outlined to the Abbess the idea he'd had when he was setting off into the forest.

The Abbess was nodding slowly. 'It seems you were right,' she said. 'But why? Why should Esyllt make secret visits into the forest? And at night!'

'They would have to be at night, if they were to be secret,' he pointed out. And, even though she'd gone at night, she hadn't managed to keep it secret from him; he'd seen her returning, yesterday morning.

'Quite, quite,' Helewise was saying impatiently. 'But for what purpose? And why should Sister Caliste know about it, whatever it was, and be prompted to follow her?'

'Abbess, there's something else,' Josse said. 'Something which, unless I'm very much mistaken, is more dreadful than a young woman going off into the forest at night.'

A sudden terrible thought struck him. Caliste was safely back within the Abbey walls, but Esyllt wasn't.

Oh, God, what if that appalling, long drawn-out scream of agony had been hers?

What if it was she who now lay insensate in the forest, hidden in some place off the main track?

'What? Josse, *what*?' The Abbess was shaking him. 'Tell me! Dear God, but you've gone ashen!'

He stood up. 'Abbess, when I was still deep in the forest, I heard a dreadful cry. I'm very much afraid that the killer has struck again. And that—'

'Esyllt!' Now she, too, was ashen. 'Oh, no! Oh, sweet Jesus, no! Not—'

'There were others abroad!' he said, grabbing her by her hands. 'I fear there's no doubt but that there's been another attack, but, Abbess, it is by no means certain that the victim must be Esyllt!'

She was staring at him wide-eyed. 'We must go and look!' she cried. 'Whoever the victim is, we must search for them. Now! All of us!'

And, before he could even try to stop her, she had rushed out of the room, skirts of her habit flying, calling out to her senior nuns. Very soon afterwards, she had made her arrangements; efficient even in such a frightful crisis, she had organised and dispatched the search parties more quickly than Josse would have thought possible.

He waited for her to come back and tell him what she wanted of him, and at last she returned to her room. Wiping sweat from her brow – the night was close – she said, 'Sir Josse, will you come out and search with me?'

Making her a bow, he said, 'Gladly I will.'

*

Marching off into the forest, Abbess Helewise was more glad than she would have admitted to have Josse's steady tread at her side. And she had made sure that Sister Euphemia, Sister Basilia and Sister Martha also had strong men with them in their search parties; moreover, every man of them armed with stout staves. Few of the lay brothers, she reflected, would have much sleep this night.

The darkness under the trees was more profound than she had expected. But then, the night was wearing on, and the moon no longer so high in the sky. Full moon, she mused. Full moon again, and now a second murder.

To take her mind off her fears over who the victim was, she said to Josse, 'Sir Josse, do you realise that—'

But she never asked her question. For at that moment, flying towards them with her skirts raised high around her bare thighs, blood on her outstretched hands, on her chin and on her gown, hair awry and face as pale as death, came Esyllt.

Seeing them, she screamed, 'He's dead! And there's so much *blood*!'

Then she rushed into Helewise's arms.

In the first few seconds, Helewise could do nothing but hold the girl tightly against her breast, cradling her, quieting the harsh sound of her sobbing.

'Hush, child,' she murmured, dropping a kiss on the wild hair, 'you're safe now. We won't let any harm come to you.'

Esyllt pulled away from her, craning round to look back over her shoulder down the path along which she had just come.

'He's in there,' she said, with a shudder. 'Way back there. Lying deep in the underbrush, and he's dead, I'm sure he's dead, he *must* be dead!' She was rapidly losing control again.

Josse said gently, 'Who is dead, Esyllt?'

She spun round to look at him, staring at him wide-eyed as if she did not recognise him. But then a shadow of her usual smile touched her lips. 'Sir Knight,' she said. 'Are you going to come and see my old dearies?'

'Soon,' Josse said. 'I promise.'

She nodded. 'Good. They'll like that.' Then, as if awareness of her present distress, momentarily put aside, had come flooding back, her face crumpled and she whispered something.

'What was that?' Helewise asked, rather too sharply.

Esyllt shook her head, tears flowing down her face. 'Nothing,' she muttered.

'Esyllt,' Helewise persisted, 'something terrible has happened, and, for the moment, our Christian duty is to find this poor man who has been attacked and do what we can for him.'

'You can't do anything, he's *dead*, I keep telling you, dead, dead!' Esyllt moaned. A great shiver went through her, and her sobbing began again. 'And, oh, God, it's so awful! I – he – you see, we . . .'

'Then we must take him back to the Abbey for decent burial,' Helewise replied implacably, cutting off whatever Esyllt had been trying to say. 'Then – and only then – will we set about trying to discover what lies behind all this.' She gave the girl a gentle shake. 'Do you understand, Esyllt? You are in no condition to be questioned now, but we will be doing so when you have recovered yourself.'

Helewise wondered if Josse would realise what she was trying to do. Wondered, too, if he had noticed what Helewise had seen, when Esyllt had first rushed out of the trees towards them. No, she told herself. Don't think about that now. Time enough to get to the bottom of that later, when they were safely back inside the Abbey walls.

By speaking firmly to the girl – in effect, shutting her up – the Abbess was hoping to make sure that, in her shock and confusion, Esyllt didn't blurt out something she would later regret.

There was always the danger that, if she spoke up now, she might somehow incriminate herself. And the one thing Helewise was quite sure about was that, whatever else she might have done, Esyllt was no murderer.

Josse must have been sure, too. For he said, 'No, Esyllt, no more questions for now. We shall call out and attract the attention of one of the other search parties. Then you will be taken back to the Abbey, where they will look after you. Just tell me where to find the victim, then you can go into the warmth and the light, wash, change your clothes, then sleep until you feel better.'

Esyllt's eyes were fixed on him as he spoke, and, when he had finished, she smiled at him.

'You have a kind heart, Sir Knight,' she said. 'Doesn't he, Abbess Helewise?'

'Indeed,' Helewise agreed.

'May I do that?' Esyllt asked her. She was, it appeared, sufficiently herself to remember that it was Helewise, not Josse, who ordered her actions.

'You may,' Helewise said.

Josse had trotted off down the main track, calling out as he went. Presently he had an answer, and, shortly after that, Brother Saul, Sister Euphemia and the other two lay brothers in their group came into sight.

When they had finished exclaiming and offering up thanks over Esyllt's having been found alive and safe, Sister Euphemia put her arm round the girl and the group set off with her back towards the Abbey.

'Brother Saul?' Josse called after him.

He stopped. 'Sir Josse?'

'We have an unpleasant duty to perform,' Josse said. He shot a look at Helewise, who had a good idea what was coming. 'Esyllt has told us where to find the man who was attacked,' Josse went on, 'and I wonder, Brother Saul, if you would come with me, so that the Abbess can go back to—'

Yes. It was exactly what Helewise had expected. 'Sir Josse,' she interrupted, 'I am leading this expedition, and I shall not return to the Abbey until we have accomplished what we set out to do.' She added, dropping her voice so that Brother Saul would not hear, 'And I'll thank you to remember that it is I, not you, who is in command here!'

He looked suitably reprimanded, and for a brief moment she felt a rich satisfaction. Then she thought, but he was trying to help! Trying to spare me a possibly – no, a definitely – terrible sight. I should not have bitten his head off for that impulse to charity.

'I am sorry,' she whispered.

But Josse was already turning to set off down the path, and she didn't think he had heard.

The moon had set now, and they had to use the flares which had been hastily prepared before the search parties had set out. Even so, it took a long time to find him.

Esyllt had left quite a clear path for them to follow wherever she had pushed her way through undergrowth; there, it was a relatively easy matter to find the broken twigs and branches, the flattened bracken, that marked her flying feet. But, when she had run across clearings, they had to spend many minutes looking for the point at which she had entered the open space.

It was Brother Saul who first spotted him.

'Sir Josse!' he called, his voice strangely uncertain. He, too, thinks to spare me, Helewise thought swiftly, rushing ahead, since he only calls Sir Josse.

She and Josse arrived at the scene together.

And the three of them stared down at the dead man.

He was dead, there could be no doubt – nobody could lose so much blood and still live. Besides, there were savage, deep cuts to his neck and chest, and another that ran right through his left eye. Any one of those cuts could have penetrated to brain, or heart, or lung, bringing inevitable death.

Helewise realised slowly that she was very cold. Her teeth were chattering, and her fingers felt numb. She tucked her hands into her sleeves.

She became aware that Brother Saul had turned

aside and was vomiting into the undergrowth.

She felt Josse's hand touch her arm. Tentatively. Then he said, in a matter-of-fact voice that did a great deal to bring her back into control – and stop her taking the same route as Brother Saul – 'No wonder the girl had so much blood on her. I would think, wouldn't you, Abbess, that she must have knelt down to look at him, and the blood seeped into her skirt?'

Helewise swallowed. 'Er – yes, indeed, Sir Josse. Perhaps, in the darkness, the extent of his wounds was not as apparent as it is now, to us, and she felt compelled to see how badly hurt he was.' Oh, the thought of it! That poor, poor girl, kneeling down, feeling the warm wetness seep into her gown, through to the flesh of her legs! Then putting out her hands to touch him, and coming across those dreadful cuts. 'She – er, she must have known immediately that he was dead.'

'Hmm,' Josse said reflectively. He, too, was kneeling down now, but being more careful than Esyllt and avoiding the worst of the blood-pool. He held the torch just above the body. 'Aaah.'

'You know who he is,' Helewise said. 'Don't you?'

'Aye. His name was Ewen. He was one of Hamm Robinson's poaching and thieving gang.'

'You are sure of that?'

'Aye.' He hesitated, bending to look more closely at the wounds on the chest. Then added, 'I saw him earlier. He and Hamm's cousin had gone back to the place where they were digging up treasure.'

Treasure, Helewise thought vaguely. Men digging for it. Whom Josse must have been watching, at some previous point in this interminable night, when he had been about business of a very different sort.

What was that, now? She wondered why it was suddenly so difficult to remember. Why had Josse gone into the forest?

Caliste. Yes, of course, he'd been looking for Sister Caliste.

Suddenly it all seemed a lot to take in. Helewise felt her head swim, and, stepping back from the corpse and the stink of blood, she leant back against the smooth trunk of a beech tree. She took several deep breaths, then, hopefully before either Josse or Brother Saul had noticed her momentary weakness, she said, 'We must get him back to the Abbey. And, I think, Sir Josse, I must notify Sheriff Pelham that there has been another murder.'

Josse and Brother Saul carried the corpse out of the forest between them. It was not a pleasant task, especially as, with dawn now well advanced, there was sufficient light, even under the trees, to see the dead man all too clearly.

The Abbess, Josse noticed, had not, as she might have done, suggested that she hurry on ahead to notify the sisters at the Abbey of what they must prepare themselves to receive. Instead, she paced along beside the corpse, her rosary beads in her hands, her lips moving in silent prayers.

Ah, but she was a determined woman! Josse thought, partly in admiration, partly in frustration. There had been no need for her to subject herself to this horror, not when he and Saul had been there, ready and willing to go and look for the body on their own!

Still, as she had been at pains to point out, she was in command here. And, like a good commander, she didn't make her troops do anything she wasn't prepared to do herself.

'Stubborn woman,' Josse muttered under his breath.

The Abbess, quietly intoning her prayers, didn't hear. But Brother Saul, walking ahead of Josse and bearing the dead man's feet, turned and gave Josse a very fleeting grin.

They laid him in the crypt, a chilly, stone-walled chamber beneath the Abbey church. Its floor space was broken up by the massive stone pillars that supported the incalculable weight above; it was a dank and gloomy place.

This was not the first time it had housed the recently dead.

In the more adequate light of several torches, Josse confirmed what he had already suspected concerning Ewen's manner of death.

Then, while Sisters Euphemia and Beata went about the ghastly task of preparing the corpse for burial, Josse went up to the Abbess's room to await the arrival of the sheriff.

'Did he have relatives?' Josse asked the Abbess, resuming his seat on the wooden stool.

'Hm?' She turned to him, and briefly he wondered what she had been thinking about that he had just interrupted. 'Relatives? Ewen Asher? I believe . . . He lived alone, I think. He used to board with his widowed mother, if indeed this is that same man. But she died last year. He had no wife and no children, as far as I know.'

'That's as well, now,' Josse remarked.

There was a short reflective silence. Then the Abbess said, 'Was he, too, killed by the Forest People?'

'No,' Josse said instantly.

'How can you be so sure?'

'Because – well, I won't go into that.'

'But—'

He went on, determinedly ignoring her interruption, 'I've been thinking, Abbess, that the most likely killer is Seth, since, on the face of it, he's the only person with anything to gain by Ewen's death.'

'A larger share of whatever it is they've discovered in the forest, you mean.'

'Aye. In fact, with both Hamm and Ewen dead, Seth can have the lot. Only . . .' His brows came together in a fierce frown.

'Only what?'

'Only that's not right, either.'

'What do you mean?'

Josse raised his head. Meeting her eyes, he said, 'Unlikely as it seems, Abbess, there must have been a third party out in the forest last night. Besides the poachers and Esyllt, I mean. Well, in fact a fourth party, if you count me. And, since neither the Forest People, Seth nor I slaughtered Ewen, and we must surely agree that Esyllt didn't either, then we can only conclude that it was this mysterious fourth party who did.'

Chapter Ten

Sheriff Harry Pelham, Helewise observed, had made about as favourable an impression on Josse as he had done on her.

Josse had given the sheriff his seat when the officer had come into the room; on the surface a courteous gesture, but she had realised – as surely Josse had done – that, for the sheriff to squat on a low and insubstantial stool while Josse stood over him, nonchalantly leaning against the wall, put the sheriff at a distinct disadvantage.

'It's those damnable Godless Forest People again, you mark my words,' Harry Pelham was saying, shaking an aggressive, finger at Josse. 'First one murder, then another. And both on the night of the full moon! I ask you, what more proof do you need?'

'Hmm,' Josse said. He glanced at Helewise, and she thought that he, like her, was probably wondering if Sheriff Pelham had noticed the moon himself, or had had the fact of its being full again last night pointed out to him.

Probably, she concluded, the latter.

'You see,' Harry Pelham went on, 'they *do* things, when it's full moon.'

'They do things,' Josse repeated tonelessly. 'What sort of things, Sheriff?'

'Oh, you know. Ceremonies, and that.'

'Ah, I see. You make it so clear, Sheriff.'

Surely, Helewise thought, Harry Pelham must hear the sarcasm?

Apparently not. The sheriff went on, 'They're an old – um – tribe, if you like, see, Sir Josse. Live according to their own laws, live that sort of odd outdoor life when things like the moon are important. And, like I said to the good Sister here this time last month, when what's-his-name was murdered—'

'Hamm Robinson,' Helewise supplied.

'Thank you, Sister.'

'Abbess,' Josse corrected expressionlessly.

Harry Pelham shot him a glance. 'Huh?'

'The Abbess Helewise is in command here,' Josse explained, with what Helewise thought was an admirable lack of anything in his tone that could have been construed as patronising. 'We should do her the courtesy, Sheriff, of addressing her by her proper title.'

'Oh. Ah.' Harry Pelham looked from Helewise to Josse and back again, and, fleetingly, both anger and resentment crossed his face. 'Where was I?' he snapped. 'You've gone and made me lose my thread, Sir Josse.'

'Oh, dear,' Josse said.

'You were speaking of the Forest People,' Helewise said gently, taking pity on the wretched man. 'Explaining to us that they live an outdoor life, which includes elements of nature worship such as an awareness of the moon and its cycles.'

Harry Pelham looked as if he could hardly credit he'd said all that. 'Was I?' Recovering quickly, he went on, 'Aye, well, like I said, they – the forest folk – don't like what they'd probably see as trespassers on their territory. Specially not at full moon. It'd make them angry, would that. Make them take savage action against intruders, likely as not.' He folded his arms, smiling grimly as if to say, there! Case solved!

'I see,' Josse said thoughtfully. 'You maintain, Sheriff, that there are well-documented rites associated with these people's worship of the full moon, which, when observed by outsiders, are so secret that those outsiders must be put to death?'

'Er—' Harry Pelham scratched his head. 'Aye,' he said firmly. 'Aye, I do.'

'What are these rites?' Josse moved closer to the sheriff, bending down and putting his face close to the other man's. 'Can you describe them?'

'I – well, not exactly, I—' The sheriff took some well-needed quiet time in which to think. 'Course, I can't describe them in *detail*,' he said, giving Josse a triumphant grin. 'They're secret.'

'Ah, how perceptive, Sheriff,' Josse said softly.

Harry Pelham was in the act of puffing out his chest with pride when, at long last, Josse's mild sarcasm breached his defences. 'Well, perceptive or not, I've solved your murder for you,' he snapped.

'*My* murder?' Josse echoed faintly.

'It has to be them, those dirty wretches up there.' He jerked his head towards the forest. 'Two dead now, and I reckon I might just go up there and round up the lot of them, hang a few and teach the rest a lesson.'

'I shouldn't do that, if I were you,' Josse said.

'And exactly why not?'

He seemed so confident, Helewise thought, watching him. It was almost a pity, when he was about to be rather firmly demolished.

'Because,' Josse shot her a look, then returned his eyes to the sheriff, 'because, although it's possible the Forest People killed Hamm Robinson – although I've yet to see or hear anything that remotely resembles proof, without which you can hardly hang one man, let alone a whole tribe – I can tell you for certain that the Forest People didn't kill Ewen Asher.'

The sheriff emitted an expletive which Helewise hadn't heard for years. People did not normally employ that sort of language within the walls of a convent. 'You're talking rot!' he went on, getting to his feet and lurching towards Josse. 'How can you be *certain*?' His repetition of the word mocked Josse. 'Just tell me that!'

'Because Ewen was killed with a dagger, and because his killer was both a very different man, and in a very different frame of mind, from whoever slayed Hamm Robinson,' Josse said coolly. 'Hamm's murder was clean and quick, performed with considerable expertise, by someone who was an excellent shot and used to his chosen weapon. The spear tip, I understand, pierced the heart.'

'All right,' the sheriff acknowledged. 'So what?'

'The man who killed Ewen – and I am quite sure it *was* a man, because of the force behind some of the wounds – was in a panic. Possibly he had tried to make it a quick, clean kill, too, but whichever of the cuts he made first wasn't deep enough, and failed to penetrate a vital organ. With Ewen screaming and writhing at his feet, the murderer, perhaps beginning to be overcome with the horror of it all, slashed out again and again, throat, chest, face, until at last, realising the man was quite dead, he stopped.'

The sheriff was staring at Josse, mouth open. 'How can you tell all this?' he said, a sneering tone entering his voice.

'For one thing, by the wounds,' Josse replied. 'And for another—'

'Well?'

Josse glanced across at the Abbess. 'Never mind.'

The sheriff looked as if he was about to press him, but apparently decided against it. 'Well, if it wasn't the Forest People, then it was that poacher. That other fellow who used to go about with Hamm Robinson. His cousin.'

'Seth?' supplied Josse.

'Aye. Seth Miller.'

'I don't believe Seth killed him either,' Josse said. 'Although I admit he had a motive.'

'Well, won't you enlighten us as to why it wasn't Seth?' It was the sheriff's turn to sound sarcastic. 'Not the type of man to panic, perhaps? Arms too weak to make such cuts?'

'I've no idea,' Josse said mildly, not, Helewise noticed, rising to the bait. 'The reason that I doubt Seth was responsible was because he carries a knife, with a fairly short blade. The wounds on the dead man were made by a dagger.'

'Knife or dagger, what's the difference?'

Josse shook his head gently. 'Oh, dear,' he murmured. Then, before the sheriff's anger could come to the boil and erupt, said, 'A knife has one sharp surface and a dagger has two. Seth carries a common-or-garden knife, which he probably uses for everything from gutting rabbits to picking his teeth. The wounds on Ewen Asher show very clearly that they were made by a weapon with two sharp edges. Therefore, the killer is unlikely to be Seth. Unless, of course, you think that Seth was carrying a special dagger last night, purely to kill Ewen with, which is perfectly possible, I grant you. Except that Ewen was killed in a sudden fit of panic, or temper, and for Seth to have armed himself beforehand with this hypothetical dagger would have meant the murder was premeditated.'

Helewise, not at all sure that the sheriff had grasped all of that, suppressed a smile as, sinking down again on to his seat, Harry Pelham muttered, 'Hypothetical dagger. Premeditated. Panic.' After a few moments' thought, however, he rallied.

'I'm going to arrest Seth Miller,' he announced. 'Right now. Whether he planned to murder Ewen or not, I reckon he did it. He can sweat it out in my jail for a while and think about his sins. Then I'm going to ask him a few questions.'

Harry Pelham stood up, took a couple of paces

towards Josse and, snarling at him as if he wished it were to be Josse rather than Ewen he would be interrogating, finished, 'And, God help him, he'd better have some good answers!'

Helewise and Josse listened to the repeated echoes of the slammed door. As the sheriff's furious footsteps faded away, Josse said, 'Pleasant fellow.'

Helewise smiled. 'Indeed. I wouldn't be in the shoes of any of his minions, at least not for the next few hours.'

'Has he a wife?'

'I've no idea. I hope not.'

'The man's a dullard,' Josse pronounced. 'The kind who jumps at the first obvious solution in order to save himself the trouble of seeking out the truth.'

'I fear you are right,' she agreed. 'Or, in this case, the second obvious solution. Which means that he'll probably hang Seth for the murder of Ewen.'

'And, although Seth is a poacher and a thief, and perhaps deserves to hang for those and other crimes, I don't think he killed Ewen,' Josse said slowly.

'You're certain? That talk about the knife and the dagger was true?'

Josse grinned at her. 'You thought I might have produced all those arguments merely to annoy Sheriff Pelham?'

She smiled. 'No, I didn't think that. Although I could have understood it if you had done.'

'No,' Josse said. 'It was true. Those cuts on poor Ewen were without doubt made by a dagger, moreover, a very sharp one. The edges of the slashes were so clean, and I doubt they could have been so had they been made with Seth's knife. Anyone's knife, come to that – it's not practical, is it, Abbess, to carry stuck in your belt something with two such keen edges?'

'No.' She looked at him thoughtfully. 'How do you come to know so much, Sir Josse?' she asked. It was something she had wondered about before. 'Has your life been so wild, that you are well acquainted with death by violence?'

He returned her gaze for some moments without speaking, as if he were thinking back. Then he said, 'I was long a fighting man, Abbess. For better or worse, I did as I was ordered. In that time, I saw many dead men. Although I didn't realise it, I must have been taking in more than I thought.'

'I—' she began.

But he had rested his hands on her table, and, leaning towards her, went on, 'I should not wish you to imagine that I spent my fighting years hanging around the wounded and the dead, poking and prodding at their wounds like some ghoul.'

'I didn't imagine that for one moment!' she protested. 'I comment on it merely because, as in other things, it is proof that you are a man who keeps his eyes open. Who observes, who uses his wits. As, indeed, God intended that all men should.' She sighed. 'Clearly an intention that did not penetrate into Sheriff Harry Pelham's head.'

'Too much thick bone in the way,' Josse said dourly. 'Abbess, how come such a man is sheriff? Who appointed him? And do they not realise that he is a fool?'

'The office of Sheriff of Tonbridge is, I believe, a matter for the Clares,' she replied. 'And – but this is only hearsay, Sir Josse, so please accept it as such – I do hear it muttered that the Clares prefer a malleable man, and, possibly, one without too much mother-wit, in order that the true authority shall remain with them.'

Josse was nodding. 'I see.'

And, although he asked no more questions and made no further comment on the matter, she was quite sure that he did.

She rose to her feet. 'Sir Josse, if you will excuse me, I wish to speak to both Sister Caliste and to Esyllt.' She hesitated, watching him. 'I know that you do, too, but will you allow me to interview them alone, to begin with?'

'Of course!' He looked surprised. 'I hadn't expected anything else, Abbess. Apart from any other considerations,' he added with a grin, 'you're likely to get far more out of them than if I'm there looming behind you.'

Helewise walked off in the direction of the retirement home, leaving Josse to fetch his horse and set out to find out anything more that there was to find about Ewen. He said he would return via the forest, and have a good look in daylight at the scene of the killing.

Helewise composed her thoughts and put

herself in the right frame of mind for questioning Esyllt.

Entering the retirement home, she was impressed, as always, by both the calm, contented atmosphere and by the scent of flowers. It was, in her experience, rare for the elderly to be housed in a place where either of those conditions prevailed, never mind both of them.

But, then, other old people were not lucky enough to be cared for by Sister Emanuel. Who now, observing her superior's quiet entry, came gliding to greet her, making the usual reverence with a simple grace.

'Good morning, Sister Emanuel,' Helewise said softly.

'Good morning, Abbess.' Sister Emanuel's voice was low and mellow, and, even when she was issuing commands or speaking up so that some deaf old soul could hear, she never became strident. It was not so much that she insisted others spoke gently when they entered her domain, more that they automatically adopted Sister Emanuel's own custom because it was considerate and kind. And it made sense.

'Is it a convenient moment for me to speak to

Esyllt?' the Abbess asked as, side by side, she and the sister walked slowly down the long room. On either side were narrow cots, bearing ample bedding for cold old bodies, and each with its own little table for the placing of treasured mementos. The cots were divided by hangings, so as to give a measure of privacy, but, around most of the beds, the hangings were now neatly tied back. With a few exceptions, the old people were up, dressed and either sitting at the large table at the far end of the room, or else taking a turn in the warm sunshine outside.

'Esyllt,' Sister Emanuel said after a pause, 'is perfectly ready to speak to you, Abbess. When Sister Euphemia brought her back here last night – well, it was very early this morning, in fact, a couple of hours before Prime – the girl had been largely restored by her ministrations. Certainly, she had been cleaned up and dressed in fresh clothes.' She gave a sudden sound of distress. 'I understand Esyllt had knelt down by the body, and was covered in blood. Terrible.'

'Terrible indeed,' Helewise agreed. 'Did she manage to sleep?'

'Yes, I believe so. I looked in on her on my way

out to go to Prime, and she seemed to be asleep then.'

'You had a disturbed night,' Helewise remarked.

'I am quite used to that, thank you, Abbess.'

'What is Esyllt doing now?'

'She is laundering bedding. Although she is very good with the old people, always patient and kind, with a smile and a pleasantry for those who respond to such things, I did feel that, today, with all that she must have on her mind, it would be better to keep her segregated.'

'Quite.' And that consideration, Helewise was sure, was for the old people's benefit more than for Esyllt's. 'She is out in the wash room?'

'She is.' Silently, with a small bow, Sister Emanuel stepped in front of the Abbess and opened the door of a small lean-to where there were large stone vessels for the washing of garments and bedding, and smaller jars of fresh water. There was a hearth in which a well-stoked fire was burning, over which was suspended a pot of hot water.

Sister Emanuel pointed to the figure of the girl, bent over the wash tub, sleeves rolled up to reveal strongly muscled arms, scrubbing hard. Helewise nodded her thanks, and Sister Emanuel departed, closing the door behind her.

The little room was very hot. It was a warm morning, and the fire plus the steam from the boiling water had raised the temperature by many degrees. Esyllt, as might be expected, was sweating freely as she went about her work. And, unusual for her, she wasn't singing.

'Hello, Esyllt,' Helewise said.

The girl jumped, dropped her washing in the tub and spun round. Her expression was difficult to read, but, before she had wiped it away and replaced it with a smile of welcome, Helewise had thought she looked guilty.

'Good morning, Abbess.' Esyllt put up a wet hand and pushed her hair out of her eyes.

'Shall we step outside?' Helewise suggested.

Esyllt smiled briefly. 'Yes. It's a bit close in here, isn't it?'

'You have been working hard,' Helewise observed as, outside the lean-to, she noticed several freshly washed items hanging out to dry.

'Yes.' Esyllt led the way to one of the benches used by the old people, and, waiting while

Helewise seated herself, then sat down beside her. 'Sister Emanuel is very wise, she believes hard labour is a good medicine for – well, for what I'm suffering from.'

It was said without self-pity. But, nevertheless, it was with concern that Helewise asked gently, 'And what is that, Esyllt?'

Esyllt's dark eyes met hers. 'I can't exactly tell you, Abbess.'

'But, Esyllt, you—'

Esyllt put out a hand. 'Abbess, you're going to ask me what I was doing out in the forest last night, since, if I'd been tucked up here like I should have been, then that poor man wouldn't have . . . I mean, I wouldn't have seen . . . what I saw.' She turned to face the Abbess, expression intense. 'I was preparing a story to tell you – I was going to pretend I'd gone to pick wild flowers to make posies for the old ladies, I was even going to sneak out and fetch some, to make my story convincing.' She looked down at her hands, now reddened and sore from the hot water. 'But I find I can't. I can't lie to you, when you've been so good to me.'

Helewise was stunned. She tried to assimilate

all that Esyllt had just said, and, equally, implied; she had, it seemed, been out in the forest last night for some reason that she wasn't prepared to divulge.

What on earth could it be?

'Esyllt,' Helewise said eventually, 'you are not a professed nun, nor even a postulant. It is true that we have found you work here, when otherwise you might have had to leave and face the perils of the world outside, but you do that work conscientiously and well. Sister Emanuel says you have the gift of knowing just how to treat your elderly patients, and she is satisfied with you. More than satisfied!' Sister Emanuel was a little grudging with her praise, but Helewise, who had seen for herself how Esyllt carried out her duties, was not. 'What I am saying is that, as a member of the Abbey who is not in holy orders, your position is a little different. Of course, you owe Sister Emanuel obedience, and, naturally, we should not condone any wrongdoing that you committed. But, if you choose to go walking in the forest at night, then, apart from reasons concerning your own wellbeing, we can hardly stop you.'

Esyllt's head and shoulders were bowed, and she appeared intent on the fingernail she was picking at. Helewise waited, but she didn't answer.

'Esyllt?' Helewise prompted.

At last Esyllt raised her eyes and met Helewise's. 'I keep seeing him, Abbess,' she whispered. 'All that blood! Oh, God!' She covered her face with her hands.

'It was a frightful thing to have seen,' Helewise said, putting her arm round Esyllt's shaking shoulders. 'It's better not to fight the reaction, Esyllt – the dreadful images will haunt you for a while, but, believe me, if you try to suppress them, then you will take longer to get over this.' She gave Esyllt a quick hug. 'You're strong. I know that. You *will* get over it.'

For a brief moment, Esyllt leaned against the Abbess, allowing herself to be comforted. But then she pulled away.

Staring into Helewise's eyes, she said, 'Don't be kind to me, Abbess!'

'But—'

Esyllt began to cry. Brushing away the tears, she stood up. She was half-way back to her wash house when she turned, gave Helewise a brave attempt at a smile and said, 'Save your kindness for others. Much as I wish I could accept it, I can't.'

The smile faded as, in a whisper, she added, 'I'm not worthy.'

Then she went back inside and closed the door.

Helewise sat on for a while in the sunshine, thinking hard. She was tempted to call Esyllt back there and then, and face the girl with one or two very pertinent questions.

But would it do any good?

Would it not be better to give Esyllt a chance to calm down, come to her senses? Goodness, the child was probably still suffering from shock!

Helewise was becoming more and more convinced that she knew why Esyllt had been in the forest, and why she couldn't – wouldn't – explain herself. She was, the Abbess reflected, an honourable girl, in her own way.

With a sigh, Helewise got up and went in search of Sister Caliste.

A short while later, going into the Abbey church a good half hour before Sext to give herself time for some private prayer, Helewise tried to quell her irritation with Sister Caliste.

Because, despite Helewise's probings, despite having the paucity of her version of events thrown in her face, Caliste was sticking stubbornly to her story.

She went into the forest the previous day for a little walk. And, entranced by the flowers and the trees, she forgot the time.

Falling to her knees, Helewise began quietly, 'Dear Lord, please help me to find the truth.'

The one thing about which she was absolutely sure was that she had got nowhere near it yet.

Chapter Eleven

Josse met with as little help in his search for Ewen's killer as he had when he tried to investigate who might have slain Hamm. Ewen had indeed lived with his mean-spirited and whingeing widowed mother until her death, which was, according to the old man who was Josse's only faintly useful informant, 'a right blessing for the old misery-guts, Ewen being the wastrel and the worry that 'e were.'

A picture emerged of a youth who, without a father and with a nagging, narrow-minded mother, had absented himself from home as much as possible, never putting his shoulder to even the least demanding of wheels, either physically or symbolically, and who had earned his meagre livelihood by a bit of desultory poaching and thieving. Who, according to the same old man, 'didn't do a 'and's turn iffen someone else'd do it for 'im.'

Until, Josse thought, filling in the many blanks, life took on a new turn. When Ewen joined forces with Hamm Robinson and Seth Miller in the venture that killed him. Killed Hamm, too, come to that.

And, like Hamm, Ewen Asher did not, on the face of it, seem a great loss to the world.

But that, Josse told himself firmly, is thinking as Sheriff Pelham would think. Ewen is dead, cut to death in a brutal assault.

And Josse himself had heard the man's screams. It had not, as Josse was all too well aware, been either a quick death or a painless one.

He spoke last to a couple of men herding their pigs back towards some miserable-looking dwellings half a mile up the road from where Hamm's widow lived. They could add little more to Josse's knowledge of Ewen, except to remark that 'it were more'n likely Seth Miller did for 'im, 'e's always 'ad a temper on 'im.' And, echoing Josse's own shameful conclusion, 'We're well rid of 'im, aye, and that 'amm Robinson 'n all.'

If Sheriff Pelham speaks to those two, Josse thought, thanking the men and riding away, then Seth will be strung up on the nearest gallows the very next day.

Heading up the track into the forest, Josse's mind was already concentrating on what he should look out for at the murder scene when he saw a mounted figure coming towards him.

Coming out of the forest.

'Good day, Sir Josse!' the man called when he was within hailing distance. He was young, no more than thirty, and bareheaded. Dressed well, he rode a fine horse, with what looked like new harness, beautifully crafted. On one wrist he wore a heavy leather glove, on which, tethered by jesses, perched a hooded hawk.

Josse said, 'Good day to you, Tobias.'

'Fine morning for hawking!' Tobias exclaimed. He glanced at the bird. 'She's caught a rabbit and two voles, and we haven't been out more than an hour!'

'She's beautiful,' Josse said. 'What is she?'

'A peregrine falcon.' Tobias had come to a halt,

and now, as his horse stood patiently, he stroked the falcon's head with his free hand. 'Do you know why they're called that?'

'I don't.'

'It means pilgrimage hawk. Because they're caught on their passage from their breeding places.'

'Oh.' Was the young man deliberately setting out to charm, so as to distract Josse from wondering what he was doing there? If so, he wasn't quite succeeding. 'You have come from home this morning?'

'This morning?' A fractional hesitation. Then, with a wide smile, 'No, indeed! I have friends hereabouts, good fellows who share my – my interests, who kindly offer me hospitality when I am this way.'

'Men with whom you hunt?'

Again, a flashing smile. 'Hunt? Aye, Sir Josse.' Turning from interviewee to questioner with a ruthless speed that almost caught Josse unawares, he said, 'And you, Sir Knight? Where are you going?'

Since the track led straight into the forest, there was really only one answer. Josse said, 'Into the forest. A man was killed there last night. Murdered. As the King's representative, I am investigating the death.'

King Richard, Josse was well aware, had no idea either that there had been a killing or that Josse was even in the vicinity. But there was no need to reveal that to Tobias Durand.

The young man, however, did not react, or not, at least, in the way Josse had expected. Not even a look of mild apprehension. Instead, Tobias was turning his horse, as, with an eager expression, he said, 'How terrible! You must let me help you, Sir Josse! For one thing, two heads are better than one, and, for another, if there is a murderer abroad, then you should not go into the woods alone!'

Company was the very last thing Josse wanted. Firmly he put out a restraining arm. 'It is good of you, Tobias, but I prefer to work alone. Those inexperienced in such matters can unwittingly disturb significant clues, if you'll forgive my bluntness. Footprints, you know, that sort of thing.'

Tobias was nodding understandingly. 'Yes, I see. You don't want my clumsy great feet trampling the evidence!' He laughed. 'Then I'll bid you good day, and good hunting, and let you go on your way.' He bowed, smiled, and, wheeling his horse again, set off once more down the track leading away from the trees.

As Josse went on into the forest, he reflected that it would have been a shame to have dampened the young man's spirits by confronting him with Ewen's place of death. The body might be gone, but the blood would still be there.

It was not a sight for a happy, carefree fellow out hawking on a sunny morning.

In the end, there was very little evidence for Josse to find at the murder scene. The blood was indeed still there, and that which had not seeped down into the ground was now congealing slowly. There were signs of a struggle – broken branches, trampled undergrowth – and Josse thought he could tell which direction Ewen had come from. But he'd known that already, since he'd seen the man leave the clearing where the fallen trees were.

And that was about all.

Thinking hard, Josse paced around the place of

death. Ewen came from here, he thought, walking back a few yards and then returning, and someone jumped him. From where, though? From behind? Or in front?

If it *had* been Seth, and Josse was wrong about the knife, then, since Josse had witnessed him leave the clearing after Ewen, he must have leapt on him from behind. There could be no way that Seth could have overtaken Ewen and come at him from the front. Trying to be objective, Josse studied the ground again. There were no tracks approaching the place where Ewen had been killed from either side; the underbrush was quite undisturbed. And the tracks that led away from it had been widened, even if not made, by those who had found and borne away the body.

So in which direction did the murderer go?

Ewen had been cut down as he fled along a minor path, little more than an animal run. Referring to his mental map, Josse realised that the man must have been heading for home, cutting off into the thicket because he wanted to take the shortest route. It was not the easiest way, though, and so not the route that anyone lying in wait for him would have expected him to take.

Seth would have known, though. Because Seth was coming after him.

Josse sat down on a fallen log, puzzling. And the more he puzzled, the more it seemed likely, much as he hated to admit it, that the sheriff's swift and ill-thought-out conclusion must be the right one.

Seth and Ewen had gone back last night, by the light of the full moon, to fetch the last of whatever valuables they'd discovered in the clearing. With Hamm Robinson conveniently dead, the treasure could now be shared between the two of them. Ewen had taken fright and rushed off, and Seth, the braver of the two, had stayed behind. Found something else – something large and bulky, Josse recalled, picturing Seth cramming it into the sack.

Yes! he decided abruptly. That's it! Seth found the last object, perhaps the most precious thing in the whole hoard, and he didn't want to share it with Ewen. Why should he, indeed, when Ewen had already fled in fright? It was Seth's and Seth's alone! the man would have reasoned. So off he went in pursuit, and, catching Ewen up as he ran for home, Seth knifed him to death.

Leaving Seth as sole possessor of whatever it was they had dug up.

Slowly Josse got to his feet, brushing leaves from his tunic. He untied Horace's reins from the branch where he'd slung them, and, mounting, tried to suppress his pique.

A man is dead, he told himself severely. And his killer must be brought to justice. If it is indeed Seth, then the sheriff is acting correctly, and I, much as it will pain me, must tell him I think so.

As he rode off in the direction of Hawkenlye and the distant Abbey, Josse reflected that he would also have to break the news of his findings to the Abbess.

Now that, he thought ruefully, was *really* going to hurt.

She watched him with a hint of compassion in her grey eyes.

'It is manful of you to admit that you were wrong,' she said when he had finished.

'Well, I suppose even someone as dense as Sheriff Pelham has to get it right sometimes,' he replied, trying to smile.

'You're certain that he has done, in this instance?' the Abbess said.

'Certain?' Josse stared out across the sunlit Abbey courtyard. 'No. I'm not certain. But it's logical that Seth is the killer. He must, I can only conclude, have used a weapon he did not normally carry. Which, I assume, he threw away afterwards.' Briefly he met the Abbess's eyes. 'I'm quite sure Sheriff Pelham would have informed us, had he discovered a bloodied dagger in Seth's possession. Aren't you?'

'Indeed.' She held his eyes. 'He would probably have raced up here to tell you in person.'

There was a brief pause. Then: 'I hear that his men did find, if not a dagger, then an assortment of other objects in Seth's cottage,' the Abbess said. 'From what little I've been told, it seems to be a collection of coins and metal objects; plates, I believe. Seth is protesting his innocence, saying he found them under his hen run.'

'Roman coins?' he asked.

'I have no idea.' She glanced at him. 'I imagine that the few people who have seen the things so far wouldn't know a Roman coin if they were to be hit in the eye by it.'

'Hmm.' He would very much like to have a look at the hoard, although it was hardly relevant to the investigation.

He was still nursing the wound to his pride of having to acknowledge the sheriff had been right, when the Abbess said tentatively, 'Sir Josse?'

'Hm? Yes?'

'It may be agreed that Seth killed Ewen. But can he, do you think, also have killed Hamm?'

Josse got up, paced as far as the end of the cloister, then returned to where they had been sitting. No, of course not, he thought. And why didn't I think of that?

'No, Abbess,' he said. 'Even if I have to admit I was wrong, and that Seth did own a dagger, then I'm quite sure he possessed neither a spear nor the skill to throw it so accurately. A flint head,' he mused. 'I'd have liked to see that.'

The Abbess got to her feet, and, without a word, walked swiftly along to her room. Presently she returned.

Carrying in her hands a long-shafted, flint-headed spear.

'I've cleaned it thoroughly,' she murmured as he took it from her.

After some time he asked, 'Why did you keep it?'

She shrugged. 'Oh – I don't really know. I suppose I thought it might come in useful as evidence, although that makes little sense.' She met his eyes, and her expression seemed bashful. Ashamed, almost. 'No. That's not the truth.' She took a breath, then said, 'I kept it because the workmanship is so fine. For all that this thing was the means of a cruel death' – she stroked a careful finger down the central spine of the flint spear-head – 'it is so very beautifully made.'

Josse studied it. 'Aye,' he said softly. 'It is.' He gave a snort of laughter, instantly recognising it as inappropriate.

She looked up at him questioningly. 'Sir Josse?'

'I was just thinking that I can't see Seth Miller making such an object.'

The ghost of a smile twised her lips. 'Neither can I.'

Some time later, Josse reluctantly got to his feet and announced he should be on his way; although he and the Abbess had been arguing the merits of various possible next steps regarding Seth Miller, they had reached no conclusion.

Josse was aware that he was holding something back. But he didn't know that she was, too.

He said to the Abbess, who was walking beside him as he went to collect his horse, 'I'm wondering if there's any value in putting a watch on Seth's cottage, if indeed it could be arranged discreetly.'

'I suppose it could,' she said after a moment's pause. 'But why? What would be the point?'

'I have an idea—' He hesitated. 'Because,' he said instead, 'it might be revealing to see if anyone went to the place to look for the treasure trove. It would tell us whether Hamm, Ewen and Seth had let anybody else in on the secret.'

'But—'

'Abbess, I've been thinking,' he went on urgently. 'What possible good would Roman coins and plate be to a band of petty thieves? They're simple countrymen, the three of them, born and bred not a mile from here. How could they realistically have hoped to gain by their treasure trove, unless they knew someone who would buy it off them?' Someone rather more sophisticated, he added silently. Someone who knew his way around the rich and the wealthy of this world. Who might, say, know exactly which clandestine patron of the historic arts would be prepared to pay a small fortune for genuine Roman silver and gold. Who, more importantly, had not sufficient respect for the law to worry that two men had been murdered in the process of acquiring the precious goods.

The Abbess was nodding. 'I understand,' she said. 'And, in principle, your idea is good. But, Sir Josse, the treasure is in Sheriff Pelham's keeping. And, before you ask, no, I doubt very much that he would be prepared to give up one or two items with which to bait your trap.'

'Oh.' And, Josse thought, annoyed with himself for even mentioning the plan, anyone sophisticated enough to peddle antique treasure would, equally, be sufficiently worldly to know perfectly well that there would be nothing left to find in Seth Miller's little hovel.

'You have, I believe, someone in mind for this shady role of middle man,' the Abbess said softly.

'I have.'

Typically, she did not press him. And he,

wondering why he did not want to implicate in this crime, even to her, a man who might well be innocent, kept his peace.

It was not until he had one foot in the stirrup and was about to mount that he remembered to ask her: 'Abbess, I all but forgot! You learned nothing from the girl, from Esyllt?'

'No,' she agreed, watching him settle in the saddle. 'But how, Sir Josse, can you be so sure of that?'

'Because if you'd discovered anything of value, you'd have said so.'

'Indeed,' she murmured.

'No sinister explanation for her presence in the woods last night?'

'No explanation at all.' The Abbess looked worried. Turning her face up to look at him, she added, 'But something hangs heavy on her conscience.'

He pictured Esyllt. Well-built, strong . . . Strong enough to have made those savage cuts?

His eyes still on the Abbess's, he guessed she was thinking the same. 'No,' he said quietly. 'No, Abbess, I cannot believe it. The girl has a loving heart, I'd stake my reputation on it.'

'Even the most loving heart can be roused to fury,' she whispered. 'If —' She did not go on.

'If what?' he pressed.

She looked at him now with, he thought, almost a pleading expression in the grey eyes. After a small infinity of time, she said, 'Nothing. I'm sure – I pray – you are right.'

He reached down and briefly touched her sleeve. 'Count on it.'

But she was still looking worried. 'I think —' she began.

'What?'

Lifting her chin as if reaching a difficult decision, she said, 'Another is involved here, Sir Josse.'

Could she, he wondered, be thinking about Tobias? Surely not, for she had no way of knowing that he had been seen in the vicinity this morning. Had she? 'Go on,' he said.

'Sister Caliste,' she said simply.

'Caliste!' He had forgotten about her. 'Yes!' All he knew, he now thought, was that, when he had arrived back at the Abbey soon after midnight, it was to find that the novice had returned. 'When *did* she get back?'

'She was waiting outside the church when we came out of Compline.'

She had returned, then, some three hours before Josse.

'And with no explanation for her absence, either?'

'Only this ridiculous story of walking among the trees and forgetting the time.'

Josse slowly shook his head. Caliste, Seth, Ewen, Esyllt. And, if he was right, Tobias, waiting near at hand to receive the treasure. Hoping swiftly to pay off his work force and be on his way to his wealthy buyer.

Caliste, Seth, Ewen and Esyllt had all been in the forest last night, though, deep within it. Hadn't they? *How* did they all connect?

With a sound of impatience, he jerked Horace's head up and said to the Abbess, 'There's a complicated story here and no mistake, but I'm all at sea, I can't make head nor tail of it.'

She murmured something: '. . . afraid to . . .' and more words he didn't catch.

'Abbess?'

'Nothing.'

'I'm going home,' he announced, not without a

certain edge to his voice; if the Abbess could not bring herself to share her thoughts with him, then there was little point in pursuing the matter. 'If there are any developments, will you let me know?'

Her face once more turned up to his, she gave him a thin smile. 'Of course.'

'Until then . . .' He left the sentence unfinished, and, kicking Horace into a trot, headed off along the road for New Winnowlands.

Helewise, left to the pain of her unspoken anxiety, made her way slowly back towards her room.

Then, changing her mind, instead she went into the church.

But not, this time, to pray, unless it was for God's guidance in this matter. Instead, she settled on a narrow bench at the back of the great building, and, in its atmosphere of power combined so affectingly with peace, tried to straighten out the tangle of her thoughts and her emotions.

She had noticed – as it had become obvious that Josse had not – that, as Esyllt had come flying through the trees towards them last night,

211

bloodied and terrified out of her wits, there had been something else unusual about her.

She had raised the long, full skirt of her gown, the better to run through the forest.

And, underneath that gown, Helewise had seen that Esyllt had been naked from the waist down.

Oh, dear God, it didn't mean, did it, that Ewen had come across her and attacked her? Stripped off her underclothes, tried to rape her? Succeeded?

And that Esyllt, in her horror and despair, had grabbed his own weapon and killed him? She was strong enough, heaven knew, with those well-muscled arms of hers, those powerful shoulders . . .

Head bent over her folded hands, Helewise was praying in earnest now. 'Dear Lord, if that is what happened, then please, of Thy mercy, give Esyllt the courage to speak out. If she was defending herself, then surely it is no mortal sin to have killed him?'

It was that – the judgement that would fall on Esyllt – that was holding Helewise back. Because, if she were wrong and such a killing *was* to be viewed as a mortal sin, then Esyllt would hang for murder.

And, once dead, her soul would go to hell.

In the silence of the Abbey church, Helewise covered her face with her hands and tried to decide what to do.

Chapter Twelve

Arriving back at his new home, Josse was unsurprised to hear the sound of hammering. No doubt, he thought wearily, there had been yet another delay. Even now, the foreman was probably wondering how best to inform Josse that the work on New Winnowlands wouldn't be completed this side of Christmas.

But, other than that – in fact, matters weren't quite that bad, since the foreman promised everything would be finished in a week, two at the most – Josse's welcome home was all that a man could wish for. Will came out to take Horace, and, as Josse well knew, the man would care for the horse as diligently as Josse himself would have done. Furthermore, Josse's swift but penetrating look around the courtyard and outbuildings of his new domain was sufficient to indicate that everything was neat and tidy.

Inside the house, it was the same. Ella had clearly busied herself clearing up after the workmen, and not so much as a small pile of sawdust marred the polished sheen of the flagstones in the hall. She had rubbed beeswax into the fine wood of Josse's table, chair and benches, and bowls of flowers stood in the deep stone window embrasures.

Greeting him, she said, 'Will you eat, sir? I have a pot of stew simmering, duck, it is, and Will's pulled some lovely young onions, white and smooth, they are.'

Josse's mouth was watering. 'That sounds wonderful. Yes please, Ella.'

He was relaxing in the mid-afternoon heat – not asleep, he told himself firmly, merely resting with his eyes closed – when he heard someone ride into the yard. Getting up, he crossed the hall to the open doorway and looked down the steps into the courtyard. Will was in conversation with a mounted messenger.

Josse thought immediately of the Abbess, but,

since he didn't recognise the messenger, it was not likely that the man came from Hawkenlye. He watched as Will came hurrying up the steps towards him.

'Sir Josse, this man brings word from someone calling himself Tobias Durand,' Will reported. 'He says you know his master, and that he – the master – invites you to visit him and his lady.'

'Does he indeed,' Josse said softly.

'Sir?'

'Thank you, Will, I shall speak to the man myself.'

He went down the steps and across to the mounted man, who, well-schooled in manners, slipped off his horse's back and made Josse a courteous bow.

'Tell your master and his good lady that I accept their invitation,' Josse said.

The man – he was actually little more than a boy – raised his head. 'When shall I say, sir?'

'Say—' Josse thought. 'Say the end of the week.'

'The end of the week,' the boy echoed. Then he said, 'I'd better tell you the way.'

Josse set out mid-morning of the following Friday;

the ride to the house of Tobias Durand would, the boy had said, take well over the hour.

As he rode, he distracted his main train of thought – why Tobias should suddenly have expressed a desire for Josse's company – by recalling what the Abbess had told him of the man. Which was, in fact, precious little.

Ah well, he would just have to see for himself.

The house was a grand one. Not all that big, but expensively built and, as Josse discovered when a tall and dignified man-servant ushered him inside, beautifully furnished in the latest style.

No expense had been spared, it was clear.

What was not quite so clear was where Tobias had come by the money to pay for it all . . .

Tobias came bounding across the hall to greet his guest.

'Sir Josse, how wonderful to see you!' he gushed. 'We're in the solar, enjoying the sunshine. Won't you join us? Paul!' he called to the man-servant. 'Bring wine – draw a jug of that new barrel we broached last night.'

Josse followed Tobias back across the hall and up a spiral stair that led off it. At the top, the stair opened out into a sunny room with, Josse noticed in faint surprise, glass in its modest window.

Glass!

In front of which, stitching at a framed piece of embroidery with every appearance of calm, sat a woman.

Straight away, as the woman turned her head, Tobias said, 'Dearest, may I present Sir Josse d'Acquin, King's knight and lord of the manor of New Winnowlands?' And, to Josse, 'Sir Josse, my wife, Petronilla.'

It was just as well, Josse reflected swiftly as, moving forward, he bent to kiss the woman's outstretched hand, that Tobias had introduced her immediately, and so clearly.

Because, otherwise, Josse might have taken the woman for Tobias's mother rather than his wife.

'Please, Sir Josse, sit down,' Petronilla was saying, indicating a leather-seated chair. 'In the sunshine, by me.'

'Thank you, lady.'

Tobias busied himself with pouring the wine that the manservant had just brought, and Josse, listening to the lighthearted comments he was exchanging with his wife, took the chance to study Petronilla Durand.

She had a thin face, and had a bony look about her, so that she appeared to be all angles. She must, he thought, trying to be charitable, be at least forty-five. At *least*. And the greying hair visible at the temples, under the smoothly starched linen of her barbette, made her look older, as did the thin lips surrounded by a network of tiny lines. Lines which, Josse observed, all seemed to run downwards. If she could manage a less severe look, put a little flesh on those bones, he thought, then it might take a few years off her. As it was . . .

If he had been right in his estimate of Tobias's age, then Petronilla was about fifteen years his senior. Perhaps not quite old enough to be his mother, but it was a close-run thing.

'. . . making an embroidery to celebrate our first three months in this gracious house,' Tobias was saying. 'See, Sir Josse, how fine is her work?' He pointed to the stitched linen in Petronilla's hands; she appeared to be working on a design of pansies, the purple and the egg-yolk yellow making a dramatic but pleasing contrast.

'Fine indeed, my lady.' Josse looked up into the pale face, noticing the maze of small wrinkles around the deep-set eyes. 'Such stitching! This must have taken you hours.'

'I like to sew,' she said. Her voice was pleasantly low-pitched. Her lips made a gesture which, Josse was to realise, was typical of her, a sort of folding-together which made them all but disappear. It was not, he thought with some pity, a mannerism that did anything for her appearance. 'It is a pastime I have always enjoyed.'

'I see. I—'

'Petronilla was lady-in-waiting to Queen Eleanor,' Tobias butted in. 'They are old friends, my wife and the Queen.' Possibly *old* had been tactless, Josse thought, as had the implication that Petronilla and the Queen were contemporaries. 'Petronilla was a member of the Queen's court, both here in England and in France.'

A faint blush had stained Petronilla's white and slightly greasy-looking cheeks. 'I hardly think—' she began.

'Oh, dearest, don't be modest!' Again, her husband interrupted. 'Sir Josse would love to hear of your days in court circles, him being King Richard's man! Wouldn't you, Sir Josse?'

'Aye, that I would,' Josse said, with as much

enthusiasm as he could muster.

'Why, you'll probably discover you have a friend or two in common,' Tobias went on. 'Don't let me stand in the way of some enjoyable reminiscences!'

Was he, Josse wondered, testing? To see if Josse was really what he had claimed to be? Had Tobias primed his wife to pose some searching questions?

If so, then Josse was more than ready to field them.

Petronilla had turned towards him, and was saying politely, 'Sir Josse, my husband exaggerates. I did indeed have the honour to serve the Queen, and I like to believe that we became friends. However, my time in her court was but brief, and amounted to the relatively short years between Queen Eleanor's emergence from her residence at Winchester and the death of my father.'

'I am sorry for your loss,' Josse said sincerely. 'A recent one, I take it?'

'Yes,' she said quietly. 'Some six months ago.'

There was a brief and, Josse thought, awkward silence. Perhaps, he thought, it's just my guilty conscience that makes it seem awkward.

He did indeed feel slightly guilty. Because he

couldn't suppress the possibly unworthy thought that he now knew exactly why a young, lively and very handsome man like Tobias Durand had married a tight-lipped woman fifteen years older than himself.

It was – it *had* to be – because she had inherited richly from her late father.

As if Tobias knew very well what Josse was thinking, he said smoothly, 'It was to me that, I am humbly happy to say, Petronilla looked for comfort in her loss.' He gave his wife a warm smile. 'And, since we became man and wife, together we have set about turning her father's house into our own home.'

Nice for you, Josse thought. But, despite himself, his cynicism was being undermined. Covertly observing Petronilla, he watched as her face lit up in response to her husband's smile. And, flicking a glance back at Tobias, he could see nothing but affection. And was there the briefest suspicion of moisture in the young man's eyes? Could it really be that his emotions regarding his elderly wife were that strong?

Perhaps it was true, then. Perhaps he really loved his bride, despite her years.

Josse decided he would reserve his judgement.

But, whether Tobias had married his wife for love of herself or of her wealth, it still undermined Josse's case against the man. Because, if Tobias had access to the sort of money that had so clearly been spent on this house, then he hardly had need to risk his freedom – risk his life, even – involving himself with the shady thieving of the likes of Hamm, Ewen and Seth.

Unless some sense of chivalry aroused in Tobias the desire to acquire his own wealth, that was.

Was it likely? Josse couldn't be sure.

He was still pondering that, while at the same time engaging in superficial conversation with Petronilla concerning various mutual acquaintances in the Plantagenet court, when, shortly afterwards, the manservant returned to summon them to table.

The food was excellent, and the manservant Paul remained at hand, answering Petronilla's quiet orders and frequently replenishing Josse's and Tobias's goblets with more of the sweet wine. Petronilla, Josse observed, drank but little.

When they had eaten the last of the small, round

honey cakes that followed the fish and the game, Petronilla stood up and announced she was going to her chamber to have a short rest. The man-servant also having disappeared, it was left to Tobias to share what was left in the wine jug between Josse and himself.

'A superb meal, Tobias,' Josse said, stretching his full stomach. 'You and your lady keep a fine table.'

'We live well,' Tobias agreed.

Josse was trying to kick his somewhat fuddled wits into order and come up with a diplomatic way of asking some more penetrating questions about Tobias's household when, as if suddenly impatient with sitting still, the young man tossed back the dregs of wine in his goblet, leapt up and said, 'Come, Sir Josse! Let us take a turn outside in the sunshine!'

Josse managed the necessary admiring comments as, with an almost childlike pride, Tobias showed off his estate, from barns and paddocks to hunting birds and fine horses. As the two of them were about to go back into the hall, someone called out to Tobias – to judge by his clothing and by the mud on his feet and lower legs, he was an outdoor worker – and, with a brief apology, Tobias went back across the yard to speak to him.

Josse went into the empty hall alone.

He glanced around. There was a tapestry hanging on one wall, its colours too fresh and vibrant for it to have hung there long. And, on a long wooden table that stood against the opposite wall, there were several decorative objects . . . a carved ivory statue of the Madonna, a wooden triptych depicting the Crucifixion on its central panel, with angels and cherubs on the two outer panels. The paintwork, to Josse's fairly experienced eye, looked well executed and, considering the strong, rich blues and golds, had probably been expensive.

He glanced over his shoulder. Tobias was still in conversation with the labourer. He had a few moments in hand . . .

He opened the first of the wooden chests ranged beneath the table; it contained a quantity of white cloth, which he thought might be household linen. No incriminating Roman treasure *there*. Moving on to the next chest, he was in the very act of raising the lid when a quiet voice said, 'What are you doing, Sir Josse?'

He spun round. Petronilla stood a few feet behind him.

There was nothing he could say, no possible excuse he could offer; he bowed his head and said, 'Lady, forgive me.'

For some moments she did not speak. Then, when finally she broke her silence, it was not to say the accusing words that Josse had both expected and deserved.

Instead, she said, 'We made a bargain, my Tobias and I.' She had moved to the doorway, from where she could look down at her young husband as he stood in the courtyard. 'I know, Sir Josse, what you think. What they all think. That it can only be my wealth that attracted a fine man like Tobias.'

She turned to meet Josse's eyes; the expression in her own was surprisingly calm. 'It is true that his marriage to me gives him riches he had never hoped to possess. He was orphaned young, you see, and raised by an elderly aunt, the sister of his mother, who kept a meagre household with no aspirations either to style or to comfort.' With sudden passion, she said, 'Is it any surprise that Tobias should have fallen into dishonourable ways? For pity, Sir Josse, a young man must have *some* excitement!'

'I—' Josse began.

But Petronilla hadn't finished. 'No, Sir Knight, let me speak. It was the truth when, earlier, Tobias told you that it was he who comforted me in the loss of my dear father, and, not being the fool you and the world take me for, naturally I suspected his motives. However, while he admitted freely that it would gladden him immeasurably to help me manage my fortune, he promised that he would, in return, make me an affectionate, if not a passionately loving, husband.' She moved a step or two nearer to Josse, so that he could see the fervour in her dark eyes. 'He promised me, *promised*, Sir Josse, that, if I agreed to marry him, with all that such an undertaking involved, then he would forsake his – forsake the ways of his misspent youth.' A faint smile briefly twisted the narrow lips. 'And I accepted.'

Josse opened his mouth to speak, but, unable to think what to say that could in any way express his feelings, he shut it again.

'You may search my house if you wish,' Petronilla went on, her voice distant now. 'You will find many rich objects, and all are gifts from me to my husband. Or, since naturally he is free to spend as he sees fit, gifts from him to me.'

His shame beginning to abate, Josse found that he was now filled with a different emotion: the stirrings of anger. Petronilla might be prepared to take Tobias's word that he had mended his ways, but Josse had too clear a mind-picture of the elated young man who emerged from the forest the morning after Ewen Asher was killed. Was it really to be believed, that Tobias had left his thieving ways behind him?

'My lady,' Josse said, making his voice as mild as he could 'you have your husband's word that he is now a model of respectability. But—'

'But how do I know I can believe him?' she finished for him. To Josse's surprise, she laughed. Only a short laugh, with more than a touch of irony in it, but a laugh nevertheless. 'Sir Knight, I had him followed. When first he would announce he was off on some early hawking expedition, I asked my faithful Paul to follow him.' She put her face close to Josse's. 'To *spy* on him. Not pretty, is it, for a new wife to resort to such tactics?'

'Perhaps not pretty,' Jose replied tersely. 'But necessary.'

'*Not* necessary!' she cried. 'Those expeditions, every one – even when he was from home for a day and a night together – were as innocent as if I had been there to accompany him! He was, just as he said, hawking.'

'You no longer have him followed?' Josse asked, although he thought he already knew the answer.

She studied him for a long moment. Then said: 'Rarely.'

Was that the truth? Or had she made that reply merely to make Josse think she was not the infatuated, blinkered wife he took her for?

There was, he realised, no way of knowing.

He watched as, Tobias having finished his conversation, he turned back towards the house. Catching sight of Petronilla at the top of the steps, he gave her a wave and then blew her a kiss. With a sharp intake of breath, Petronilla responded.

Then she picked up her long skirts in one hand and, a beaming smile spreading over the pallid, lined face, she ran down the steps and went to meet him.

It is time I left, Josse thought.

Following Petronilla down into the courtyard, he began his speech of thanks and farewell.

Chapter Thirteen

Helewise did not forget her undertaking to notify Josse if any developments occurred. But, other than Seth Miller being charged with the murder of Ewen Asher and the trial set for some six weeks hence, there *were* no developments.

She tried again to get Esyllt to talk. Tried to persuade her to go to Mass, but the girl's eyes had widened with horror at the thought. 'I *can't*!' she whispered.

Can't because you are in a state of mortal sin? Helewise wondered, worried to her very depths. 'Make your confession, child!' she had urged. 'Whatever you have done, the Lord will understand!'

But Esyllt, with an expression that had wrung

the Abbess's heart, had shaken her head and turned away.

Helewise went to see Seth Miller, in the stinking cell where the sheriff had locked him away. Sheriff Pelham, apparently surprised to see a nun in his gaol, tried to deter her – 'In there's not fit for a lady nor a nun, Sis— I mean, Abbess!' he said – but she insisted.

'We are enjoined by Our Lord, are we not, Sheriff,' she pointed out, 'to visit the sick and imprisoned? Did not Jesus Himself say that for as much as it is done for one of His children, it is done for Him?'

'Yes, but – Oh, very well, Abbess, but only for a few moments.' He leaned confidingly towards her. 'He's dangerous, see. Done a man in.'

But Helewise, allowed to go as far as the wooden door set with stout bars that kept Seth penned in his cell, apart from the rest of humanity, didn't think he looked dangerous. He sat crumpled against a stone wall that ran with moisture and with unknown slimy matter, and the fetters around his ankles had raised angry red welts. The mouldering straw that covered the stone floor smelled rank with decay. And with other, more malodorous stenches; it was apparent that Seth must relieve himself where he sat.

'Seth?' she called.

He raised his head. 'Who's that?'

'Abbess Helewise of Hawkenlye,' she said. 'Will you pray with me?'

'Aye, lady.' He struggled on to his knees, and followed her in her prayers, responding, when required, with a heartfelt fervour.

When they had finished, she asked, 'Seth, do you wish me to send a priest to you?'

'Priest?'

'To hear your confession,' she said gently.

'Confession?' The light dawned. 'I didn't kill him, Abbess, he were dead when I reached him! That's God's honest truth, I swear!'

'I see.' Was he telling the truth? He sounded earnest enough, but then a man who stood to hang for murder was bound to deny the crime, as convincingly as he could. 'But, Seth, what of your thieving?' she went on. 'You, Hamm and Ewen were all involved in digging beneath the fallen oak in the forest, weren't you? And you cut down a healthy tree, too, to help you in your treasure seeking. That's true, isn't it?'

'Aye, aye,' Seth muttered. 'I wish to God I'd told Hamm what to do with his coins, I do that! Begging your pardon, lady,' he added.

'It was Hamm who found the hoard?'

'Aye. Setting traps, he were, for game and that. He dug down under the fallen tree because he saw something glinting. It were a coin, and, soon as he started digging a bit harder, he saw that there was more, much more. He got me and Ewen involved because it were too much for one man to do alone – it were the three of us cut down the second tree, which stood right in the way, and no easy job it were. I'm his cousin – Hamm's cousin – see, we've always worked together.'

'No, Seth, you've always *stolen* together,' she corrected him.

He looked at her, his face pitiful. 'Aye,' he sighed. 'And now they've got me for something I never did, and I'm going to hang.' A sob escaped him. 'Aren't I?'

She wished she could say otherwise, but she had to agree; it certainly looked like it. Slowly she nodded.

Seth sank to the floor again, leaning his hopeless, filthy face against the wall. 'Then I reckon I'd better have that priest.'

When almost a month had gone by, and, once more, the moon was waxing towards the full, Helewise was woken from deep sleep.

She sat up in her narrow bed, wondering why she had awakened. All around came the sounds of women asleep: faint murmurs, regular breathing, a few snores.

All sounds to which she was well accustomed.

What, then, had disturbed her?

She got up and crept through the hangings around her cubicle. All was still, there was nobody creeping about and—

Yes. There was.

Someone was standing by the door to the dormitory, and, as Helewise watched, the slim figure descended the first two steps.

Helewise, barefoot, hurried across the floor, stopping in the doorway and holding on to the door post. The figure was now on the third step down, slim hands clutching at the guard rail, her body leaning forward, tense, as if she yearned with her whole being towards the object of her fierce attention.

Towards the forest.

And, as Helewise watched, Caliste again began her weird, unearthly humming.

It was not, Helewise thought, any the less affecting the second time; in fact, it was possibly more so. The eerie sight of bright moonlight over the sinister darkness of the trees, combined with the still-vivid memory of recent events, created in the Abbess a profound dread.

But, dread or not, it was quite a chilly night, and it would do neither her nor Caliste any good to stand out there on the steps.

Her fanciful thoughts dispersed by common sense, Helewise took a firm grip on herself and went on down the steps until she could take a gentle hold on Caliste's arm. 'Come, child,' she said softly, 'back to your bed. It's too cold to be out here in nothing but your chemise.'

Caliste's humming faltered, then ceased. Turning wide eyes to Helewise, she seemed to stare straight through her.

'Are you awake, Sister Caliste?' Helewise whispered. There was no reply. Pulling steadily at the girl's arm, Helewise led her back into the dormitory and along the room to her bed. There, like an obedient child, the novice lay down and shut her eyes. Helewise arranged the covers over her, then, drawing the hangings across the opening, left the girl to sleep.

Helewise noticed that she had left the dormitory door open; with a mild tut of annoyance at her own carelessness, she went back to close it.

As she did so, she heard the humming again.

Now it was fainter, and, if anything, even more unsettling.

Because, although it was the same wandering tune that Caliste had hummed, in the same unearthly key, it came from the forest.

Somewhere out there in that vast darkness, someone had heard Caliste's strange song. And they were sending back a reply.

The Abbess's ability to concentrate on her devotions and her duties the following day was, she soon discovered, severely impaired. For one thing, she had resolved to keep a watchful eye on Sister Caliste, which in itself was disturbing since the girl had a vacant look about her; wide-eyed and anxious, she was far from being her usual serene and smiling self.

When Helewise asked her gently if she felt all right – and, more relevant, if she had slept well – the girl gave her a puzzled frown and replied, 'I am quite well, thank you, Abbess. And, yes, I slept deeply. Why?'

'Oh – I thought you looked a little pale,' Helewise improvised.

Caliste gave her a sweet smile. 'How well you care for us,' she said softly.

Helewise couldn't answer. Just then, she felt she was failing at least one of her little community quite badly. Leaving Caliste to carry on with her work – she was washing out soiled bandages and hanging them to dry in the strong sunshine, which, according to Sister Euphemia, was the best thing for making them wholesome and fit for re-use – Helewise went back to her room. It appeared, she reflected as she paced across the courtyard, that Caliste had no recollection of her sleepwalking.

Which somehow made it all the more strange.

Helewise's preoccupation with Caliste meant that, try as she might, she had not been able to rid her mind of memories of the chilling scene she had witnessed last night. At times, she even thought she could still hear echoes of that inhuman humming . . .

And, as if all that were not enough to worry about, in addition there was Esyllt. A very different Esyllt since the murder in the forest, and Helewise's conscience nagged her continuously to find out why.

Paying another visit to her in the old people's home, Helewise realised that Esyllt had lost weight. She was still a fine, strong young woman, but her face was thinner. And there was something else . . . Yes. Helewise, watching Esyllt walk to greet her, nodded faintly.

Esyllt had lost the proud carriage which had thrown back her shoulders and displayed her fine figure. Now, she moved as if a yoke lay across her back. A yoke, moreover, that bore a heavy load.

'Abbess?' Esyllt said, having made her reverence. 'Did you wish to speak to Sister Emanuel? Only she's just gone outside with old Brother Josiah, and—'

Helewise held up her hand. 'No, Esyllt. It is you I wished to see.'

'Oh.'

It was amazing, Helewise reflected briefly, how so much feeling could be put into that small response. 'I wondered if you might want to talk about—' she began.

Then she stopped. She had tried that approach before, and it had failed. Why should she expect it to work now? Instead, stepping closer to the girl, Helewise opened her arms and enfolded her in a hug.

For a moment, Esyllt seemed to respond. Sagging against Helewise, she emitted a sob.

'There, child,' Helewise murmured. 'There, now.' She reached up a hand and smoothed the girl's hair. 'Let me help you,' she went on, keeping her voice low, 'I do hate to see you suffer so, and—'

But Esyllt's brief collapse was over.

Straightening up and pulling herself away from Helewise, she wiped her hand across her eyes and said, 'I thank you, Abbess, but there is nothing you can do.' Turning away, she added under her breath, 'Nothing *anybody* can do.'

Helewise watched her walk away.

Then she went outside to look for Sister Emanuel.

The nun was sitting on a bench next to a very old man in monk's habit. She was holding his hand, and occasionally reaching up to wipe tears from his cheeks with a spotless piece of linen.

Seeing the Abbess, Sister Emanuel began to detach herself and get up. Helewise motioned for her to stay where she was; the old monk, she observed, didn't appear to have noticed her.

She went to sit down on Sister Emanuel's free side. 'What is the matter with him?' she asked quietly.

Sister Emanuel gave the old man an affectionate glance. 'Nothing, really,' she replied in her normal voice. 'It's all right,' she added, 'Brother Josiah doesn't hear very well. Nor, indeed, does he see very well.' She sighed. 'His eyes run in the bright light, Abbess, that is all.'

Helewise nodded. She could, for the moment, think of nothing to say.

'He likes to feel the sunshine on his face,' Sister Emanuel remarked. 'That, really, is his one remaining pleasure, so I like him to enjoy it as often as is practical.'

There was a short silence. Then Sister Emanuel said, 'Were you looking for me, Abbess?'

Helewise, too, had been enjoying the sun on her face. With an effort, she brought herself back to the matter in hand.

'Yes, Sister. I am concerned about Esyllt.'

'As am I,' Sister Emanuel said. 'She is —' She frowned, as if not sure how to proceed. After a few moments, she went on, 'It is as if she were pining. She does not eat, does not, I think, sleep well. I have no complaint about the quantity of her work; indeed, she is almost working herself *too* hard. However, the quality of it has changed.' Sister Emanuel gave a small sigh. 'It is not charitable of me to criticise someone whom, I am sure, is in deep distress, but, Abbess, I feel that I must report to you any observations I have made.'

'Yes, please do,' Helewise urged. 'Go on.'

'Esyllt has lost her touch,' Sister Emanuel said sadly. 'There used to be such a sense of joy about her that it communicated itself even to people such as he, who can barely see nor hear.' She indicated Brother Josiah, sitting mumbling to himself by her side. 'But now . . .' She did not finish her sentence.

'As if she were pining,' Helewise repeated.

'Abbess?'

'That's what you said. But pining for what, Sister Emanuel?'

Sister Emanuel shot her a sad look. 'Abbess, I really could not say.'

At Sext, after a morning in which she felt she had accomplished absolutely nothing except to give herself a headache, the Abbess took a firm hold on her emotions. Praying for fortitude and wisdom, she forced her own problems out of her mind and opened herself up to the Lord. With the result that, as she left the Abbey church, at last she knew what she must do.

There might still be time . . .

Josse, disturbed in the middle of a warm and lazy afternoon, was surprised to see Brother Saul ride into the courtyard of New Winnowlands. Even more surprised when Saul delivered his message.

'Now?' Josse exclaimed.

'Yes,' Brother Saul said. 'Well, if it is not an inconvenience.'

'Why the hurry?'

Brother Saul shrugged. 'She did not say.'

'Hmm.' Strange, Josse thought as, sending Saul on ahead to say that Josse was on his way, he packed up the few belongings he would need for a night or two away from home. Still puzzling – and not a little intrigued – he yelled out to Will to prepare his horse, and, not long after Saul had gone, he was on the road behind him.

Josse was no more nor less interested in the phases of the moon than the next person. He had noticed, a couple of nights ago, that it had not been far off the full, but, since his observation had been fleeting, he could not have said whether the moon was waxing or waning.

As he rode towards Hawkenlye, catching up with Brother Saul so that they rode the last few miles in companionable conversation, Josse did not give the lunar cycle even a single thought.

But, whether Josse was aware of it or not, tonight the moon would be full.

And, even if Josse didn't know, others did.

Chapter Fourteen

'You propose we do *what*?'

Josse could hardly believe it. Was the Abbess Helewise sick? Had she suffered some strange aberration? He stared at her, trying to detect any sign of it, but she looked pretty much as usual. A slight frown seemed to have settled between the wide grey eyes, but, other than that, she appeared calm and in control.

'I intend to go into the forest tonight,' she said, 'and, as I just suggested, I think it would be a good idea for you to accompany me.' Her eyes rested on his and, briefly, she gave the shadow of a smile. 'If, that is, you are prepared to, Sir Josse, given its recent violent history. I should, of course, quite understand if you refuse, and I—'

'I haven't refused!' He thumped his fist against

the wall of her room with suppressed anger. Great God, but she was leaping ahead of herself here! 'Of course I won't let you go alone, Abbess, but—'

'Oh, good,' she said mildly.

'What's good?'

She turned an innocent face up to his. 'That you've agreed to come with me, of course!'

'Abbess, just wait a moment!' He tried to think rapidly, tried to work out how best to put his huge disapproval into words that might have a chance of stopping her in this folly.

Moving across the room and standing with his hands resting on her table, he said, 'Abbess Helewise, there is great peril in the forest. Two men have been killed there, and, for all that Sheriff Pelham believes he has one murderer safely under lock and key, there is still the matter of the first death!'

'I am aware of that,' she said, with a new coolness in her voice. 'However, I—'

'And yet you're telling me that, despite all that, the two of us are going to sally out into the forest tonight!' he exploded. 'For what purpose, pray? To have a good nose around and see how long it takes for us to get a spear in *our* backs?'

'You did not listen when I used that same argument to try to prevent you from going into the forest a few weeks ago,' she observed. 'You said, if I recall, that, since you would be armed *and* on the look out, you would be perfectly safe.'

'And I was!' he replied heatedly.

'So why will you not be as safe now?' she demanded.

'Because—'

He stopped. Yes, of course. This was the crux of it. And, having realised it already, this was, naturally, why she was being so belligerent.

'*I* would be as safe,' he said, after a pause. 'But I am not prepared to risk *your* wellbeing.'

'It is not up to you to make that decision,' she said coolly. 'As Abbess of Hawkenlye, I am in charge of my nuns and my lay servants. Two of my women are suffering, and suffering deeply, and it is my duty to do all that I can to alleviate their distress.'

'By making some ill-prepared and reckless venture into the forest by night?' he shouted.

'Yes!' she shouted back. 'Do you not see, the forest holds the key to all this?'

He wasn't at all sure that it did. And, even if she was right, he had to stop her in this wild idea. Good Lord, it was impossible! 'It will not help your young women for you to be killed!' he cried.

'I have absolutely no intention of being killed,' she said. 'Why should anyone kill me, in any case?'

'They killed Hamm Robinson.' He could not help the righteousness in his voice.

She gave a sigh of exasperation. 'Hamm Robinson was different!'

'Why, pray?'

'He—' She stopped. Then, in a more placatory tone, 'Come with me tonight, Sir Josse, and I will show you!'

Come with me! Dear God, but she was determined! If he wasn't careful, he'd find himself left in the safety of Hawkenlye Abbey tonight while she went off by herself into the forest.

'Is there nothing I can say that will dissuade you?' he asked quietly.

'Nothing.'

He ran his hands over his face. 'Very well, then.'

'You will come with me?' She sounded as if she could hardly believe it.

He removed his hands and looked at her. 'Aye.'

He wasn't entirely sure, but he thought he saw her relax briefly in her relief.

Helewise had thought he would not give up without one last attempt to dissuade her, and she was right. He kept his peace as they ate the evening meal – her conscience hadn't troubled her over ordering good portions of the braised hare with vegetables for Josse and herself, bearing in mind the night's work that lay ahead for them – and, as they drank a fortifying cup of wine back in the privacy of her room, he had managed to restrict himself to the sort of remarks habitually made to one another by courteous strangers meeting on the road.

She excused herself and went across to the Abbey church for Compline, making a great effort to empty her mind of all thoughts of the forthcoming adventure. In the powerful atmosphere of the church in the late evening, she felt a sudden flow of courage come coursing through her; had she not already firmly made up her mind that what she was doing was the right thing, this sign of almighty approval would surely have convinced her.

'In Thy wisdom, Thou hast put these troubled women in my care, oh, Lord,' she prayed softly. 'Dear Lord, let me not fail them now.' After a moment's pause, she added, 'Let me not fail Thee.'

Returning to Josse some time later, she found he had come out into the cloister to wait for her. And, as she approached, he was already saying the words he must have been rehearsing: 'Abbess, won't you please reconsider?'

She let him make a brave start, then gently put up a hand to silence him. 'Sir Josse,' she said quietly, 'this is pointless.'

'But—'

He was glaring down at her, face close to hers. As if, at long last, he read her determination in her eyes, he gave a faint shrug. 'Very well,' he said with a sigh. 'I wash my hands of you.'

'Oh, no, Sir Josse,' she replied. 'That you certainly do not do.' She added, aware that she was teasing him, 'If you must add a homily, what about, on your own head be it?'

His only reply was a grunt.

*

He had, she observed, been busy while she had been at Compline. He had filled a pack with a couple of blankets, some bread and some water, and, down in the bottom of the pack, was a wrapped object that she thought looked very like a small weapon; a dagger, perhaps. She stared at it for a second or two. But now, she appreciated, was not the moment to remind him of the rule about not bringing arms into the Abbey.

'You are warmly clad?' he demanded as, with the darkness now absolute and the full moon just rising, at last they set out. 'The air is still warm now, but the night will be cold later.'

'I am indeed,' she said. She had had the same thought, and had taken the time to visit her cubicle and put on a warm woollen chemise beneath her habit.

He nodded.

They left the Abbey by the main gate. The forest, into whose strange and mysterious depths they would soon be tentatively walking, loomed up ahead. Helewise noticed Josse slip into the porteress's lodge, now empty; when he returned, his heavy sword hung in its scabbard at his left side.

Even more than the dagger hidden in the pack, the sight of it gave her a shudder of fear.

He seemed to know the way.

Following close behind him – a good place to be, since, apart from anything else, it meant that, with his back to her, she was free to hitch up her skirts and still retain her modesty – she was quickly impressed by how familiar he was with the tracks and the paths of the Great Forest.

The moon was now well risen, and gave sufficient light for the journey to be fairly comfortable; this expedition would, she thought as she carefully took from Josse's hand a wicked length of bramble whose thorns could have sliced open a cheek, have been an impossibility on a dark or cloudy night. It was wonderful how one's eyes adjusted, she reflected, because, whereas on first leaving the Abbey, she had been able to make out only vague shapes, now she was seeing details. That little animal run going off into the undergrowth, for example, and that huge beech tree with its tangle of roots half-exposed on the bank, and—

Josse had stopped without warning, and she walked into him.

'Sorry!' she said. 'But—'

'Hush!' He glanced at her, looking slightly apologetic for having silenced her so unceremoniously.

'It's all right.' She, too, pitched her voice low. 'What is it?'

He was standing quite still, turning his head slowly first this way, then that. She waited. After some moments, he shrugged faintly and said, 'I don't know. Probably nothing. Shall we go on?'

'Yes.'

It was apparent to her that he was moving more cautiously now, although he had hardly been reckless or noisy before. He paused frequently, repeating his head-turning, and she realised he was listening.

For what?

Oh, dear Lord, not for that singing! Please, no!

She clutched at the wooden cross that hung around her neck, momentarily terrified.

But then a calm voice inside her head said, and what did you expect? You have heard the chanting, and you know it came from this forest. Is it not more than likely that you are about to hear it again?

She took a deep breath, then another.

It worked. She was still terrified, but at least she felt in control of herself.

Fleetingly she wondered, as she set off once more after Josse, if he was wearing his talisman. Somehow, she thought he probably was.

They were now deep in the forest. They had come, she reckoned, some two miles or more. Probably more; it was hard to tell, with the frequent stopping, but when they had been moving, they had walked swiftly. Despite everything, a part of her had been revelling in the sheer pleasure of hard physical exercise. It must, she thought, be years since she'd marched along like this, breathing deeply, arms swinging, legs striding out. Nuns in a convent just didn't walk like that.

It reminds me, she reflected happily, of outings with dear old Ivo.

Her late husband had liked to walk hard, too. Often, when the demands of their busy life had relented for a few hours, the two of them had set out and—

'Listen!' said Josse's soft voice, right beside her.

'What?'

He had stopped again, at what appeared to be the end of a long and winding little path deep within the trees; they had been following its rather well-concealed course for some time. He drew her back into the moon shadow of a great oak, and, mouth to her ear, said, 'Can you hear it too, or am I imagining it?'

She held her breath, and, trying to shut out the sounds of Josse beside her, listened.

At first, nothing. The wind in the treetops, high overhead, and a faint distant rustling, quickly curtailed, as if some small animal had been running for safety and had made it to its burrow.

She was just beginning to shake her head in denial when she heard it.

Just a short snatch, which could have been the dancing leaves up above. But then it came again. The same phrase was repeated, again and then once more, each time with a fraction more volume.

And then, in some macabre and premature parody of the dawn chorus, still many hours away, other throats took up the sound. The original phrase echoed again, but extended now, elaborate, involved, turning back on itself and going higher, higher, so high as almost to leave the range of human hearing, only to dive down into a deep, thrumming baritone that throbbed like a distant drum.

Then it stopped.

Helewise felt the sweat of fear run down her back, accompanied by a great shudder that seemed to make her hair crawl on her scalp. In atavistic dread, she wanted to crouch on the ground, curl herself up small, creep away into some dark little niche where she would be safe, where *they* could not find her. But, just as the urge to hide became all but irresistible, Josse leaned close and said quietly, 'Abbess, it seems you were right after all, and the answers to all our questions may be just ahead of us.'

She managed to say, in something like her usual tones, 'Indeed.'

Had he known? Had he picked up her huge fear, and, wanting to help her master it, spoken thus to her?

It was his having called her by her title that did it, she thought, feeling strength returning with each second. It had, in that moment of weakness, reminded her of who and what she was. Of her responsibilities. And, even more important, reminded her what she was doing there in the middle of the forest when she ought to be safe in her bed.

Answers must be found, she told herself firmly. And Sir Josse and I shall find them.

She whispered, 'What should we do now?'

Turning from his intense concentration on the open space that lay ahead, he whispered back, 'We are close to the grove where the two fallen oak trees lie, where Hamm discovered the treasure. It is, I believe, of some importance in the forest, and I think we should try to get closer.'

'Very well. I was going to tell you, I—' But now was not the moment, and in answer to his eyebrows raised in enquiry, she shook her head.

He hitched the pack higher on his back, and was about to set forth when he hesitated. With a quick look back to her, he said, 'They – whoever they may be – could be in the oak grove. We must be absolutely silent.'

She smiled in the darkness, and said, 'I realise that. I'll be as quiet as the grave.'

Only as she began to creep after him did

she wish she had used any other word but 'grave'.

The next mile seemed terribly slow. Copying him, she trod carefully, trying each footstep before committing herself to it, making sure no cracking twig gave them away. It was nerve-racking.

At last, he stopped once more. Again, they were on the edge of an open space, but this time it was a much wider one. And, peering round the comforting bulk of Josse's shoulder, Helewise could see two vast felled oak trees lying across the short turf.

But, apart from the trees, the grove was empty.

Josse was moving forward, peering into the shadows that encircled the moonlit space. Suddenly he gave a soft exclamation, and, as he came back to her, she saw that he was grinning.

'They're ahead of us,' he said softly, when he was right beside her again. 'In another clearing, through there.' He pointed.

She looked, but could see nothing. 'Where?'

He took hold of her shoulders and pushed her gently towards the open space. 'Go to where the trees thin out, and look to your left,' he ordered.

She did as he said. And, staring into the darkness of an apparently impenetrable thicket of old trees, younger trees and dense, scrubby undergrowth, she saw what he had seen.

A light.

Faint, as if a single candle had been lit, or perhaps a small and carefully contained fire. But, in the deserted blackness, a strange sight.

She was about to return to him, ask what he thought should be their next move, when something caught her eye.

That light . . . It was as if, just for a splitsecond, it had been extinguished, then, just as quickly, relit. Watching, straining her eyes, it happened again.

What was it? Could it be—

Then she knew.

The blinking-out effect had an obvious cause, when you stopped to think about it. A cause that explained, too, why it went on happening.

Somebody was moving between Helewise and the source of the light.

Out in that hidden grove, there were other beings abroad in the forest.

For all that she had known they must be out

there – what else, indeed, was the purpose of this whole enterprise but to find them? – still, the sight of human movement, so close by, set her heart thumping.

The fear came flooding back, with the speed and the unremitting force of the tide over flat sands. And Helewise, forgetting all about being quiet, raced the few paces back to Josse's side as if she herself were in danger of inundation.

Chapter Fifteen

Silent as wraiths, they moved around the fringes of the oak grove, keeping to the shadows, pressing close to the surrounding trees.

As they passed the place where he had found the ancient ruined temple, Josse thought, I have never yet been further into the forest than this.

Amid all the other causes for concern, this was a new one. And, illogical though it was, somehow it was the most frightening.

The Abbess, he thought, more to take his mind off his apprehension than for any other reason, was obeying his command to move even more quietly. Had he not been perfectly well aware that she was behind him, he would never have guessed. Moving as if she had been specially trained for silent night operations, she made not a sound. Once or twice he had to fight the temptation to turn round and make sure she was still with him.

He would never have guessed, either, that a nun would be so well adapted for hard exercise; the pace he had set had made no concession to having a woman with him, less out of deliberate consideration for her and more because it had not entered his mind. Fear and intense concentration, he had found, tended to drive courtesy and pretty manners right out of the head.

Was she afraid? He would think no less of her if she were. How could he, when he was fearful himself? If she was afraid, she didn't show it, which was in itself brave. As a commanding officer had once said long ago to Josse, there is no courage where there is no fear.

They had almost reached the far side of the oak grove. Entering the thick undergrowth, Josse strained his eyes for a sign of a path, however insignificant. If there were no break at all in the trees, then how were they going to proceed?

But there was a break. Hardly worthy of the name of path, a thin trickle of a track led away

into the thicket. Pushing at tall, abundant
bracken, which, Josse soon discovered, concealed
an equal density of bramble, he led the way on
towards the light.

After an unpleasant time of thrusting and
edging forward, whilst keeping in mind the
imperative need for silence, at last the undergrowth began to thin out. Staring ahead, Josse
could see clear moonlight; they were approaching
another grove.

The trees that led up to and encircled it were
ancient and tall, and spaced far enough apart to
allow for considerable new growth beneath them.
There was, Josse thought in wonder, almost a
sense of pattern about them, as if, aeons ago,
someone had planted them with the intention of
making an avenue. As if, wishing to honour this
pathway that led to the holy grove, someone had
marked it with a double row of the most sacred of
trees . . .

For the trees that set the grove apart from the
rest of the forest were, without exception, oaks.

Selecting one with a broader trunk than its
fellows, Josse crept up to it, and the Abbess followed. Pressing themselves against the gnarled

bark, they stared out into the moonlit space before them.

For what seemed like a long time, nothing happened.

The fire – built on a stone hearth right in the centre of the clearing – burned on brightly, sending out the occasional crackle which made them both jump. Beside it was a thick, heavy section of wood, a man's height in length, remnant, perhaps, of a long-ago fallen tree. Staring at it, Josse was struck with the bizarre notion that it did not in fact lie there from any natural event, but that it had been *placed* there, after having been cut and shaped according to the dictates of some age-old ritual.

Unbidden, he recalled Sheriff Pelham's words. *They do things, when it's full moon.* And, even more worrying, *the forest folk don't like trespassers, specially not at full moon.*

Was that what they were, he and the Abbess? Trespassers, about to witness some terrible rite? About to commit the forbidden infringement for which another man had been killed?

The folly of what they were doing – of what he had allowed the Abbess to persuade him to do –

struck Josse like a poleaxe to the forehead. Turning, he said in a whisper, 'Abbess, we shouldn't be here, it's—'

But, whatever it was, it was too late.

Someone had entered the grove.

At some time during their witnessing of what happened then, Abbess Helewise must have taken hold of his arm. He couldn't have said exactly when; all he thought, both at the time and afterwards, was how very glad he was that she had done so. Had he not had that small human contact, he might have lost even the small amount of wits necessary to stop him doing something stupid.

Something such as responding to the blood thundering through his body and, in answer to the potent summons of all that he saw, rushing out into the moonlit clearing and begging to be allowed to join in.

Sheriff Pelham, absurd though it was, had been quite right.

Before Josse and the Abbess's astounded eyes, just as he had said, things were indeed done under the full moon . . .

*

It began with a lone robed figure making a complete circuit of the grove. It was a woman, undoubtedly, for, apart from the long grey-white hair that hung down her back as far as her waist, she had a woman's slight build. She held in her hand a bunch of some sort of herbs or seed-heavy grasses, and she had set light to the dried, twiglike fronds by dipping them into the fire. Waving the smouldering bunch to and fro in front of her as she slowly paced, she set clouds of smoke wafting out into the night air. Scented smoke – strongly, pungently scented.

She made her circle of the grove three times.

Then, putting the remnants of her herb bundle on to the fire, she picked up a long, straight wand. And, stepping as if in some dance, she moved all round the fire and the big log, making a pattern of some sort in the earth.

When at last she had finished, she moved to the fringes of the clearing and, for a moment, disappeared into the trees. When she emerged again into the moonlight, she was no longer alone.

She was leading by the hand a young woman. Dressed in a long flowing garment made of some sheer fabric, it was readily apparent that, beneath its folds, the girl wore nothing else. On her head, arranged on the glossy hair, was a thickly woven garland of leaves, grasses and flowers.

As the woman led the girl into the middle of the grove, the girl stopped for a brief moment and turned her face up to the night sky. As the rays of the full moon shone down on her, in the same instant Josse and the Abbess started in horrified amazement.

It was Caliste.

Josse felt the Abbess's tension, was aware, without her having made the smallest move, that some protective instinct in her was about to prompt her into action. Bending his head so that he could speak softly right in her ear, he said, as forcefully as he could, '*No.*'

She understood. And, an instant after he had spoken, he sensed her relax.

Beckoning him close again, she said, 'It's not—'

Not what? He was not to find out, for, in the grove, something else was happening.

The humming had begun again, accompanied by a dull, steady drum beat. From the way the sound seemed to creep up on the awareness,

Josse had an idea that it might have quietly been going on for some time. The volume was increasing rapidly, and, as it grew, the nature of the music was changing. Less like chanting, more like singing now, pure and sweet, as, at first in conflict with the chanting and then overcoming it, the melody rang out as if sung by the most perfect of heavenly choirs.

More fuel must have been added to the fire, for the smoke was thick now, its pale billows spreading right across the grove, penetrating under the trees to where Josse and the Abbess stood. It smelt of . . . what? Sage, and roses, and something that was reminiscent of anointing oil. Around the hearth, appearing and disappearing as the screen of smoke waxed and waned, giving the strange illusion that they were floating, were bunches of flowers tied with grass: poppies, deadly nightshade, and some leafy plant with small white blooms which Josse thought was hemlock.

The singing was much louder now. Somewhere out of sight in the trees there must be a great host of people, and—

The noise reached a deafening climax, drowning out the very power of thought. Then, with an abruptness that hurt the ears, it stopped.

In the utter silence of the moon-bathed clearing, the woman led the girl to the log. It, too, had been decorated with flowers, and at its head had been placed a pair of tall candles, burning with a steady flame.

It looked unmistakably like an altar.

The woman helped the girl to lie down, making for her a pillow of flowers. Then, moving round to stand behind the girl's head, she took hold of the girl's outstretched hands in what looked like a gesture of kindly companionship.

At first.

Then, as the woman's grip moved to the girl's wrists, it became clear that she was making sure the girl could not escape.

The singing began again. Now it was but a single voice, a woman's, and it came from the altar.

The girl, eyes closed, was chanting.

As her voice strengthened, she began to move her body, writhing from side to side, knees bent, hips circling. Then, with a great cry, she arched her back and flung her legs wide apart.

Another figure had emerged into the moonlight. Robed and hooded, it was only the height and the breadth of shoulder that revealed it to be male; the face was hidden deep within the cowled hood.

He went to stand at the foot of the altar.

The girl had moved downwards along it and, with her wrists still pinioned by the woman, her arms were now at full stretch. The movement had made her gown ride up, so that, from the full breasts to the bare feet, she was naked. Her spread legs flopped over the edges of the tree trunk on which she lay, and her exposed groin was at waist height for the standing man.

Even as it became obvious what was about to happen, already it seemed to have begun. The man had raised the hem of his full robe so that it spread over the girl's belly, concealing what it was that he did to her, but, visible or not, it was plain what act he was performing. Resuming her chanting, but abstractly now, with frequent breaks, she pushed herself upwards to meet him. Their movements swiftly becoming frenetic, suddenly it was over.

Stepping back from her, covering himself with

his robe, the man turned and, as the thick smoke
plumed up around him, he seemed to disappear.

The girl gave a small cry, a sound which, short
though it was, yet contained a dread, desperate
longing. As if in answer, another man appeared to
take the first one's place. Taking a little more time,
he too came to a climax and then, like his prede-
cessor, abandoned her.

Another followed, and another.

While the fifth one – a taller, stronger-looking
man – was thrusting into her, meeting the savage
upward push of her hips with an equal force of
his own, at long last her need was met. Wrists still
held firm by the woman who stood at the top of
the altar, the girl raised her body, threw back her
head, opened her mouth and emitted a long,
piercing, triumphant cry that rang out through
the oak grove and across the forest like the
victory scream of some triumphant animal.

As the echoes faded and died, the girl
slumped back on her tree trunk. Spent,
exhausted, her legs fell either side of its girth,
and, had the woman not had firm hold of her
arms, it seemed she would have slipped off and
fallen to the forest floor. But the woman, solici-

tous now, was swiftly going into action, an arm round the girl's shoulders, free hand pulling down the flimsy, flung-back robe as she helped the girl to stand.

Then, supporting most of the girl's weight – for her legs seemed suddenly powerless, and the little bare feet that dragged along the ground were barely moving – the woman bore her out of the brilliant moonlight and away into the black shade of the trees.

Josse, his mind and his body seething with a powerful force that he barely understood, put up his hands and rubbed hard at his face. Then, one hand still over his eyes as if, too late, he wanted to block out what he had just seen, he slid his back down the oak's trunk and slumped at its base.

After a moment, the Abbess sat down beside him.

He couldn't speak. Didn't know what he would have said had he been able to.

But, after a soft clearing of the throat, she said, 'It wasn't Caliste. Very like her, but not her.'

And, saying the first thing that entered his

head, he breathed, 'Thank God.' Then, after a pause: 'How can you be so sure?'

'The hair,' she replied.

He pictured the girl in her wild abandon. The garland had fallen off, and the thick dark hair had flowed like a black tide over the wood of the altar.

Of course. No nun had abundant hair like that.

'Not Caliste,' he echoed.

'No.'

Silence fell once more, surrounding them, suffocating them, as if someone had dropped a soft blanket on to them.

I could sleep, Josse thought vaguely. My eyelids are so heavy, I could lie down here and sleep till daybreak. Far beyond daybreak. Sleep all day, and the night after that.

He yawned hugely.

He felt the weight of the Abbess as she leaned against him, and, making an enormous effort, he turned his head a little to look at her. She had closed her eyes, and, her lips slightly apart, was breathing deeply. She seemed to have dozed off.

And why not? he thought. It's as good a place as any. Quite comfortable, and . . .

He slept.

But not for long.

As if some sense of self-preservation were working in him, some relic of his soldiering past that, even in these extreme circumstances, had not deserted him, he went straight into a vivid dream.

He was in the clearing, right in it, exposed and standing alone in the moonlight. And, creeping up behind him, each carrying a spear whose tip was pointing straight at Josse's back, stealthily came the grey-haired woman and the dark girl.

Both now were naked.

With a start and a snort, he was awake. Panting in terror, sweat breaking out all over his body, he spun round.

And banged his nose smartly on the tree trunk.

Thank God, thank God! He was not in the grove, was not about to be pierced to the heart by twin spears.

Leaping up, grabbing the Abbess's arm, he hissed, 'Abbess, wake up! We can't stay here! We—'

His head began to spin. Faster, faster, until he had to turn away and vomit into the bracken.

When he could stand up, he risked a gentle

swivelling of the eyes to look at her. Awake now, she, too, was looking sick. 'What is the matter?' she whispered. 'We should sleep, Josse! I'm so tired . . .'

He took both her hands and hauled her to her feet, no easy task since she was not only tall and well-built but also a near dead weight. 'Come *on*!' He gave her a shake, and, reluctantly, she straightened up, instantly falling back to lean against the oak.

'Oh, dear Lord!' she whispered. 'What . . .' She frowned, then, appearing to recall where they were and what they had just witnessed, at once she seemed to come to herself. 'We must get away,' she stated firmly. 'To a place of safety.'

He hustled her off, back through the trees and towards the underbrush through which they had come, all that time ago – it seemed an eternity. Fine sentiments, he thought, but it was a shame she'd spoken them out loud in such a strong voice.

Back along the overgrown path, back through the larger clearing with the fallen oaks, and well on the way to the path leading out of it. The path that would take them home.

He should have realised. Should have foreseen that, whereas he had been sick and was already on the way to recovery, she had not. *Was* not.

But the fact that she was hurrying along behind him must have fooled him into thinking she was all right.

As they approached the relative safety of the trees on the far side of the fallen-oak grove, Josse heard the Abbess give a low groan. Spinning round, he watched helplessly as she doubled up and retched. Then, wiping her mouth with one hand and waving him on with the other, she said, 'Go on! Hurry up and get under cover!'

Picking up her urgency, he ran.

Heard her running after him, one pace, two, three, four, her footfalls sounding hollow on the firm ground.

Then, as he ducked his head and raced in under the trees, he heard a sickening thump.

He stopped dead and spun round in a single action, to see her slumped on the ground under the very first of the circling trees.

She had just been sick, and was probably feeling horribly dizzy. In no state, in any case, to run headlong through a forest where there were overhanging trees with low branches.

Josse might have had the presence of mind to duck, but Helewise hadn't. She had run slap into the stout branch of an oak tree, and she had knocked herself out.

Josse, falling to his knees beside her, could see the blood already spreading out from under the starched white linen that bound her forehead. In sudden dread, roughly he pushed aside her wimple and put his fingers to her throat.

For a terrible few seconds he could feel no pulse.

But then he could. Irregular, and quite feeble, but still a pulse.

Fervently he said aloud, 'Thank God! Oh, thank God!'

From the profound shadows beside the path, someone said, 'Amen.'

Chapter Sixteen

His head flew up. Staring around him, trying to peer into the gloom beneath the trees, at first he couldn't see anybody.

Then she was there. It was like that: one moment he could see nothing but the trunks of the trees and the tangling undergrowth, then, like an apparition, suddenly a figure was standing there.

His head felt muzzy. Josse didn't really know if he was awake or dreaming.

The robed figure moved closer, seeming to float as if she rode on a cushioning cloud of sweet-smelling smoke. Leaning over Josse and Helewise, her long silver hair brushed against his face. She smelt as sweetly as the smoke. Of flowers, and fresh green things.

A long-fingered hand stretched out, touched the Abbess's cheek, was laid flat across her forehead. 'She is injured,' a calm voice said.

'She hit her head,' Josse said, his own voice sounding strangely distant. 'As we ran in under the trees, she banged her forehead on a branch.'

No answer.

The robed figure had vanished. Then, some time later, she came back. He knew she was coming because she held a light in her hand, and it was the light that he saw.

She held it out to him.

'Make a fire,' the voice intoned. 'It is forbidden here in the forest, except by my decree, but, for this need, I allow it. Keep the woman warm.'

She was, Josse noticed then, carrying something in her other hand: it was his pack. He must have left it by the smaller grove, where they had witnessed that incredible ceremony. The light from her flare caught a glitter of response from the pack, and he remembered pinning his talisman on the pack's flap, before he and the Abbess had set out.

He said, having to force out the words as if his mouth were full of wool, 'Thank you, lady.'

The woman stood staring down at him for a few moments. Then she said, 'I am Domina.'

Watching her float off across the clearing and disappear away under the trees, Josse thought absently that he would bet money on 'Domina' being as much a title as 'Abbess'.

The moon had set.

In the utter darkness of the pre-dawn, the temperature went down sharply.

And Josse gave thanks all over again to Domina, and her fire.

Left alone with the unconscious Abbess, Josse had hastened to make some sort of shelter for her; clearly, there was no question of trying to move her very far until she awoke. If that had not happened by daylight, then Josse would have to think about leaving her there in the deep forest and going for help.

It was a disturbing thought.

Using the Domina's flare, he went in under the trees and, in the thick bracken, found a shallow dell with an earth bank at its back, overhung with hazel and holly trees. Stamping down the green fronds of bracken, he took one of the blankets out of his pack and laid it down, putting the other one ready beside it. Then he went back for the Abbess.

Had he been fully himself, then he probably wouldn't have found carrying her the short distance to the shelter such a task. As it was, he still felt sick and dizzy, and the exertion of carrying a well-built woman a dozen or so paces almost made him black out.

As he was settling her, trying to arrange her habit around her legs so as to keep her warm before tucking the blanket round her, he wondered briefly *why* he felt so ill.

But then he remembered the wound on her forehead, and, in the rush of anxiety which that recollection brought, the thought went out of his mind.

He rammed the flare into the crook made where a low branch of the hazel tree met its trunk, and, by its steady light, bent down to examine the Abbess's head. There was a wash of blood over her eyebrows now, and a thin trail had run into her right eye. Through the fuzz in his brain he thought: water. I need water to bathe her face.

It took him quite a long time to remember that he had put a flask of fresh water in his pack.

He needed a cloth of some sort, preferably clean . . . Rummaging in the pack, he came across the dagger which he had hidden away right at the bottom, wrapped in a square of linen. The cloth was not all that clean, but it would serve. It would have to.

He washed her eyes and her forehead, noticing with dismay that the blood had turned the stiff, pristine white of her linen headdress to scarlet.

I must see the wound, he decided. Hesitantly he pushed back the black veil, and untied the tapes which fastened the linen cap covering her head and her forehead, experiencing as he did so the shameful sensation that he was violating her. But I *must*, he told himself firmly, because the wound might still be bleeding, and, if so, I need to staunch the flow before—

Before what?

He decided it was better for his peace of mind not to dwell on that.

The wimple was tied at the top of her head, the ties normally sitting beneath the headdress. With that last item removed, the Abbess was bare-headed, and at last Josse could see her injury.

There was a huge bruise on the left side of her forehead, starting just under the hairline and extending almost to her eyebrow. In the centre of the bruise – which had swelled up to the size of a child's fist – was a deep cut, the length of the top pad of his thumb. Blood was slowly welling out of it.

He wiped away the steadily seeping blood, then squeezed out his cloth until it was as clean as he could make it. He tore a long strip off one edge, folding the rest into a pad; he pressed the pad against the wound, and tied it firmly in place with the strip of cloth.

He said softly out loud, 'That, my dear Helewise, is the best I can do for you.'

He looked down at her, frowning. Was it his imagination, or was she even paler? Perhaps it was just that her face *seemed* more pale, now that it was framed by her hair and not by the black veil on top of the white linen band and wimple.

Her hair, he noted absently, was reddish-gold, cut short and curling round her face, a little grey at the temples. The skin of her neck and throat, normally hidden beneath her wimple, was smooth and unlined; somehow, seeing her like this, he thought she seemed younger . . .

Looking down at her when she could not return his gaze was making him uneasy. And besides, he thought, he could be of more use to her than merely standing there gawping with his mouth open. He could, for example, do something about trying to warm her.

He made a swift search for dry and well-seasoned kindling and firewood – both of which were abundant in these wild, uninhabited depths of the forest – and, touching the Domina's flare to the base of his fire, he soon had a small but intense blaze going. He put a stack of branches within reach beside it. Then, having stared at the still-unconscious Abbess for some moments, he gently turned her on to her right side, the front of her body to the fire, and lay down behind her.

She was well wrapped-up, in her own clothes and, outside them, the blanket; there must be, he was sure, a good four or five layers of various materials between her body and his. Nevertheless, he felt that he was committing a sin.

'I've got to keep her warm,' he said aloud to nobody in particular. 'I'm doing it the best way that I can, by building the fire and by the heat of my own body. But I—'

What? But I swear I'm not enjoying it?

He grinned into the darkness. Well, perhaps he was, just a little.

Putting his arm round her waist and drawing her towards him, he closed his eyes and tried to relax. Even if he couldn't sleep, at least he could rest, try to build up some reserves of strength.

Whatever happened, he was probably going to need them.

Helewise was dreaming.

She was young again, dressed in a flowing silk gown of sunshine yellow, and someone had put a garland of flowers on her hair. It was too tight, biting into her forehead and making her head ache. But there was singing and dancing, and she was sitting on a grassy bank beneath a vast, spreading willow tree, and her sons, both babies together, were at her breast. She was plump with milk, breasts running with it, abundant, earthy. Then Ivo was there, smiling his joy, kissing her, calling her his Flora, his Queen of the May, and she was laughing too, telling him that she could only be Queen of the May for a day, for then she must return to the Abbey.

And, in the instant way of dreams, she was back in Hawkenlye Abbey, kneeling at the altar in the Abbey church, eyes closed, hands folded as she prayed, and Sister Euphemia was plucking at her sleeve and saying, Abbess, Abbess, what has become of your habit? Looking down at herself, she saw she was still wearing the yellow silk. And the garland of flowers, heavy on her brow, was making her headache worse . . .

Helewise opened her eyes.

She lay quite still, trying to work out where she was. It was dark, and, judging from the smell – of earth and greenery – and from the cold, she guessed she was out of doors. In front of her were the remains of a small fire, little more than glowing embers now, although there was a neat pile of branches beside the fire. It could be rekindled quite easily, she thought dreamily.

Her head gave a throb, and she put up her hand to ease the pain. There seemed to be something tied around her brow.

And where was her veil? Her headband? Her wimple?

Her movement had disturbed Ivo, who gave a grunt and wriggled himself into a more comfortable position. He was lovely and warm; she pressed her buttocks into the crook of his body and revelled in the comfort of him, dear old Ivo, and—

Hurled into shocked wakefulness, she remembered. Ivo was dead, dead and buried years ago! Oh, dear God, then who was she cuddling up to?

And, equally important, where was she?

She made herself stop panicking, and thought back.

And, soon, saw again that incredible scene in the clearing. Remembered running, running, as fast as she could, and remembered being sick. Feeling so ill, so dizzy.

Remembered Josse.

I must have hurt myself, she decided. And Josse, bless him, has looked after me. Tended me – she fingered the pad pressed to what seemed to be the source of the pain on her forehead – and lit a fire. Wrapped me up, lain down beside me to keep me warm.

It was, she knew, exactly the right thing, in cases of injury. Keep the patient warm.

Well, he'd done that, all right. And the sudden hot blood she could feel rushing to her face was merely a side-effect of how warm the rest of her was. Wasn't it?

She let her eyes roam across the scene before her. The greyish light was growing – it must be a little after dawn – and she could make out the big clearing with the two fallen oak trees. She and Josse appeared to be lying on a bed of bracken, in a little hollow in the undergrowth.

Oh, dear.

She must have moved again, for she knew suddenly that she had woken him up. His body against hers had been relaxed in sleep, and now there was a tension in him.

What on earth, she wondered, do we say to one another?

It was he who broke the awkward silence. In a surprisingly normal tone, he said, 'Good morning, Abbess. How do you feel?'

'My head hurts,' she confessed.

'I'm not surprised. You ran full tilt into an oak tree.'

'Oh.'

He was, she noticed, lying absolutely still, as if any movement would make an embarrassing situation even worse. Despite herself, she had to suppress a smile.

'I needed to keep you warm,' he said in a rush. 'I'm sorry, but it – this – lying behind you like this – was the best I could think of.'

'I understand.'

She felt him raise himself on an elbow, and then he was looking down at her, anxious face looming above hers. 'You're still pale,' he said.

'Mm.' There was something slightly odd about him, too. She studied him for a few moments, then said gravely, 'Your eyes are funny.'

'Funny?'

'The black bits – what do you call them?' She couldn't for the life of her think of the word.

'Pupils?'

'Pupils. Thank you. Your pupils are huge. So big that there's hardly any brown round the edges.'

He leaned closer to her, eyes fixed to hers. 'So are yours,' he said.

Then, as if the discovery had exhausted him, he lay down again.

After quite some time she said, 'I think we've been drugged.'

'I think so, too. I was just putting it all together, the dizziness, the sickness, and I don't know about you but I've been having the most incredibly vivid—'

'Dreams?'

'Dreams.' She could hear that he was smiling.

'What was it, do you think?' she asked. 'The drug. Something in the smoke?'

'I imagine so. That – that ceremony which we saw seemed to employ some fairly sophisticated potions and herbal concoctions.'

'Mm.' She hadn't wanted to be reminded of the ceremony.

He gave a great yawn, then said, 'Sorry. I can't seem to keep my eyes open.'

She, too, was sleepy. 'Nor I.'

He said tentatively, 'Shall we try to sleep again? For an hour or two, at least, until the sun rises and begins to warm the air?'

'Yes.' Absently she snuggled her hips against him, cradling her cheek on her hand. 'Good night,' she said, already dozy.

He muttered something. She heard the word 'chastity'.

'What was that?' she said sharply.

'Oh. Er – nothing.'

'Josse?'

'I said, whatever happened to the nun's vow of chastity?' he said.

She should have been angry, affronted, but for some reason she actually wanted to laugh. Controlling the urge, she said crushingly, 'And who, may I ask, said anything about being unchaste?' He began to make an apology, but she cut him off. 'Sir Knight, do not presume!'

'Abbess, please, do not take offence, I merely—'

But she was laughing now, and he, pressed so close to her, must realise it. She said, 'It's all right. I was teasing.'

'So was I,' he murmured.

She closed her eyes. 'I was a wife before ever I was a nun,' she said drowsily.

'Were you?'

'Yes.' She yawned, so widely that it made her eyes water. 'What I remember with the most fondness is not the passion of the marriage bed, but the comfort.' She wriggled again, settling into sleep. 'And,' she added in a murmur, 'the companionship.'

He said something, but she didn't hear. She was already asleep.

Chapter Seventeen

When Josse next woke, the Abbess no longer lay in front of him. The sun was shining brightly down into the grove, and, a few paces away, a figure in a nun's habit knelt in prayer.

She was, he thought, watching her, probably saying the Office. Prime, would it be? Or Tierce? It depended on how long they'd been asleep.

She was wearing wimple, headdress and veil. The garments sat a little awkwardly over the bandage round her brow, but she looked herself again. The laughing, curly-haired woman with whom he had shared his forest bed had gone.

With a faint sigh, he bade her a fond farewell.

While the Abbess was praying, he got up, folded the blankets and stowed them back into his pack, trying to move quietly so as not to disturb her. The fire was still glowing, but, now that the sun's heat was reaching down to warm up the forest, there was no more need of it. He stamped out the last of the red embers, and then took out his knife and cut neat turves from the thinly growing grass on the outer fringes of the undergrowth, with which he covered the burned scar in the ground.

He hoped his actions would be pleasing to the Domina.

Then, with nothing else to do, he sat down and waited until the Abbess had finished.

As she walked towards him, he noticed that, for a moment, she could not meet his eyes. Remembering the night, remembering how he had not only removed quite a lot of her habit but had also lain with her, body close up against hers, he understood.

We have to put that behind us, he thought. Just as if it had never happened.

He stood up. With a bow, he said, 'Abbess Helewise. I wish you good day. We should, I think, make our way back to the Abbey, as soon as you feel able to travel.'

She shot him a look in which relief and gratitude were mixed. Then she said quietly, 'Yes, Sir Josse. I am able to travel straight away.'

He shouldered his pack and stepped out on to the path beside her. Together they turned towards the track that led to Hawkenlye.

And saw, standing silently some ten paces off, the robed figure of the Domina.

For a long moment, she stared at them, unmoving, deep-set eyes fixed first on the Abbess, then on him. He felt he should speak – felt, indeed, that he should apologise, although he was not entirely sure what for – but somehow her intent gaze kept him dumb.

Eventually she said, 'The woman is well?'

The Abbess said quietly, 'I am well.'

The other woman nodded. 'It is a long journey you have, for one who has been injured.'

'I can manage,' the Abbess said.

The Domina stepped closer. When she stood right in front of the Abbess, she raised a hand and touched the dressing on Helewise's head, leaning briefly forward and apparently sniffing at the place where the cut was. 'Clean,' she observed. 'The man has done well.' She glanced at Josse.

He bowed his head.

The Domina was reaching into a leather pouch that hung at her waist, half-concealed by the cloak she now wore over her white robe. Taking out a small glass phial, she removed its stopper and held it out to the Abbess. 'Drink,' she ordered.

Josse watched the Abbess. He could sense she was reluctant – which was more than understandable, bearing in mind how they had both suffered from the smoke they had inhaled last night – but at the same time she was also, he thought, hesitant to offend someone who was genuinely trying to help her.

As if she read all of that, the Domina gave a brief laugh. 'This will not make you see the dance of the creatures of the night,' she said. 'It will not make you feel you can fly, nor create the wild pictures inside your head. It is to help your pain.'

'I have no—' the Abbess began.

The Domina gave a short *tch!* of annoyance. 'Do not deny it,' she said. 'I can feel it.'

The Abbess's mouth dropped open slightly. Then, as if making up her mind, she took the phial and drank its contents.

'Good, good,' said the Domina.

The three of them stood, not moving, not speaking; Josse felt, as probably the Abbess did too, that, here in the Domina's realm, they must take their cue from her. And she seemed to be waiting for something.

After a while, the Abbess suddenly smiled. Looking both happy and surprised, she exclaimed, 'The pain has gone!'

And the Domina said, 'Of course.'

Then she turned to Josse. 'I sense your impatience, man,' she said. 'You wish to take the woman back to her own place.'

She appeared to be waiting for an answer, so he said, 'Aye. I do.'

'All in good time,' the Domina said. 'Before you depart from my domain, I will address you.' She held out her hands towards Josse and the Abbess, and, as if pushing aside the branches of a tree, she moved them out of her way. Then, beckoning them to follow, she led them along a path which Josse had not previously noticed, one which wound away into the deep forest on the far side of the clearing with the fallen trees.

Why, he wondered, did I not notice it before?

He shook his head in puzzlement, for, now that the Domina was leading them to it, the track seemed all too obvious.

The Domina glanced at him over her shoulder, gave him a strange smile, then turned back to face the way she was going. And, quite clearly inside Josse's head, he heard the words, 'You did not see this secret way before because I did not want you to.'

Not for the first time, Josse had the alarming sensation that he was in the presence of something – someone – far beyond his experience or comprehension.

As they left the clearing, the Domina said, waving a hand towards the dead trees, 'This is the work of Outworlders. It is an abomination.'

And Josse thought he heard the Abbess mutter, 'I *knew* it!'

She did not take them far. After perhaps a quarter of a mile of negotiating the narrow path, it opened out into an open space, through which a small stream ran. Above the stream, on a bank which rose up above it, was what appeared to be a dwelling. Made of branches, bent and woven into a framework, it was roofed with leaves and turves. Inside was a stone hearth, on which a pot bubbled quietly.

The Domina indicated that they should sit down on the bank above the rippling water.

As they settled, Josse thought fleetingly how bewitching was the combination of the sounds – the stream rushing along its stony bed, the softly simmering pot – and the smells . . . some strong herbal scent, from the steam coming from the pot, the sweet smell of flowers and green grass, a sort of peatyness from the stream.

Ah, but it was powerful, this atmosphere!

The Domina did not sit down, but remained standing above them.

After a moment, as if she had been waiting until she had their full, undivided attention, she began to speak.

'Outworlders,' she said, 'are not welcome here.' She looked down at Josse, then at the Abbess. 'Outworlders do not understand our ways. They destroy and desecrate what we hold to be holy. Outworlders killed the sacred oak.'

Josse nodded slowly. 'In the grove where the old temple ruins are,' he said. 'They set traps for game, and disturbed buried coins.'

'They burrowed beneath the oldest tree,' the Domina said. 'He had fallen of his own volition, for he was tired and no longer wished to live. Out worlders took what was not theirs to take, and, not content with what came readily out of the earth, they killed a second tree.' Her face working, she said harshly, 'He was young, with centuries of life ahead of him! Yet Outworlders hacked with their blunt weapons, hacked at him until he bled, until he wept, and they brought him to the ground!'

'They did a grave wrong,' Josse said quietly.

'Outworlders trespass against us,' the Domina said, more controlled now. 'And we do not forgive.'

'The man – the Outworlder – died,' Josse said. 'The spear was skilfully thrown, and he died cleanly.'

The Domina nodded. 'It is our way. We do not deliberately inflict pain.'

'Did he die because he had killed your oak?' Josse went on tentatively.

The Domina gazed down at him for some moments. 'The trees in the sacred grove bear the golden bough and the silver berry,' she said. 'Fruit of the sun and fruit of the moon, pure white seed of the god.'

'Mistletoe,' Josse murmured. No wonder the Forest People had taken the felling so seriously; mistletoe growing on oak was a rarity indeed, and now, in a very short time, they had lost two of those special trees. One had died, but the other had been deliberately felled. Purely to serve man's greed.

'There is something else,' the Domina said. She turned away from the stream bank, paced a circle between the water and the dwelling, and then, as if having collected her thoughts, returned to address them once more.

'You saw our most secret ceremony,' she stated. 'It is not for Outworlders.'

'We had no malicious intent,' the Abbess said. 'We came into the forest because I was concerned for two of my – for two young women who are my responsibility. We came across your – your activities in the grove by pure mischance.'

The Domina stared at her. 'No malicious intent,' she repeated. 'But yet you were witnesses to what it is forbidden for Outworlders to see.'

'We did not—' Josse began.

But the Abbess and the Domina were still locked in each other's gaze; Josse, watching closely, had the sudden sensation that there was an invisible thread between them, a thread which, against all odds, meant that they understood one another. The Abbess said softly, 'Domina, what was it for?'

And, with an almost imperceptible nod of acceptance, the Domina said, 'Listen, and I will tell you.'

She drew herself up, arms by her sides, and stared out over the rushing water to the dark forest beyond. Then she began to speak.

'We are few, we who live with and within the Great Forest,' she said. 'We move from place to place, here for a season, there for the next, always the same pattern down through the years. We take what the forest freely gives, but we do not abuse her bounty. We limit our numbers, so that the Great Mother is not overstretched in supporting us.'

She paused. Then the calm voice went on: 'Under the bright night skies of summer, every two hundred moons, we assemble in the most ancient of the silver fruit groves for our sacred procreation ritual. A ripe virgin is chosen, who is the recipient of the seed of the tribe. If the Mother so decrees, the seed of the elders is successfully sown in the womb of the young woman, and, in time, the new child of the tribe is born.' Briefly she closed her eyes, murmuring some soft invocation; it was as if the matters of which she spoke were so potent, so deeply ritualistic, that to describe them was both dangerous and exhausting.

But, gathering herself, the Domina went on.

'If the procreation ritual results in a live birth and the child is male, he in turn is schooled in the mysteries, and, in time, takes his place as an elder of the tribe, to engender new life as he was himself engendered. If the child is female, she is sequestered from the tribe until, in her sixteenth year, she is led forth to be fertilised with the seed of the tribe.'

Josse, shaking his head in disbelief, could scarcely believe that here in this forest – its fringes only yards from Hawkenlye Abbey, only a few miles from roads, towns, villages – here in this forest, an ancient people still lived who worshipped the old goddesses and gods, whose lives were ruled by the moon and the sun. Who had not, it seemed, been touched by the least fingertip of late twelfth-century civilisation.

It was all but incredible.

He realised that the Abbess was speaking. Reverently, in the attitude of a supplicant, she was asking the Domina for permission to pose a question.

'Ask,' the Domina said.

'The girl, last night,' Abbess Helewise said. 'She – Domina, she looked exactly like one of the girls in my care. One of the girls, indeed, about whom I have been so concerned.' She smiled briefly. 'Sufficiently concerned to trespass into your forest.'

The Domina, eyes still on the Abbess's, gave a curt nod of understanding. Then she said, 'Selene. The girl you saw in the grove is called Selene. She was born sixteen years ago, in the silver fruit glade, but in bringing her into the world, her mother left it.' The echo of an old sorrow crossed the Domina's face, darkening her countenance; the deep, far-seeing eyes were narrowed to ominous slits, and the full mouth

became a stern, hard line. For an instant, Josse
saw the dread power of the woman.

Then, staring once more at the Abbess, the
Domina said, 'The mother died because the birth
was so hard. And the birth was so hard because
she bore in her belly not one but two offspring.
Two daughters, the one an exact copy of the
other.'

Twins, Josse thought. Some poor woman of
these primitive forest folk had carried twins.
Multiple births, God knew, were difficult enough
at the best of times. But out here, on the forest
floor, no comforts, no warmth, not even a village
midwife to help, what must the wretched woman
have suffered?

He realised that the Domina was watching
him. She said, 'The mother had care, Outworlder.
The best care. Do not imagine that she would
have fared better out there in your world, some
man's chattel in one of your great houses.'

He dropped his head. 'I apologise.' Fool! he
berated himself. First, for forgetting about this
Domina's skills with herbs and potions, which
must surely far surpass those of some peasant
midwife. And second, for overlooking her clear

ability to read his thoughts.

'Only one child was needed by the tribe,' the Domina continued. 'By our laws, if such an event occurs, the choice must be the elder child. Selene remained with us, Caliste was given away.'

'Caliste!' The Abbess breathed. 'That is what she calls herself!'

The Domina looked mildly surprised. 'Of course.'

'But—' Josse knew what the Abbess was thinking. Sure enough, she went on: 'But how did she know? She was but a babe when she was lain on Alison Hurst's doorstep! And they – Alison and Matt – named her Peg!'

'Peg,' the Domina repeated tonelessly.

'I know, it's not a very lovely name,' the Abbess agreed, 'especially when compared with the child's real name. But they didn't know the real name! And I cannot understand how the child did, either.'

'She wore her name around her neck,' the Domina said.

'But—' The Abbess frowned, then her brow cleared. 'The piece of wood!' she exclaimed. 'Yes, I remember Alison Hurst showed it to me when

Caliste wanted to come and join us.' She turned to Josse. 'The baby wore a leather thong round her neck, on which hung a pendant made of wood, carved with strange marks.' Wonderingly she turned back to the Domina. 'Was it some sort of code, which only Caliste understood?' she asked softly.

'It was our script,' the Domina said.

'How could she interpret it?' Josse demanded. 'She was only an infant when you left her with the Hursts, so where did she find the key to the code?'

The Domina was eyeing the Abbess. 'You have manuscripts in your Abbey?'

'Yes. We do.'

'Tomes on natural lore?'

'I – Yes!' Excitedly, she went on, 'I remember now! Peg – she was still called Peg, when she first came to us – particularly liked the tree lore manuscript!' She turned her eyes up to the Domina. 'And it was after she had discovered it that she asked to be known as Caliste.'

The Domina nodded, unsurprised. 'She found the key to the script,' she remarked, in a tone that seemed to say, naturally!

'What did it look like?' Josse asked. 'The

script?' He had been thinking hard.

'It was a series of notches, cut into the sides of the pendant,' the Abbess told him.

'Aye.' He glanced up at the Domina. 'The ogham alphabet.'

She shrugged. 'Call it what you will. It is our way of recording the sounds of things.'

'She always loved to spend her time out of doors,' the Abbess said. 'Alison Hurst told me how, even when Peg was tiny, she made her own little garden.' She looked at the Domina. 'It's hardly surprising, is it? Given whose child she really was.'

The Domina shrugged again. 'All of my people understand their brothers and sisters in nature. They are all the Great Mother's children.'

The Abbess was nodding. 'Human people, too,' she said eagerly. 'Caliste has the healing touch, Domina. Recently I have put her to nursing duties, and, in her care of the sick, she shows a true natural ability.'

For the first time, the Domina gave a faint smile. She said, 'Caliste is her mother's daughter.'

Josse had been aware of a steadily growing irritation in himself. All very well and good to speak of Caliste and her abilities so proudly, but had this Domina any right to pride? Look what she subjected Caliste's twin to, only last night!

Again remembering, too late, the Domina's telepathic skill, he tried to make his mind turn to some other subject. Something innocuous – the flowers, perhaps, the trees . . .

But she had overheard his thoughts, picked up his anger. In a cold voice, she said, 'You criticise our ways, Outworlder? You, who have not the least knowledge or understanding of forest life?'

He stood up, suddenly humiliated by sitting obediently at her feet like some schoolboy. 'I do criticise,' he said baldly. 'You took a young woman into that clearing last night, you held her down naked on a log and stood there watching while five men raped her! Would not anybody criticise that?'

The Domina's face changed. The deep, dark eyes seemed to light up with a bright flame, and, as her lips drew back from her strong, even teeth, she hissed like an angry snake. Josse, standing his ground, felt briefly as if flame were scorching up and down his body; a stab of primeval terror pierced him, and it was all that he could do not to fall, screaming in fear, begging for mercy, at her feet.

But, as quickly as it had come, her attack eased off.

And, in a voice that sounded quite gentle, she said, 'There was no rape. Selene went willingly to the ritual, knowing full well what would happen. She has long been aware that she would be the chosen one. And I myself administered the potion that would both arouse her and moisten her – did she not look eager, Outworlder? Did the ritual not end in a more glorious climax for her than for any of the males? And besides' – the harsh lines of the face softened – 'why should I wish to harm her?'

She paused, looking from Josse to the Abbess and then back again.

'Why, indeed, should I inflict pain or harm,' she repeated, 'on the child of my own daughter?'

Chapter Eighteen

Helewise, watching Josse, felt a wave of pity for him. He does not understand, she thought. It was as though he were still on some upper level of comprehension, where things were merely what they were, with no more profound or symbolic meaning.

But *I* understand, she realised wonderingly. For all that she had lived her life in the narrow worlds of, first, the homes of knights and, second, within the walls of an abbey, she knew, at some deep place in her mind, what the essence was of this strange, archaic, parallel world into which she and Josse had stumbled.

For a moment she felt a brief return of last night's trance state, and, as if she were dreaming while awake, she seemed to see a circle of women, chanting, creeping apprehensively through dark underground passages, emerging into some rock womb of the earth where, at last, the ultimate mystery was revealed . . .

To them. To the women.

With a start, Helewise shook her head violently – sending shock-waves of pain from her wounded forehead – and dismissed the vision. I am a nun! she cried silently. I worship the one true God and His holy son Jesus Christ, and I live my life of service and devotion in an abbey dedicated to the blessed virgin, Mary!

What have I to do with the Great Mother?

From somewhere deep within herself – or possibly from the older woman standing so still, so tense, at her side, there came the beginnings of a reply. 'We are all to do with the Great—'

But Helewise said aloud, '*No,*' and the soft inner voice was stilled.

Josse was speaking. Bringing herself back to the present – not without difficulty – Helewise listened.

'. . . another reason for killing Hamm Robinson?' he was saying, directing a ferocious frown at the Domina.

Unperturbed, she said, 'Hamm Robinson? Who is he?'

'The man you stuck through with a spear!' Josse cried.

'Ah. You wish to know whether he was similarly an uninvited witness to a secret ceremony.'

'Aye.'

A faint sneer crossed the smooth pale face of the Domina. 'He was. He stood there at the edge of the holy grove, and I could see him drooling at what he saw. His life was already forfeit because he had killed the oak in the silver fruit grove. However, we would have slain him twice over, were that possible, for his double offence against us. Yes, Outworlder. The man Hamm was witness to that other procreation ritual, which took place in the grove two moons ago.'

'You mean,' Josse said slowly, 'that the poor lass had to go through that *twice*?'

'Still you do not understand,' the Domina observed, her tone a few degrees colder. 'Selene is aware of the honour of her role. It is the epitome of forest life, to be selected as preserver of the elemental essence of all that we are. And, naturally, she knew that, if the first seed-sowing were unsuccessful, then there would be another.'

'You mention only one other ritual,' Helewise said. 'Why was there not one last full moon?'

The Domina turned her deep eyes to Helewise. 'Because—' she began.

But Josse did not let her finish. 'There *was*!' he shouted. 'I was in the forest that night, I stood in the clearing with the fallen oak trees, and I heard your damnable chanting! You were there, I know full well you were!'

Helewise, amazed at the sudden profanity, was momentarily afraid of the Domina's reaction. Slowly the older woman turned, until she was facing Josse, and, even from where she stood, Helewise felt the malevolence. But then, perceptibly, the Domina relaxed, and she said calmly, 'We were there. I do not deny it. But there was no ritual that night.' Pointedly she turned back to Helewise, as if to say, only another woman can understand these matters. 'We believed Selene to have conceived, following the first ritual,' she said. 'Hence there appeared no need for a second. However, what had been within her slipped away. Her womb did not hold new life.'

Helewise, amid everything else, was struck

with the incredible skill of anyone who could tell, so early on, whether or not a girl was pregnant. 'It's very hard to judge,' she agreed, 'in the first weeks. The symptoms are quite slow to show up.'

The Domina was looking at her with amusement. 'Symptoms,' she repeated.

'How else?' Helewise asked simply.

The Domina moved closer to her, eyes narrowed in concentration. 'There is life, or there is not life. And life sends out its own emanations.' She held out an arm, the hand outstretched so that the thumb and fingers spanned a rough circle. 'The aura of a newly conceived infant is faint but detectable, from the very moment when its life begins.' She must have noticed Helewise's incomprehension, for, lowering her hand, she said, 'Ah, well. Perhaps, like so many other things, it is a skill that Outworld women have lost.'

Incredible, Helewise thought. Quite incredible. If she understood right, the Domina was claiming that she had known straight after the first ritual that Selene had conceived, but, as often happened, the new pregnancy was not sound, and had soon failed. Now, two months later, the girl had been impregnated again . . .

'Is she pregnant now?' she asked.

The Domina smiled. 'She is. And, this time, the new life is vibrant and strong. It is a male child,' she added.

Josse, apparently, had endured enough of this. He said, stubbornly returning to the matter uppermost in his own mind, 'Why were you chanting, then, that night? If there was no ritual, what were you doing?'

Steady! Helewise wanted to say. We are on the Domina's ground, and it is neither diplomatic nor prudent for us to interrogate a woman possessing powers such as hers!

As if the Domina had heard, she turned and said to Helewise, 'Do not be distressed. I will answer the man.' Then, to Josse: 'There were Outworlders in the grove that night.' A faint smile crossed her face. 'Outworlders other than you, man. We were there to observe.'

He looked doubtful. 'Not to kill?'

'Not to kill,' she confirmed. 'The Outworlder who bled like a stuck pig on to the forest floor did not die at our hands.' She fixed Josse with piercing eyes. 'We kill cleanly. And, as you are well aware, Outworlder, that man took a time to die.'

Josse, Helewise noticed, was nodding. 'Josse?' she whispered. 'What does she mean?'

He shot her a compassionate look. 'I heard him,' he said.

'*Oh!*' He heard a man die! she thought, horrified. Heard the screams of a long drawn-out death. Oh, dear God!

'We saw you, too,' the Domina said to Josse. 'As I think you are aware. We knew you visited the grove, both that night and the night before.'

Josse gave a brief grin, which looked more like a grimace. 'Yes. I know. I felt eyes on me, both times.' He raised an eyebrow. 'You did not harm me,' he said.

'No,' the Domina agreed. 'Of all the Outworlders in our realm that night, you had some faint sense of what the forest element means.'

Josse nodded slowly. 'Aye.'

'You stood by the fallen trees, and you mourned for the life that was no more.'

'Aye.'

Helewise said tentatively, 'Josse?'

He turned to her. 'I couldn't tell you,' he said,

an apology in his voice. 'I – it – oh, it's just not something I knew how to put into words.'

'No,' she said softly. 'I see that.'

He was looking at the Domina. 'Why?' he asked.

'Why?'

'Why did you not harm me?' he said. 'I wondered then, and I wonder now. Wonder, indeed, why you are here with us, answering our questions, tolerating our presence, when you have demonstrated quite clearly before that you do not welcome strangers.'

The Domina pointed to his pack, lying on the stream bank where he had thrown it. 'That is why.'

'The pack?'

She gave a soft sound of impatience. 'No, Outworlder, what is on your pack.'

He looked. As he turned back to the Domina, Helewise knew, before he spoke, what he would say. 'The talisman,' he whispered. 'You saw the talisman.'

'It is ours,' the Domina said.

'Who put it on my pack?'

The Domina smiled. 'Who do you think?'

'Caliste,' he said, an answering smile creasing his face. 'It was Caliste.'

'It was,' the Domina agreed. 'You must have made a favourable impression, Outworlder,' she said, with gentle irony. 'Caliste understands our signs, and, by putting the amulet of the Sword of Nuada on your pack, she was saying, as plain as light, *do not harm him*.'

'Dear Lord,' Josse muttered. Then, as if a new thought had occurred to him, he glanced at Helewise and said urgently, 'Does that still hold good?'

For a long moment the Domina did not answer. She stared back at Josse, then turned her steady gaze to Helewise.

It felt, Helewise thought amid the fear, as if her very brain were being penetrated. By two thin beams of white light, which seemed to emanate from the Domina's extraordinary eyes and pierce through Helewise's pupils.

It was a ghastly sensation.

But, just as she was beginning to feel that she could endure no longer but must cry out for mercy, it stopped.

The Domina said, gazing innocently out over

the stream, 'By ancient law, you should both be put to death. It is not permitted for Outworlders to live, having shared in our secrets.' Briefly she looked again at Helewise. 'But you, woman, have taken to yourself one of our own, and she speaks for you.' Bless Caliste for that, Helewise thought swiftly. 'And you, man,' the Domina turned to Josse, 'bear the sacred talisman.' She indicated the little sword on his pack. 'Its protective magic overrides the death penalty. I could not slay a bearer of the Sword of Nuada, even if I wanted to. Not,' she added softly, almost to herself, 'without great difficulty.'

Helewise felt her rigid shoulders relax. Josse gave an audible sigh.

But the Domina hadn't finished.

'No harm shall come to you, for now!' she cried suddenly, her raised right hand pointing threateningly at Helewise, at Josse. Then, more calmly, 'For now, I release you back into your world. But you will not speak of what you have witnessed. Ever.'

'No!' Helewise agreed.

'Never,' Josse echoed.

The Domina was watching them, frowning as if

deep in thought. Then, her expression lightening, she said, 'If either of you break faith with me, I shall know. Have no doubt, I shall know.' Helewise was quite certain she would. 'And, should that happen' – the Domina walked over to Josse, staring into his eyes for a moment, repeating the process with Helewise – 'should that happen, whichever one of you has spoken of our secrets, I shall kill the other.'

In the shocked silence that followed her words, a single thought rushed into Helewise's head: how very clever!

One of them, she or Josse, might have yielded to temptation, and, one dark night, whispered of what they had seen into some sympathetic ear. After all, it was human nature to confide, and, from King Midas's poor barber onwards, the torment of carrying a marvellous secret, of keeping it for ever to oneself, was well known.

Yes, one of them might have felt it was worth the risk. Had it been merely their own safety that they were thereby putting in jeopardy.

But for each other, Helewise thought, looking across at him, that big, kind, strong man whom she had come both to like and admire. But for each other! Oh, dear Lord, *I* would not dare take the risk!

And neither, she knew equally well, would he.

The Domina was nodding in satisfaction. Knowing what Helewise was thinking, no doubt what Josse was thinking, too, she had, Helewise reflected, every right to be satisfied.

The Domina raised both hands, holding them palms-outwards towards Helewise and Josse. 'Leave the forest,' she intoned. 'Do not come back to our deep realms. We go from here now, but we shall be back.'

She was backing away, the soft, subtle colours of her cloak seeming to merge with the undergrowth and the rich green foliage behind her. She was becoming hard to make out . . .

Her voice floated softly out from the trees: 'Go in peace.'

Helewise and Josse stood by the stream for some time. Breaking the silence that had fallen around them, eventually Helewise murmured, 'We wish the same to you.'

On the long trudge back through the forest, Josse repeatedly asked the Abbess if she were all right,

or if she'd prefer to sit down by the track while
he went on ahead to fetch a horse to bear her
home.

And repeatedly she answered, 'No, Josse. I can
walk.'

He was worried about her. Her face was very
white, and the bruise on her forehead was now
enormous, the swelling bulging down beneath
her left eyebrow and half-closing the eye. She
looked, he thought with compassion, as if she had
been in a tap-room brawl, and come off the
worse.

He still felt a little dizzy, especially if he moved
his head too quickly. Whatever that woman had
been burning on her fire last night, its effects were
long lasting.

Turning briefly to check for the tenth time that
the Abbess was still keeping up, he let his
thoughts go back to the incredible events in
which the two of them had just been involved.
From which – and this seemed a cause for heartfelt gratitude and thankfulness – they had just
escaped.

No. That was wrong. It should be, from which
they had just been *permitted* to escape.

Dear God, but that had been a worrying moment, back there by the stream! *By ancient law, you should be put to death*, she'd said. How would she have done it? Spear in the back, like poor Hamm Robinson? Hardly, when he and the Abbess had been standing there in front of her – you could scarcely hurl a spear at someone not a yard away. Garrotte, perhaps? A quick loop round the throat, a swift twist, and death from a broken neck? Or a dagger to the windpipe? One neat, deep cut, then oblivion?

With an effort, he made himself stop his ghoulish train of thought.

We know now what Caliste's connection with the forest is, he mused instead. Her twin lives still with the Wild People, and, given the renowned closeness of twins, she was probably picking up emotions of some sort from her sister. Emotions, perhaps, heightened by the rituals which Selene was undergoing.

Yes. What was more natural than that Caliste would want to be with Selene? Offer her support, perhaps, her encouragement. Give the girl comfort, even. After all, had Caliste been born first instead of Selene, it might have been her out there in the glade. Given all that, the theory certainly seemed likely.

He and the Abbess would, though, never know for sure. Unless the Abbess was able to get it out of Caliste. And, somehow, he couldn't picture her trying all that hard.

The Forest People killed Hamm Robinson, for their own good reasons. That, Josse knew, was a crime that would never officially be 'solved'; the perpetrator would escape justice. Would escape Outworld justice, he corrected himself, which was rather different. To say that whoever had flung that spear at Hamm Robinson should himself be executed was, from the Forest People's point of view, like suggesting every hangman in England was guilty of murder.

Ah, well.

He glanced round to look at the Abbess again. Still marching along, face set. Not far to go now, thank heaven.

He was just beginning to relax, to enjoy the picture of a good dinner and a mug or two of wine which he was conjuring up, when his peace was shattered by an unwelcome thought.

The Domina said they did not kill Ewen Asher.

Josse had already known that, although it would have been a pleasant surprise if she had confessed to it after all.

But she hadn't.

With a faint sigh, he hefted his pack higher up on his shoulders. Tired though he was, there would be more work ahead when he and the Abbess reached Hawkenlye.

This appalling business wasn't over yet.

PART THREE

DEATH IN THE HALL

Chapter Nineteen

Raising her head to return the greetings of those eagerly awaiting them at Hawkenlye Abbey, Helewise noticed that, standing at the back of the little clutch of anxious nuns, was Caliste.

Oh, child, I must speak to you! Helewise thought, giving the girl a quick smile.

'Abbess dear, your *forehead*!' Sister Euphemia was crying, trying simultaneously to wring her hands and put out an exploratory finger to touch the wound. 'That dressing looks filthy! You must come with me at once, and I will see to you!'

'Sister Euphemia, I thank you, but—'

'Abbess! Oh, Abbess, a night spent in the woods, and no proper, hot food inside you all that time!' Sister Basilia moaned, taking hold of Helewise's sleeve in a firm grip as if she would drag her bodily over to the refectory and stuff her with simmering stew and good new bread.

'Abbess, I wish audience with you,' Sister Emanuel's quiet voice said in Helewise's left ear. 'A matter of urgency—'

'*Please!*' Helewise burst out, drowning the clamour. 'Sisters, thank you for your welcome and for your concern. You cannot know how it gladdens my heart to be among you again, and, in due course, we shall all go to pray, to give thanks to the Lord for His care. Now, then.' She turned to them one by one. 'Sister Euphemia, my wound was tended adequately by Sir Josse, and the pain is not great. I will, I promise, present myself at the infirmary and ask for your ministrations, just as soon as I am able. Sister Basilia, both Sir Josse and I would benefit from a hot meal; will you please take Sir Josse to the refectory straight away? I will join you in a little while. Sister Emanuel, what . . .'

But Sister Emanuel had silently slipped away.

Making a mental note to seek her out as soon as she was free, Helewise caught Sister Caliste's eye and, with an all but imperceptible gesture, indicated that the girl should follow her.

Then, with a good deal of relief, she extracted herself from her fussing, well-meaning nuns and fled for the privacy of her own little room.

When she and Caliste were safely behind the closed door, Helewise said without preamble, 'I have seen your sister. She is well, and she is pregnant.'

Sister Caliste's hand flew to her mouth. 'Abbess, I am so sorry!' she said from behind it.

'Sorry?' Helewise sank down in her chair. 'For what, Sister?'

'What must you think of it all!' Caliste cried. 'And Selene is my sister, my own flesh and blood!'

Helewise thought for a moment. Then: 'Caliste, we do not choose the family into which we are born. Whoever they are, of whatever station in life, indeed, of what faith, is not within our power to control. What we *do* have to do, however, is to make our own choices, guided by our heavenly Father and in the hope that we do what is right.' She paused. 'Your sister has, through no fault of her own, lived her life in a society whose standards are very different from our own, and whose people have not had the benefit of God's holy light.'

In a sudden flash, she was back in the forest. And the age-old wisdom – the feminine wisdom – in the Domina's intelligent eyes seemed once more to flood through her.

She did not live with the blessings of God's holy light. And yet . . .

I am back in my Abbey now, she told herself – told the Domina – firmly. Things are not the same, here.

Sister Caliste was waiting patiently for her to go on, but she seemed to have lost her thread.

She smiled feebly at the girl. 'All is well,' she said.

'Oh!' Caliste looked surprised, as if she had expected more. After a moment, she said, 'Abbess, I shall not see Selene again.'

'You cannot be sure,' Helewise said gently. It seemed a hard thing for a young girl to accept. 'After all, the Great Forest is but a step away!'

'Yes, but it extends across hundreds of miles,' Caliste said, 'and the Wild People roam its entire length and breadth.'

'Nevertheless—' Helewise began.

'Abbess, forgive me for interrupting you, but it is not that.' Caliste's smooth brow wrinkled in a frown. 'How to explain?' she muttered. Then: 'You said before that I should wait a while before taking my final vows,' she went on.

'I did,' Helewise agreed. 'I wondered if you were entirely sure you knew what you were doing.'

Caliste smiled. 'You were right, Abbess Helewise. I *thought* I was, but that's not good enough, is it?'

'No.'

'But it's different now.' The girl's face grew serious, earnest. 'It's as if – that is, I think—' She paused, collected herself and said, 'I was worried about Selene. It felt as if a part of me was being drawn out of me and away into the forest, to share in what she was doing. That's why I went off to look for her that day, because I needed to see her. Oh, we were only together for a moment – it took a very long time to find her, even though she was actually looking for me, too – but it was enough. I didn't tell anyone where I was going, only that old dear, Hilde, in the infirmary, and I thought I could slip out and be back again before anyone noticed I was gone. I felt she needed me, you see. Selene, I mean. I felt that she was apprehensive.'

Helewise said quietly, 'That is only natural, under the circumstances.'

Caliste threw her a grateful look. 'I knew you would understand. But things have changed. She's no longer calling me, she's happy. She's done what she wanted to do, and now she's gone away from me.' This was said totally without self-pity. 'And it means, Abbess – oh! it's so wonderful – it means I can be whole again. And *that* means I'm ready.'

Mentally, Helewise went through the hurried, breathless little speech again. Ready. Did she mean ready to take her vows? She looked up at the radiant, beautiful face, even lovelier now that the worry of uncertainty had gone.

You *are* ready, Helewise thought. Ready, with God's help, to make a very good nun.

She rose, went round to stand in front of Caliste, who, fully appreciating the gravity of the moment, fell to her knees. Taking Helewise's outstretched hands, she bent her head over them. Softly Helewise heard her say, 'Thank you.'

'It is I, or, rather, the community at Hawkenlye, who should thank you, Sister Caliste,' Helewise replied. 'Already we appreciate your talents with the sick. You are loved by your patients, and you are steadily earning the respect of your fellow nuns, especially those of them who are also nurses. As one of the fully professed, we will from now on be assured that you will continue to be with us.' She helped Sister Caliste to her feet, and, on impulse, leaned forward and dropped a soft kiss on her cheek.

'Oh!' Caliste said. Then, a wide smile of pure joy spreading over her face, she said, 'Abbess, may I go and tell Sister Euphemia the news?'

And Helewise said, 'Of course.' Realising as she spoke that she was echoing the Domina's benediction, she added, 'Go in peace.'

Josse, having eaten rather too well of Sister Basilia's splendid meal, took himself off down to the monks' quarters in the vale and begged a quiet corner and a bed roll from Brother Saul. With a sympathetic look, Brother Saul obliged.

As Josse settled himself down in the shade behind the pilgrims' shelter, Saul said, 'I will see that you are not disturbed, Sir Josse.'

'Thank you, Saul.'

It was not Brother Saul who awakened him, but the sound of running feet.

Opening his eyes, Josse saw Brother Michael pounding down the track from the Abbey, habit flying, arms waving. Josse, instantly wide awake, leapt up and went to meet him.

'How did you know,' Brother Michael panted, 'that I was coming for you?'

'Intuition,' Josse replied. 'What is it, Brother Michael?'

'I was up at the Abbey,' Brother Michael said, 'getting some liniment for one of the pilgrims taking the water – he's been carrying a sick child for two days and he's ricked his back, really painful, it is, makes him walk all sideways, and I thought I could—'

'Brother Michael,' Josse prompted.

'Sorry, Sir Josse. While I was there, this rider came in, horse all lathered up, and he says he must see the Abbess, he has terrible news.' Brother Michael's eyes rounded with the drama of his tidings.

'And?'

'He was directed to Abbess Helewise, he disappeared into her room, then, before you could say a Hail Mary, the two of them came out again and she – the Abbess – sees me and says, Brother Michael, go and get Sir Josse!'

'And here you are,' Josse observed. 'Well?'

Brother Michael's simple face looked mystified. 'Well what?'

'What was the rider's message? Why does the Abbess need me?' Josse said patiently.

'Oh! Didn't I say?' Michael smiled in relief, as if overjoyed that Josse's question could be so easily answered.

'No, Brother Michael, you didn't.'

Brother Michael leaned towards him, face grave. 'There's been a death,' he whispered. 'Another death!'

Helewise had been hoping for the same little post-prandial rest that Josse had enjoyed. Having seen the radiant Sister Caliste on her way, she had submitted herself to Sister Euphemia's tender hands, and now wore a fresh dressing over the cut on her forehead. Sister Euphemia had given her a cloth soaked in the infirmarer's special marshmallow solution, her specific for bruising, and Helewise, when she remembered, was pressing it periodically to her head.

Sister Basilia had totally overridden Helewise's protests that she really wasn't very hungry, and stood over her while she ate her platter of hot meat and gravy.

Then, at last, with a whole hour until it was time for Nones, Helewise had slipped away to her room. But, just as, settled in her chair, she was gratefully closing her eyes, she remembered Sister Emanuel.

It is my own fault, she told herself sternly as she stood up again. Rushing off like that, spending a night out in the open, away from the safety of the Abbey walls, it is hardly my nuns' fault if, when at last I return, there are matters about which they need to consult me.

Sister Euphemia's pad of lotion pressed to her throbbing forehead, she set off for the retirement home.

Sister Emanuel was standing by the bed of one of the oldest residents, an ancient, sour-faced nun who, in her working life, had been superior of a convent up on the North Downs. Demanding, never satisfied, it was, Helewise reflected, a tribute to Sister Emanuel's devotion that she never let the old woman get under her skin.

'. . . leaving me here all morning with a soiled pillow,' the thin, scratchy voice was saying, 'why, in *my* day, things were different, let me tell you, young woman!'

Sister Emanuel's murmured reply was inaudible. Catching sight of Helewise, she made an excuse to the old nun and approached the Abbess.

'Good afternoon, Abbess.' She made a deep reverence.

'Good afternoon, Sister Emanuel.' Helewise paused. Then, since it was her policy to leave her nuns in no doubt that she understood the various crosses they had to bear, she said softly, 'The Abbess Mary is a great perfectionist, is she not? And, as such, not your easiest patient.'

'She is quite right to complain,' Sister Emanuel replied. 'Her porridge was spilled, and the mess was not properly cleaned up until I returned from Tierce.'

'That, I should have thought, scarcely constitutes all morning,' Helewise observed.

Sister Emanuel shot her a brief look of gratitude, swiftly supplanted by her usual expression of lofty calm.

'You wished to speak to me, Sister?' Helewise said.

'I did, Abbess.' Sister Emanuel looked down the ward, and, spotting another of the nuns who worked in the home, made a small gesture and then pointed to the door. The nun nodded her comprehension. Sister Emanuel said, 'The Sister will take charge. Shall we go and sit outside, Abbess?'

'As you wish.'

Sister Emanuel led the way out to the bench where she and Helewise had sat before. Then, when they had settled themselves, she said, 'The girl Esyllt has been absenting herself.' She paused, as if still uncertain how much of Esyllt's aberrant behaviour she must reveal to her Abbess. Then she went on, 'I realise that I – we – do not have control over her comings and goings out of working hours, but . . .' She trailed off.

'But she has been absent when she should be

working,' Helewise finished for her. Yes. That probably explained the dirty pillow that wasn't changed quickly enough.

Sister Emanuel gave a brief nod. 'Yes.'

'Is she here now?' Helewise asked.

Sister Emanuel's face showed her inner struggle. 'Well . . . Abbess, I am quite certain she has been delayed somehow, and that very soon she will return. I'm sure that, once she is here, she will work twice as hard and make up for the lost time.'

'I see.' Helewise thought briefly. Esyllt, she was well aware, was a godsend to the devoted and hard-pressed Sister Emanuel, and the Abbess understood the Sister's conflict. Reporting Esyllt's absence might mean some sort of disciplinary action that would rob Sister Emanuel of her best assistant, but, on the other hand, Sister Emanuel really couldn't go on allowing Esyllt's flouting of the rules, which actually meant that the retirement home often had to do without her anyway.

Helewise said carefully, 'Sister, when Esyllt returns, would you please send her straight to me? I do not wish to usurp your authority within your own area of responsibility, but will you let me deal with this matter?'

'Gladly!' Sister Emanuel said. 'But, Abbess, do you—' She broke off. The most disciplined of nuns, it was alien to her training to ask a question of her superior.

Understanding, Helewise said quietly, 'I do have an inkling of what this may be about, Sister Emanuel.'

'She is deeply troubled, poor girl,' Sister Emanuel said, shaking her head. 'If she can be helped, Abbess . . .' Again, she left the sentence unfinished.

'I pray that she can be,' Helewise said. She glanced at Sister Emanuel. '*If* that is the case, Sister, and there is a way out of her troubles for Esyllt, am I right in assuming that you would wish her to continue working here with you and your old people?'

'Oh, *yes*!' Sister Emanuel said, with uncharacteristic fervour. 'Abbess, she is the best worker I have ever had.'

The afternoon was lazy with midsummer heat. Small blue butterflies flittered about the rosemary bushes that formed a hedge on the southern side of the cloister, and Helewise, reluctant to shut herself away in her room, sat down instead on the stone bench that ran along against the wall.

Esyllt, she thought sadly, is in torment. And, unable to come to me with her trouble, she appears to be trying to sort it out by herself. Oh, but she is so young! And, for all the happy confidence she used to possess, she is in truth but an inexperienced girl.

Helewise's late husband had been wont to say, 'Don't go out looking for trouble, nor waste time worrying about things that might never happen.' However, the Abbess, not being quite such an optimist, had always been a great believer in facing up to the worst that could happen, and planning what to do if it did. Usually, she had found, it didn't. Nevertheless, having decided what to do if it did meant that those terrible four-in-the-morning anxieties, that ate at one's peace of mind and took away any chance of sleep, could more readily be dismissed.

The worst that could have happened to Esyllt, Helewise was more and more convinced, was that, in the forest for some as yet unknown

purpose on the last full-moon night, she had
come across Ewen Asher, fleeing from his treasure-
seeking activities in the fallen oak grove. And
that he, full of the various thrills of finding valuables and being scared out of his wits, had been
unable to resist the armful of well-developed
womanhood that had literally tumbled against
him. He had stripped Esyllt of her under-
garments, been on the point of raping her –
perhaps even succeeded, poor lass – when, in her
horrified disgust and her terror, she had drawn
the man's own knife and stuck it into him.

As if that were not enough, Helewise thought
miserably, now the poor child has to sit up here
knowing that another is in jail awaiting trial for
the murder.

What would happen if, as seemed highly likely,
Seth Miller were found guilty and sent for execu-
tion? Would Esyllt let him hang, or would she
come forward?

Helewise already knew the answer to that. Not
that it was in the least consoling.

Trying to banish from her mind the dreadful
images of a well-developed female body jerking
and twisting on the end of a rope, while the face

blackened and the swollen tongue began to pro-
trude, abruptly she got up, went into her room
and firmly closed the door.

She was on the point of going across to the Abbey
church for some quiet moments of prayer before
Nones when, from somewhere outside, she heard
raised voices, followed by the thump of running
feet. She was actually moving across to the door
when someone's fist began banging on it;
opening up, she was met by the face of a stranger.

'Abbess Helewise?' the man gasped.

'Yes?'

'Abbess, do you have Sir Josse d'Acquin,
King's knight, putting up here?' he demanded
urgently.

'Indeed. He is resting at present, down in the
vale. Where the monks tend the pilgrims who—'

'Abbess, forgive me, but please will you send
for him?' The man's distress was evident. 'We
need his help!'

'Of course,' Helewise said, already leading the
man back outside and looking round for someone
who could take a message to Josse. 'Ah! Brother
Michael!' she called. 'Will you come here, please?'

Turning back to the man, she said, 'Now, where do you come from, and what is the trouble?'

The man watched Brother Michael come hurrying across from the infirmary. His face intent, at first he didn't answer.

'Who sent you?' Helewise repeated, rather more firmly.

'Eh? Oh, yes. I'm Tobias Durand's man, I serve him and the Lady Petronilla. And, oh, God!' Momentarily his face crumpled, as if overcome all over again by whatever dire happening it was that required Josse's help. 'Abbess, we shall need your prayers, yours and all the sisters',' he said.

'Why?' she demanded.

He swallowed, and, making a very evident effort to control himself, said, 'There's been a death at the hall.'

Chapter Twenty

Helewise, watching Josse as he waited with ill-concealed impatience for his horse to be brought, thought that he did not seem any more fit for a fairly long ride with, at journey's end, a serious problem to face, than she was herself.

'Will you not rest for this night, and set out in the morning?' she suggested, knowing he would say no but unable to let that prevent her from asking. 'You and I both inhaled that wretched smoke, we are both, I am quite certain, still suffering from the after effects of whatever narcotic was in it.'

He looked down at her. 'I am grateful for your consideration. Helewise, but—' He looked away. Then, as if he had remembered where they were, and that, back in the Abbey, the informality which had relaxed their relationship out in the wild forest must be forgotten as if it had never been, he said, 'I am perfectly well, thank you, Abbess. And it is my duty to go when I am summoned.'

'Very well.' She stood back, feeling the twin emotions of being grateful for his courtesy and his consideration, while, at the same time, missing his warm friendliness.

Sister Martha at last led Horace out of the stables; the horse's coat shone as if she had spent all afternoon grooming him. She handed the reins to Josse, and he swung up into the saddle.

Helewise went to stand at his stirrup. 'Send me word,' she said softly.

His eyes met hers, and, as if he understood her anxiety, smiled. 'Aye,' he said. 'That I will. That, or I'll return and tell you myself.'

Then, kicking Horace into a trot he set off out through the Abbey gates.

The messenger had gone on ahead to say that Josse was on his way. Riding swiftly, his mind busy with conjecture, the long miles of the journey passed by scarcely noticed.

He rode into the walled and well-tended courtyard of Tobias and Petronilla Durand's fine
house. This time, it was not the master who
greeted him, but the manservant, Paul.

Solemn-faced, eyes dulled with some wearying
emotion, he said in a low voice, 'This way, Sir
Josse. The body lies where it fell.'

The messenger, appearing from the stables,
rushed over to take Josse's horse. Josse, straightening his tunic with a determined tug, followed
Paul up the steps and into the house.

After the sunshine, the light within seemed
very dim, and it took Josse a moment or two to
make out clearly the scene that awaited him.

Then, as his eyes adjusted, he saw what they
had called him to see.

Stretched out at the foot of the short flight of
steps that led from the dais, where the dining
table stood, down into the main area of the hall,
lay a body.

A long body, dressed in the best, the rich
colours of the fabrics glowing in the soft light.
The corpse lay face down, and, from the blood
staining the stone slabs beneath, it appeared that
death had come as a result of some catastrophic

injury to the front of the head.

Josse said quietly, 'When did it happen?'

'This morning,' Paul replied mournfully. 'Just this morning,' he repeated, as if he could hardly believe his own words. 'They hadn't even sat down to breakfast.'

As Paul crossed himself and muttered a prayer, Josse knelt down and put his hand on the already-cold temple of Tobias Durand.

Moving his hand so that his palm cupped the forehead, gently he raised up the head. The abundant hair, glossy with health, fell forward over the dead face, and Josse had to push it aside before he could see the wound.

The damage was terrible. The wound, deep, and shaped almost like a pyramid, must, Josse thought, have been caused by a hard point of some sort . . . Looking down at where Tobias's face had lain, he saw the edge of the bottom step. Newly constructed, presumably as part of the renovations which had been carried out following Petronilla and Tobias's marriage, the step was sharp-edged and unworn, and the riser, tread and side came together to form the corner of a perfect right-angled cube.

'The lady Petronilla said he tripped over his hound,' Paul said, his voice breaking. 'He – the master – was larking about, she said, jumping down from the dais to take her hand and lead her to table, and the hound, excited by all the fun and games, started barking, then it bounded up and tangled itself in the master's legs.' He sniffed, wiping his nose with his sleeve. 'I heard voices, I heard the barking, then there was the sound of something heavy falling. Then there was this terrible silence.' He sniffed again.

'And you came hurrying into the hall and found him lying here?' Josse asked gently.

'Aye.' Weeping openly now, Paul said, 'My lady is heartbroken, sir. She sets such a store by him, I don't know how she'll manage without him, truly I don't.'

And what of you? Josse thought. Whatever she decides to do, will the lady Petronilla still have need of her faithful manservant? Or will she, like so many widows above a certain age, decide that she has had enough of the world and retire behind the walls of some tranquil, welcoming convent?

Now was definitely not the time for such

questions, even in the privacy of his thoughts. Judging that it was probably a good idea for Paul to have something to do, Josse began, 'Paul, this death comes as the most dire shock, to you and the household, indeed, to us all.' His eyes returned to the long, elegantly clad body, which, death having so recently come, still bore the outward semblance of life.

Death. So final. So terribly final.

Josse recovered himself, not without effort, and turned back to the grieving manservant. 'The rest of the staff must be almost as upset as you,' he said gently. 'Could you, do you think, organise them into doing some sort of work?' He cast round in his mind for a suitable task. 'What does Tobias usually do in the afternoons?'

Paul scratched his head. 'I don't rightly know, sir. He's often from home. He does take his hounds out sometimes, that I can tell you.'

'Well, that's one thing, then.' Josse tried an encouraging smile. 'And there's his horse, presumably, needing exercise and then a good rubdown. And, even in this grief-stricken house, there will be need of food. Could you ask the household servants to prepare a meal?'

Paul drew himself up, as if, regretting his lapse, he was concerned to show that he had now resumed the mantle of his authority. 'I shall do all that you ask, sir.' With a formal little bow that briefly wrung Josse's heart, Paul walked stiffly away.

Alone with the dead man, Josse felt all round the head for any sign of further injury. No. There was nothing.

But wait! What—

'You have come, Sir Josse,' said a quiet voice behind him. 'I thank you for answering my summons.'

Spinning round, he saw Petronilla Durand, standing not two paces off and looking down at him.

She was already dressed in some flowing, dark mourning garment, which served to remove the last vestige of colour from her normally pale cheeks. Her eyes were red-rimmed, the lids swollen. Her headdress of starched white had been tightly fastened, and over it she wore a thin black veil. The flesh of her jaw and chin, in cruel contrast to the smooth linen of the barbette, was sagging and faintly yellow-looking, like that of a recently plucked chicken. Her thin-lipped mouth had taken on a deep downward curve, on either side of which were heavily marked semicircular creases which, Josse was almost sure, hadn't been there before.

She had aged ten years.

Josse stood up, moved across to her and, kneeling once more, took her icy hand in his and kissed it. 'My lady, my deepest condolences on your loss,' he said. 'If there is anything I can do, you have but to name it.'

She took her hand out of his grasp. Turning away so that he could no longer see the ruined face, she said, with a moan, 'Bring him back!'

Josse moved to her side. Had she lost her wits? He said gently, 'That I cannot do, lady.'

She shook her head. 'I know, Sir Knight. I know.' She sighed.

'Console yourself with the knowledge that he can have felt little pain,' Josse said. It wasn't much, he knew, but grieving widows had been comforted by such remarks in the past; he had uttered the facile comment many times himself. 'The wound is deep, and death would have been instantaneous.' He couldn't be sure – not as sure as he was pretending to be – but, if it helped her, then it scarcely seemed important.

'Little pain,' she repeated. There was a moment of silence, then she said, 'How poorly you understand.'

Ah.

'My lady?' Josse said.

The pink-rimmed eyes turned to meet his. 'This house has ever been filled with pain,' she murmured. 'And, for all that my husband lies dead, that pain will never cease.'

It was a strange thing for a widow to say. Did she mean that Tobias's death had caused the pain? Perhaps, Josse thought, perplexed, but it hadn't sounded that way. 1t had sounded as if Petronilla was referring to some deep distress, ongoing, something that had been a constant element in her life.

Trying to console her – the most hard-hearted man in the world would surely have wanted to bring comfort to that deadly pale, ravaged woman, with her destroyed face – Josse said, 'Lady, there was joy in this house! Why, I saw with my own eyes the love that was between you and Tobias. Why do you speak of pain?'

As if Petronilla were regretting her words, she made a visible attempt to undermine them. With a ghastly smile that looked more dreadful on her face than her expression of misery, she said, 'How right you are, Sir Josse! Indeed, Tobias and I *were* happy. The pain is in his—' She glanced briefly at her husband's body, screwed her eyes shut, and whispered, 'The pain lies here, at our feet.'

Josse was very nearly convinced. He would have believed her, thought no more about her odd remark, had a certain line of thought not suddenly arisen in his mind. Looking carefully around to make sure that they were alone, he said quietly, 'Petronilla, I believe that, when last we met, you may have told me not the truth, but what you would have liked to be the truth.' No answer. 'Lady?' he prompted. 'Would it not be a relief to unburden yourself?'

She lowered her head. In a muffled voice, she said, 'Sir Knight, what *can* you mean?'

If she wasn't prepared to bring it out into the open, then he was. 'You told me,' he said, careful to keep his voice down, 'that Tobias had put aside the ways of his misspent youth. That his side of the bargain which you struck was that he would be a model husband, as respectable as a man married to a lady such as yourself ought to be. And that, my lady, was a lie.' Again, she kept her silence. 'Wasn't it?' he hissed.

She rounded on him. 'All right, *yes!*' she hissed back. 'Are you satisfied now? Do you wish to witness my humiliation as well as my grief? For shame, Sir Knight! For shame!'

Humiliation was not the word he would have used; intent only on finding out all that there was to find out, he probed on. 'I know that he was in the habit of visiting the Great Forest,' he said, 'because I saw him there, on two occasions. Indeed, he made no secret of his preference for the forest fringes as a fine place to fly his falcon. But that was merely a cover, wasn't it?' He wanted to take hold of her, give her the comfort of his touch even as he interrogated her. 'He was in league with Hamm Robinson, wasn't he? Hamm, and his fellow thieves Ewen Asher and Seth Miller. The three of them took the risks and did the dirty work, and passed on the valuable objects they found for Tobias to sell. Isn't that right, Petronilla?'

She had been watching him as he spoke, mouth opening in a silent gasp. She was going to deny it all, he thought grimly, tell him he was mistaken. What would he do then?

In tones of ice, she said, 'I have never heard of any of those men.'

Well, there was no reason for Tobias to have mentioned their names. But, on the other hand, she sounded so convincing! Josse would have sworn she was telling the truth! With the distinct feeling that he was racing off down a dead end, he said, 'Maybe not, but all the same, lady, it's my belief that Tobias knew them, nevertheless.' Frustration surging through him, he said, 'I could have proved it, I know I could! I still can, maybe, there must be a way to trace the things they took from the forest, and—'

She did not let him go on. Disdain making her voice harsh, she said, 'My husband had no dealings with petty thieves.' Fixing Josse with a furious stare, she went on: 'In God's name, Sir Knight, he married a rich woman! What need had he to go peddling trinkets?'

It was a good question. Frowning, Josse began, 'Well, I would scarcely call them trinkets, and—'

Again, she interrupted. 'How *can* you!' she cried, her thin hands twisting together in her distress. 'My husband's body is scarcely cold, and here you stand, accusing him of some crime more suited to forest *peasants* than to the gracious, noble man that he was!'

Josse bowed his head. Poor woman, he thought, she is in shock. The terrible events of this morning still overwhelm her, and here I am with my small accusations, pursuing a matter which, to anybody but me, must appear trivial by comparison. Guilt flooding through him, he raised his eyes and said, 'Lady, forgive me. My remarks are inappropriate. This business can wait until a later—' No. He must not even say that. Putting all the sincerity he could muster into his voice, he said gently, 'Petronilla, I came to help you. Tell me, if you will, how I may.'

She was staring at him, and, in the light from the open door, he could see her face clearly.   The angry, offended expression slowly cleared, and for a moment she looked the proud, haughty noble-woman bearing her pain with dignity. 'I thank you, Sir Knight,' she began, 'there will be matters to attend to, decisions to be made as to . . .'

Slowly she trailed, to a halt. As if drawn by some force she could not resist, her eyes returned to Tobias's body. With a tiny whimper, she knelt down, her full skirts pooling around her, and, with the tender touch of a mother on the face of a sleeping child, she smoothed the thick hair back from the ruined forehead.

'He is dead,' she whispered. 'Dead.'

Then, bending low over the corpse, she began to sob.

Josse stood the heartbreaking sounds for a moment, then, leaning down, took firm hold of Petronilla's shoulders and raised her to her feet. 'Lady, you must be brave,' he said. 'Come, sit with me, and we shall send for some heartening drink, something to give you the strength to cope with what you must endure.'

She allowed herself to be led only a few paces away from the steps where Tobias lay. Then, turning back, she murmured, 'I do not want to leave him.'

'You need not, lady,' Josse said, 'for now, we shall remain close by him, and—'

As if she had not heard, Petronilla said, 'He cannot leave me now. He must stay here, in my hall, and I shall have his bright company all the time.'

A shock ran through Josse, the frightening sense that, suddenly, he was in the presence of madness. 'He must be tended to properly, Petronilla,' he said gently. 'He cannot remain here long. It is not—' He searched for a word with sufficient weight, gave up and ended weakly, 'It is not *fitting*.'

She was still staring at Tobias. Crooning gently, a faint smile crossed her face.

'Come, we'll plan together where he is to be buried,' Josse suggested. 'Somewhere close, think you, so that you may often go to visit the place, and recall your happy times? Or—'

She had spun round, and now her attention was fully on Josse. 'Happy times?' she echoed. Some violent inner struggle evident in her face, she began to speak, then stopped. But, as emotion seared through her again, the words she was trying to hold in burst out of her.

'There was *pain* in this house!' she cried. 'I *told* you that!' Pushing her face close to his, her terrible anguish as readable as an illuminated script, she said, 'You said you knew my husband visited the Great Forest, and you asked me why. Do you want to know? *Do* you?' She was all but spitting at him. 'Well, Sir Knight, you shall know! I will tell you what he did in the forest.'

She paused, drawing in a sudden sharp breath. As if bracing herself, she briefly shut her eyes, clasping her hands on her breast as if in silent prayer.

Then, quite calmly, she said, 'He lay with a woman. A young and vivacious woman whose soft flesh yielded to his caresses, whose moist body opened to his, whose full lips kissed his eager mouth.' A violent sob broke out of her, shaking the thin frame. She added, her voice a mere whisper, 'A beautiful woman, who could give him all the passion he wouldn't take from me.'

Josse was shaken to his very core. Was she right? Could she possibly know, for sure? He said, 'How can you be certain of this?'

Her face took on a look of cunning. 'You forget,' she said. 'You asked me did I still have him followed, and I said—'

'You said, rarely,' Josse concluded for her.

Dear God. Poor, miserable soul! Was it the womanising that she had suspected, all along? Had it only been Josse's prejudiced view, already branding Tobias as being in league with Hamm Robinson, that had led him to misread her comments? To believe that she meant her husband had been a thief, when in fact, handsome and comely man that he was, his offence was that he had been unable to resist a pretty face?

I was wrong, Josse thought, guilt flooding through him. And, because I was wrong, a man lies dead in his own hall. He shot a glance at Petronilla. If I had guessed earlier, he berated himself, then maybe I could have spoken to Tobias. Persuaded him that it was folly to persist in what he was doing. Tell him that he must make a clean break from the loving bonds that held him, and be true to his wife. True to his promise to her.

But I didn't.

He said, although it was not really relevant, 'Whom did he meet?'

Petronilla looked surprised. 'You ask me that, Sir Knight? For all your cleverness, you have not worked it out?'

He shook his head. 'No.'

A faint smile briefly quirked the thin lips. 'I told you, did I not, that Tobias was raised by his old aunt?'

'Aye.'

'Yes. Well, the aunt lived a mean and penny-pinching life, but the one thing that shone like a jewel in her household was her maidservant. A jewel, indeed, that the old woman must herself have much appreciated. The girl was young and joyful, and she used to sing as she went about her work, even though, given that her days were long, the labour was hard, and the old woman gave never a word of praise, one would have thought she had little to sing about.' A soft sigh. 'She was irresistible to Tobias, naturally, and he to her. They fell for one another and they became lovers. In time, the old aunt fell sick, and, possibly in some gesture of repentance for her unkind ways, she demanded to go on a pilgrimage to take the holy waters. The girl took her off to Hawkenlye Abbey, where, in the Lord's good time, He took her to himself.' Another brief smile. 'No doubt everyone was pleased to see the back of her, although the kind thoughts any good soul might have had about her would soon have flown out of the window when her will was read, since she left not a sou to Tobias, or to anyone else who had cared for her. She left the lot to that wretched Abbey.'

But Josse was hardly listening. He was thinking, remembering. In his head he heard the Abbess Helewise's voice . . . *She arrived with her late mistress, who died when she was with us.*

Esyllt was left with nowhere to go.

'He was in love with Esyllt!' he said. 'It was she who had been the old aunt's servant, wasn't it? And it was to visit her, the love of his youth whom he couldn't forget, that Tobias kept going up to the forest!'

Carried away by the lovely, romantic picture, he hadn't paused to think that it would scarcely appear lovely to Petronilla. Hastily he said, 'Lady, forgive me, I forgot, for the instant, that it was of your husband that we speak. He was, of course, false to you, an adulterer and a liar. And that was a sin, a grave sin, both against holy law and against you, madam.'

But she wasn't listening. She was humming to herself, an incongruously bright little tune which Josse thought he recognised, although the good Lord alone knew from where.

' "It is love he doth bring, And the sweet birds do sing, And my love he loves me in the spring," ' the faint, reedy voice sang. Petronilla's eyes turned to Josse. 'She sang that to him, you know, and I would hear him singing it when he thought I couldn't hear. But I could. Then I knew he had been with her again.' Tears were running down the ashen face. 'He promised,' she whispered. 'After the last time, he *promised*.' She grasped Josse's sleeve. 'He did love me, you see, really he did, and, when I said he must stop seeing her or else I would turn him out, he promised that he would.' Her face softened suddenly. 'I couldn't have turned him out, though. I loved him far too much.'

Josse patted the hand knotted tightly in his sleeve. 'I understand, lady.' He did, all too clearly. The elderly wife, knowing her husband's nature, trying to pen him into a bargain, only to find he was unable to keep to its terms. Reneging, being found out, promising to do better, tempted back again to the sweet and joyous young woman waiting for him.

Had Tobias really loved Petronilla? Seen her as a woman – a wife, indeed – and not just as a wealthy provider?

It seemed as unlikely as it had always done.

But then Josse recalled the young man's face as he had looked at his wife, smiling at her so affectionately as he spoke of how he had comforted her when her father had died, how, together, the two of them were having such a grand time improving her late father's house.

I don't know, he confessed to himself. I just don't know.

'He told me this morning that he had been with her again,' Petronilla said softly. 'He had just come in, and I imagined he had been out riding in the cool of the early morning. He summoned me to the breakfast table, and I remarked on the glow in his face.' She sobbed, choked on her emotion, then, after a pause, went on. 'A terrible dread took me, and I said, oh, Tobias, tell me it isn't true! Tell me I'm wrong, and that you haven't been back to her! And, at first, he swore he hadn't, and I believed him, believed all was well, so I threw myself into his arms and hugged him, and – oh – and I – he—'

For a moment, she couldn't go on. Then, as if she knew she must, she said, with a touching dignity, 'He did not return my embrace. He tried to, but his arms were so stiff, and he held his beautiful body away from me. As if, despite his best efforts, he couldn't help but compare my thin bones with the luxury of her warm, soft flesh. And, finding me wanting, be unable to hold me to him as he had done her. And then I knew.'

The tears were now drenching the breast of her dark gown, but she did not try to mop them up. And, Josse thought, she could no more have stopped them than flown through the air.

'My lady, I am so sorry,' he murmured.

She looked at him. 'Thank you,' she said. 'It is, I dare say, a matter for sorrow.' She sighed. 'I could not stop myself, Sir Knight. All those broken promises, all those times when he had sought his joy with her, and now – oh! now! – he was turning away from me.' Belatedly she drew a tiny, embroidered handkerchief from her sleeve and, although it was clearly inadequate for the task, began to wipe her eyes, her nose and her wet face. 'I picked up the footstool that stood beneath table, and, as he moved out of my arms and went to go down the steps, I hit him with it.'

'Caught him right on the back of his head,' Josse murmured. 'Aye, lady. I know.'

She eyed him steadily. 'I killed him,' she said. 'Did I not, Sir Knight? I killed the love of my life, because he could not be true.'

There was a long silence between them. Josse stared down at the dead man lying at their feet, then, furtively, up at the wrecked face of the man's widow.

She had suffered, poor soul. Would go on suffering, bereft as she was of her handsome young husband, left alone to grieve. And, combined with the grief, the guilt. The blow to the back of the head might not have been the one which killed him, but it had led to that terrible fall on to the corner of the step. Enough reason, surely, to give rise to a guilt powerful enough to eat away at mind, soul, and, eventually, body.

Surely that was punishment enough.

Briefly he allowed himself to imagine what would lie ahead for her, if he did as he ought and summoned a sheriff. Arrest, imprisonment, trial. And, after a terrible time in some foul jail, she would, if they found her guilty, be led out one bright morning and hanged.

No.

It was unthinkable. And, besides, it wouldn't bring Tobias back.

Josse had, throughout Petronilla's quietly

spoken confidences, been standing on her left side. Now, with growing ostentation, he began tweaking at his right ear.

'Dear me,' he said, quite loudly, 'this ear of mine!'

After some time, she turned to look at him. 'What ails you, Sir Knight?'

He met her eyes, held the gaze. Would not let her look away. Then, very carefully, he said, 'It's funny, but I just don't seem to hear well on my right side. Do you know, lady, I haven't picked up a word you've said, not since you entered the hall and thanked me for coming.'

She looked astonished. 'But—' she began.

He held up his hand. 'No,' he said softly. 'Lady, let it be.'

For a moment, the grief, the shock and the horror left her face, and she looked as she must have done long ago, before the doomed love for Tobias had awakened in her. She whispered, 'Oh, Sir Josse. There is still some kindness in this world.'

Leaning forward, she put a light kiss on Josse's cheek.

Then, straight-backed and dignified, she

turned, crossed the hall and disappeared through the doorway that led to her chamber.

He stood in the hall for a long time after she had gone, staring down at Tobias.

Then, abruptly, he, too, left.

Going out into the soft, late sunshine of evening, he called for Paul, and, when he arrived at the foot of the steps, told him that Tobias had died as a result of his fall down the steps, and that, in the summer heat, Paul should now make all haste to have the body coffined and buried.

Advanced though the hour was, Josse decided to set out for Hawkenlye. He was tired, hungry, and faced a long ride, but that, he thought, was preferable to the alternative.

He would have endured far worse, in order to escape from the corpse and the desolate widow he had just left behind.

Chapter Twenty-one

Hawkenlye Abbey was in total darkness when Josse got back, which, given the hour, was hardly surprising. Heading down into the vale, he unsaddled Hector, put a hobble on him to stop him roaming far, then, slapping the horse's rump, turned him out into the sweet grass of the little valley.

Then he made straight for the bed-roll he had abandoned in such a rush all those hours before. Wrestling around till he'd got himself comfortable, he closed his eyes and was soon deeply asleep.

Brother Saul woke him with bread, a slice of salty cheese and a mug of weak ale.

'You were late back last night, Sir Josse,' he said as Josse ate.

'Aye.'

'I have taken your horse up to the Abbey stables,' Saul went on, 'where Sister Martha is again tending to his every whim.'

Josse grinned. 'A fine touch with horses, that woman.'

'And with a particular fondness for yours,' Saul agreed.

'Thank you, Saul,' Josse added, 'both for seeing to old Horace and for bringing me my breakfast.'

Saul bowed his head in acknowledgement. 'Sir Josse, I also bring a message from the Abbess, who says that, when you are ready, would you please—'

'—go and see her,' Josse finished, getting up and brushing food crumbs off himself. 'Aye, Saul, that I will.'

He found the Abbess seated at the table in her room. She looked up at him, compassion in her face. 'You look tired,' she observed.

'I'll do,' he replied, grinning. Then, straightening his face, he told her what had happened in the Durand hall.

'Tobias dead!' she whispered. 'By such a mishap!'

He had been trying to decide all the way home the previous night if he would tell her the truth. Now, looking down at her, this wise, understanding woman, with whom he had shared so much, he decided he couldn't have her go on believing a lie.

So he told her how Tobias Durand had died.

She made no comment. He felt strangely robbed, as if he had been expecting her affirmation that, in not revealing Petronilla's part in the death, he had acted right.

As if, perhaps, he had needed that affirmation.

But, after a silence that he, for one, was beginning to find uncomfortable, she said, 'It just goes to show, Sir Josse, does it not, how unwise it is to have unruly hounds free to trip a man at the top of his own steps?'

And he had all the affirmation he could have wished for.

Then he told her of Esyllt's involvement.

'A *lover!*' she said, astonished. 'Dear Lord, Josse, why didn't we – I beg your pardon, why didn't *I* – think of that? A young woman such as she, so lovely, so ripe, so at ease with life, why, it stands to reason that she was as she was because she both loved and knew herself to be loved in return. That, with him out there in the forest, she—' Abruptly she stopped. With a faint blush, she said, 'Well, best not to think of that, with the poor young man dead.'

'It is charitable of you, Abbess, to think kindly on him, considering how he sinned,' Josse said.

She looked up at him. 'Who are we to judge?' she asked. 'And, in truth, he has paid dearly for his sin.' She shook her head. 'Such a waste, and—' She stopped. Aghast, she whispered. 'Does Esyllt know he is dead?'

'Good God!' Josse had uttered the blasphemy before he had stopped to think. 'Your pardon, Abbess, I did not mean to offend.'

Frowning, preoccupied, she waved her hand in dismissal. 'I know that, Josse, I know. She – Esyllt – was absent from the Abbey yesterday, and, as far as I know, has not yet returned. Sister Emanuel is gravely concerned about her, as indeed am I.' She gave him a brief but sweet smile. 'May I prevail upon you once more, and ask you if you will go and look for her?'

'Of course.' He smiled back.

'Naturally, I will help,' she said, getting up. 'As soon as we have said Sext, I will set out.'

But Josse, who did not have to wait until after Sext, began to look for Esyllt straight away.

They met, those two lovers, up in the forest, he thought, walking out through the Abbey gates. In some clearing, probably not very far in, just far enough to be safe from the world's eyes.

And—

He would not, after all, have to go back into the forest. For, walking slowly down one of the smaller tracks, on a route that would take her round the side of the Abbey and in at the rear gate, was Esyllt.

He ducked back through the front entrance, turned, and started walking, in no special hurry; it would take the girl more time to reach the old people's home than it would him. At the far end of the infirmary he stopped, and, his body hidden by its stout walls, peered round to look out at the rear gate.

A few moments later, she appeared.

She still moved slowly, almost like a sleepwalker. Her head was bent so that he couldn't see her face, but her whole demeanour spoke of misery and dejection.

As she drew level with the infirmary, he emerged from his hiding place and fell into step beside her.

Hearing his footsteps, she looked up.

'Hello, Sir Josse,' she said. Her voice was low.

'Hello, Esyllt.'

They walked on towards the door of the retirement home.

'Have you come to see my old dearies?' she asked, with a faint shadow of her former sparkle. 'You promised, you would, you know. And a true man doesn't break his word, unless he cannot help it.' A spasm crossed her face.

'I haven't forgotten,' he said. 'I will come, Esyllt, but not today. For now, I have to talk to you.' He took hold of her arm, and they went round to sit on one of the sun-bathed stone benches.

He said gently, 'I have come from Tobias's house, Esyllt. I know about – I know what you and he were to one another.'

She nodded slowly. 'Yes.' Then: 'What we

were.' Her eyes flew to his. 'Oh, dear sweet Lord, then I was right!'

He put his arm around her. 'Right about what, my dear child?'

'He's dead. Isn't he?'

As kindly as he could, Josse said, 'Aye, Esyllt. I'm afraid he is.'

'How?'

'By sheer accident. A hound tripped him, and he fell and hit his head.'

She gave a soft laugh. 'Those hounds! I used to tell him he should train them better, they were always . . .'

But, as if she realised it didn't matter any more, she stopped.

Then she said, 'I knew. When he didn't come last night, I knew.'

'You were that close?' Josse asked wonderingly.

'Yes. And, you see, nothing would have kept him away. Nothing ever did.'

'Except death,' he said.

'Except death.'

He waited, knowing what would happen. And sure enough, after a while, as the ill tidings sank in and she began to realise that, from now on, she

would have to face life without him, gradually
the strength went out of her. Crumpling, she
sagged against Josse and cried as if she would
never stop.

But, as people always do, she did.

And, later, when talking of Tobias was all she
wanted to do – all she could do – she told Josse.

Told him much that he already knew, but, in
addition, something he hadn't even guessed.

It was the one thing, Josse surmised, listening
to her, which would allow her to derive some
faint comfort from her lover's death. Because,
now that he was beyond harm, beyond the reach
of all earthly justice and retribution, Esyllt could
reveal that Tobias Durand had killed Ewen Asher.

And that, on the full moon night when she had
come running out of the forest straight into Josse
and the Abbess, bloodstained, naked from the
waist down, she had been running from the tryst-
ing place which Tobias had found for them.

'We were making love,' she told Josse with a
reminiscent glow of joy. 'He was deep inside me,
we were so enthralled in one another that we
never even heard Ewen racing and crashing

through the undergrowth until he was almost on top of us. Then Tobias leapt up, all bare, his manhood still stiff and proud, and that Ewen, he said, Tobias Durand, by my faith! What are *you* doing here?'

'How did they know one another?' Josse asked.

Again, a brief smile. 'Ewen sold Tobias a hawk once, but it took sick and died.'

'Ah.'

'Then Tobias picked up his dagger and killed him,' her quiet voice went on. 'He had to kill him, you see,' she said earnestly, 'because otherwise he'd have told her. Told Petronilla. And Tobias didn't want that.'

'It's hardly surprising,' Josse said wryly. 'Clever people like Tobias don't slay the goose that lays the golden egg.'

Esyllt took a moment to work that out, then, turning to him, said, 'No, Sir Josse. You're wrong. Oh, Tobias liked being a rich woman's husband, of course he did. So would any man, brought up in miserable poverty like he was. But the reason he didn't want Ewen Asher telling Petronilla was because he didn't want to hurt her.'

'You're telling me,' Josse said slowly, 'that

Translation

Ashes of the Elements

Tobias cared for his wife?'

'Oh, yes,' Esyllt said easily. 'He had a loving heart, did Tobias. There was room for us both in it, her and me, only she didn't see it that way.'

'No, she wouldn't,' Josse murmured.

'Hm?'

But the remark hadn't really been intended for her ears. He said, 'Nothing.'

He sat on with her for some time, still with his arm around her. She seemed calmer now, and it encouraged him to ask her what she would do now.

'Now? Now, I'm going down to Tonbridge to tell that Sheriff Pelham he can let Seth Miller go. There's no reason for me to keep my secret, now Tobias is beyond the reach of the law.' Briefly her face fell, but then, rallying, she gave a fleeting smile. 'Not that folks will thank me for getting Seth set free, it's been nicer hereabouts since the three of them, Hamm, Ewen and Seth, were out of the way. Still,' she sighed, 'you can't execute a man just for being a rascal and a nuisance, can you?'

'No,' Josse agreed. 'Just as well, there'd be

bodies hanging from every gibbet in the land if we could.'

It was a feeble joke, but she gave an obliging chuckle.

He said, after a while, 'I didn't actually mean now, this minute, Esyllt. I meant, what will you do with your life?'

She sighed. 'What a question, sir knight. I have no idea.'

'You are valued here in the Abbey,' he said.

'You think I should become a nun?'

'No, Esyllt, heaven forbid! I certainly do not!' he exclaimed. This time, her laugh sounded more like the Esyllt of old. 'I meant that I think you might consider staying right where you are, working with your old dears.'

She drew a sharp breath. 'Stay here! Without him! Oh, but I don't think I could do that.'

'My lovely girl,' Josse said gently, 'you will miss him wherever you are. But here, although the memories will be more poignant, at least you will be engaged in valuable work, and work, moreover, for which you appear to have a singular aptitude. Would not that be a consolation, to be needed?' He hugged her to him. 'And, too, at least here you would be surrounded by familiar faces – friendly faces – to help you when you grieve.'

'They'll still be my friends?' she asked, astonished, pulling away slightly and staring at him in disbelief. 'Even when they know what I've done?'

'Aye, child.' He gave her a little shake. 'Many of the good nuns, despite what you may think, probably have hidden memories of long-ago love, passion, even. Some of them may understand. And I don't believe they would condemn you, not when Our Lord Himself, whom they worship and serve, taught us that we should love one another. And, although I know that the Abbess looks and, on occasions, sounds like a lion, I can assure you that she's got a kind heart and a forgiving nature.'

Esyllt shot him a shrewd look. 'And you speak as one who knows,' she murmured.

'Eh? What was that?'

At last, she gave a wholehearted smile that actually put a dimple back in her cheek. Laughing, she said, 'Never you mind.'

Chapter Twenty-two

It was many weeks before Josse went back to Hawkenlye Abbey.

With the solutions to both murders now found, there had been no excuse for a visit. And Josse found that the prospect of calling on the Abbess purely for a friendly chat was, since that night in the forest, distinctly embarrassing.

We were not ourselves, he repeatedly told himself. We had been drugged, although nobody had intended it to happen. And anything we did or said under the influence of whatever that powerful potion was, we can scarcely be held responsible.

But, reason as he might, he found it hard to banish from his mind the image of a suddenly young-looking woman with reddish curly hair, whose throat was unexpectedly smooth and who nestled her bottom into his crotch as if she had been wed to him for a decade or more . . .

He took himself off to France, and paid his family in Acquin a prolonged visit. He stayed with them well into October, long enough to celebrate bringing home the last of the apple harvest and to enjoy with them the few days of leisure they allowed themselves after all the hard toil.

Sitting next to his sister-in-law Marie one evening, after a prolonged meal at which rather too much cider had been served, he found himself telling her all about Hawkenlye Abbey. And its Abbess.

'A formidable woman,' Marie commented, when, his lengthy reminiscences at last over, she could get a word in.

'Formidable? No!' he began, the protest instinctive. But, on reflection, that was probably how the Abbess *would* seem, to someone hearing about her at second hand. 'Well, maybe,' he amended. 'But a good person to have at your side in a crisis.'

'Evidently,' remarked Marie. The baby at her breast ceased its suckling and gave a strangely adult-sounding little sigh. Marie looked down, her face full of love. 'Had enough, *ma petite*?' she asked softly.

'She's a beautiful child,' Josse said, smoothing his smallest niece's soft baby hair with his fingertips. 'I'm glad I was here to attend her christening.'

'As a good uncle should,' Marie said. She shifted the baby on to her shoulder, rubbing the little back, and the child emitted a belch. 'Ah, there's a clever girl! Well done, my Madoline.'

The christening had taken place over a month ago. Thinking back, it made Josse realise how long he had been staying with his family.

'I think I shall return to England soon,' he said. 'If I delay much longer, travelling will become steadily more uncomfortable.' Wet roads that became like quagmires, and the ever present threat of autumnal gales in the Channel, were not an attractive prospect.

'You won't stay for Christmas?' Marie asked.

Christmas! Good Lord, that was two months away! 'No,' Josse said vehemently. Then, since that was hardly courteous, added, 'Tempted though I am, Marie *ma chèrie*, I really want to be back in my own home well before that.'

She shot him an understanding look. She could, he was well aware, have made a far fuller response, but all she said was, 'Very well.'

The country to which Josse returned, in a rare spell of warm, fine weather in the late autumn of 1191, was a land which had already begun to suffer from having an absentee king.

A land whose people were starting to feel uneasy. Or, at least, those of its inhabitants whose daily round took them to places where they heard the gossip that filtered down from the country's centres of power.

Josse met a merchant on the boat that took him from France to England, and, within minutes of striking up a conversation, the man was complaining.

'Mixed news from Outremer, so they're saying in high places,' the merchant remarked. 'And we'll all have to pay for it, I shouldn't wonder, in the end. Victories and setbacks, so I was told.'

'Oh, yes?' Josse responded neutrally.

'Aye.' The merchant, leaning against the deck rail, shifted his position and made himself more comfortable. There was a brisk wind blowing from the south-west, right up the Channel, and the ship was bouncing like a lively horse. 'Our King Richard, God bless him, thought to make a bigger difference than he actually managed, so I've been led to believe.' He sniffed, hawked and spat over the rail. 'Seems Acre's still holding out tight against our Holy Christian army.'

Josse wondered where the man had acquired his information. Even a merchant with contacts throughout court circles surely had no magical way of divining what was going on half a world away. Did he? Yet, Josse had to admit, what the man said sounded unpleasantly likely.

'King Richard is a great soldier and a fine leader of men,' he replied, trying not to sound as if he were disapproving; the voyage across the Channel would be long and probably uncomfortable, and a decent bit of gossip would certainly help to pass the time. It wouldn't do to give his sole fellow passenger the brush-off so soon after setting sail.

'Aye, aye, I'm not saying he isn't,' the merchant said impatiently. 'Still, there's other things for a king to do, isn't there?' He gave Josse a sly look.

'Other *duties*, if you take my meaning.'

Josse was quite sure he did. 'You speak of the King's marriage?'

'Aye, I do that. Some exotic beauty, they say, from a hot southern land where oranges fall off the tree into your hand, where the sun burns a man's skin to black, and where the women are wild-blooded and passionate.' He swallowed, recovered himself and said more calmly, 'Least, that's what I heard. Lucky old King Richard, I say.'

Josse decided it was unlikely the man had ever travelled to Navarre. The lurid description of that country's people didn't accord at all with what Josse knew of them. 'Queen Berengaria is said to be one of the beauties of the age,' he observed.

'Well, they say that about every lass ever crowned queen,' the merchant said. 'Still let's hope for our good King Richard's sake that they're right this time, eh?'

'Indeed,' Josse mumured.

There was a brief and fairly companionable silence. Then the merchant reached down into a large pack at his feet, drew out a flask and, removing its stopper, offered it to Josse. He

accepted gratefully – it was getting cold out on
deck, and the wind was carrying spiteful drifts of
hard, icy raindrops – drank, and felt the pleasant
warmth of spirits flow down his throat.

'Thank you,' he said, returning it to the merchant, who took a rather larger sip.

'To the King and the Queen,' the merchant said,
raising his flask. He shot Josse a look. 'And to the
fruit of their marriage bed.'

Josse said, with deep sincerity, 'Amen.'

'Been out of England long?' the merchant
asked presently.

'Hm? Oh, a few weeks.'

'You'll not know what the King's brother's up
to, then,' the merchant said, the sudden glint in
his eyes suggesting he was looking forward to
enlightening this innocent stranger.

'You speak of Prince John?'

'Aye, I do.'

'What has he done?'

The merchant chuckled. 'Seems he's made up
his mind the King's never coming back,' he said.
'Thick as thieves with that half-brother of his,
Geoffrey, the one they made Archbishop of York,
although for the life of me I never knew a man

less suited to high church office, that I didn't.'

'They're plotting, Prince John and the Archbishop?' This was worrying news. 'I understood that the King had banished his half-brother Geoffrey, banned him from ever setting foot in England again?'

'Aye, he did, and a sensible move it was. Mind, he made the same ruling about Prince John, only his lady mother, the Queen Eleanor, persuaded him to relent.' He gave a faint sigh. 'Far be it for me to question the great and the good, but I do wonder what the dear Queen had in mind, bless her heart. Still, mother love knows no reason, does it, sir?' Josse agreed that it probably didn't. 'Archbishop Geoffrey now, he came back even without being told he could – seems he put it about that it was ridiculous, him being archbishop of a city in a country he wasn't allowed to live in!'

Yes, Josse thought, it was absurd. But, in the light of this new and disturbing information, how right King Richard had been, to try to keep his meddlesome, dangerous brothers out of his kingdom. Especially when he was so far away.

He was just about to ask the merchant to

elaborate on what Geoffrey and John were up to when the merchant said, 'Mind you, the King himself slipped up over that weasel Longchamp.'

'His regent? Why, what's *he* been doing?'

'Pride's gone to his head and lodged there, tight as a boot in a muddy ditch. Walks about with a sneer on his face, he does, like there's a constant bad smell under his nose. Probably is, come to think of it.' The merchant laughed briefly, and Josse joined in. 'Our dear Prince John's not the only one as finds him pompous and stuffed up with airs and graces.'

'Oh, dear,' Josse said lamely.

The merchant laughed again, a short bark that caused an answering squawk in a seagull hovering nearby. 'You'll not have heard what happened between them, Longchamp and Archbishop Geoffrey, when Geoffrey sneaked back into England? Stop me if you have, but it makes a good tale.'

'I haven't,' Josse agreed. 'Go ahead.'

The merchant shifted his position again, bracing one foot against the ship's increasing motion. 'Well, it was like this. When the Archbishop arrived at Dover, Longchamp's men were waiting for him, and, being good and faithful King's men, they didn't hesitate in applying their absent King's ruling.' He grinned. 'With more zeal than King Richard might have wished, I dare say, they seized Archbishop Geoffrey and flung him into Dover jail.'

'A fine way to treat an archbishop,' Josse said, with mock disapproval.

'Aye, you're right there! And Prince John, he didn't hesitate to use it for his own advantage. Pretending to be outraged, he summoned all them bishops and justices and what-have-you to Reading, and persuaded them that Longchamp had no business being so high-handed with the half-brother of the King, and should be called to account straight away, and kicked out of office as soon as possible.'

'He's gone? Longchamp has gone?' Josse demanded.

The merchant held up a finger. He was, it seemed, going to tell his tale his way. 'Just you wait,' he said, 'and I'll tell you. Longchamp, see, he isn't anybody's fool. He has his spies, everyone knows that, and he got advanced warning which way the wind blew. He told all them high-ups at Reading that he were too sick to travel, then he hid himself in the Tower of London. The bishops and that decided they didn't need him present to deal with him, so they did. Deal with him, I mean. He's out, out on his ear, and there's not a man regrets it. And guess what Longchamp did then! Go on, guess! Bet you can't!'

'I'm not even going to try,' Josse said, grinning. 'You tell me.'

The merchant guffawed. 'He only flees off out of England dressed as a woman!' he said. 'Him that hates the whole female sex! He's a tiddly little fellow, and they say he made a fine woman, all done up in a green gown!'

Josse found himself joining in the laughter. He had met William Longchamp, briefly, and could imagine him dressed in woman's clothes. Almost.

The merchant's mirth was growing. Chuckling again, he said, 'Just let me tell you what happened next, friend, then I'll give you a chance to do a bit of the talking.'

'I doubt if I could match you,' Josse remarked, but the merchant didn't seem to hear.

'He gets to Dover, our Lady Longchamp, see, and starts looking round sharpish for a ship to take him across to France,' the merchant said, interrupting himself with renewed laughter. 'He's standing there on the quay, looking this way and that, and up comes a sailor fresh from a long voyage, desperate for a woman to warm his bed, and the sailor puts his arm round Longchamp and says, good day, my pretty, fancy a bit of fun?'

'Ha!' Josse could picture it. 'And did he? Fancy some fun?'

With a feigned frown, the merchant said, 'I'm quite sure he didn't. Not that sort of man, for all his unpleasant ways.' Then, reaching once more for his flask, he gave Josse an encouraging look and said, 'Now, sir, it's your turn. Tell me what news you have of France.'

Josse's homecoming to New Winnowlands was cause for celebration. Will and Ella, who had been expecting him for weeks, had taken a lot of trouble to make his welcome a thorough one, and, since Will had made sure that even the meanest household on the estate knew what a good master they had, Josse found himself hailed and cheerily greeted by everyone he met.

Sitting in his own hall, feet on a footstool in

front of a huge blazing fire, a jug of Ella's excellent mead to hand, Josse decided it was great to be home.

He went to pay a courtesy call on the community at Hawkenlye a fortnight before Christmas.

Sister Martha came out to take his horse, Brother Michael looked up from his sweeping to pass the time of day, Brother Saul, spotting Josse from some way off and actually running over to him, wrung his hand with pleasure.

It was, Josse thought happily as he went across the cloister to the Abbess's room, as if he had never been away.

The Abbess, too, greeted him warmly. She asked him what he had been doing since the summer, and listened to his accounts of his family in Acquin and of his homecoming to New Winnowlands. He, in turn, asked after the Hawkenlye community, and she assured him that everything went well.

He said, after a small silence, 'Is Esyllt still here?'

The Abbess smiled. 'She is. I wondered when you would ask.'

'May I see her?'

'Of course. You know where to find her.'

As he approached the door of the retirement house, he heard Esyllt singing.

Ah, he thought. Then she is better.

He let himself in, quickly closing the door after him; there was a vicious easterly wind. He could see Sister Emanuel at the far end of the large room, bending over a patient who was inhaling the steam from some hot potion in a broad, shallow bowl. Esyllt was folding clean sheets.

She looked up and saw him.

A slow smile spread over her face as, putting down her laundry, she came to greet him.

'I promised I'd come,' he said softly.

'You did,' she agreed. 'I knew you would, one day.'

Taking his hand, she led him right round the room, introducing him to her old people, stopping for a chat with those of her patients who were alert enough to want to talk to a stranger, passing by those who didn't with a brief nod. One sweet-faced old nun, whose bright blue eyes gave the impression of missing absolutely nothing, took hold of Esyllt's hand, squeezed it and said to Josse, as her loving glance bathed Esyllt, 'She's our delight, this lassie. She has a touch as gentle as a mother's. Is it any wonder we love her?'

Esyllt, with a becoming blush, bent and dropped a kiss on the yellowing, deeply wrinkled flesh of the old woman's cheek and muttered something that sounded like, 'Pish!'

When Josse and Esyllt had completed the circuit, they went to stand just inside the door.

'You decided to stay, then,' he said.

' Yes.'

'A good decision, Esyllt,' he murmured.

'For now,' she replied swiftly.

'Only for now?'

She raised her face, and he looked into her bright eyes. For an instant, he felt he knew exactly what she was thinking: she was young, she had won and lost one love, but there was a world of lovers out there. Was it the only future for her, to stay shut away with her old dears, no matter how much she might care about them?

Aye, he thought sadly, aye.

But neither she nor he spoke of what must have been in both their minds. Instead, after a pause, she merely echoed his and her own words: 'Only for now.'

He went back to sit with the Abbess, who had promised him a jug of mulled wine. As he knocked on the door and entered her room, he caught the aroma of spices.

'That smells delicious,' he said, sitting down.

'It *is* delicious,' the Abbess replied. She filled a pewter goblet, handed it to him, then, raising her own, said, 'Welcome back.'

'Thank you.' He sipped at the wine. Wonderful! Then: 'Young Esyllt will not, I fear, remain an old people's nurse for ever.'

'No, indeed,' the Abbess agreed calmly. 'She will marry, raise a large family, and then, God willing, remember her skills and return to the work she does so well.'

'You think so?'

She smiled. 'I pray so. Such a woman as she will always be needed.'

'Hm.' He paused, drank again, then said, 'And Sister Caliste? What about her?'

'Ah, Sister Caliste! Yes. For all that she is one of the youngest nuns ever to embark on her first

final vows here with us, it was right, I think, to
have admitted her as one of the fully professed.
She is so happy, Sir Josse!'

'I am glad,' he said simply. One thought led to
another, and he asked, 'Did anything further
happen, following that business in the summer?
Seth Miller was released, I presume?'

'Indeed.' She frowned briefly. 'No great cause
for celebration, but I do hear tell that his near-
miss with the hangman has had the effect of
making him mend his ways.' She sighed. 'One
can only pray that the improvement will be permanent, but I have my doubts.'

'Have faith, Abbess,' he said, in mock admon-
ishment.

Her eyebrows shot up. 'I do, Sir Josse. But I also
have experience.'

'Ah, yes.' He inclined his head. Then, returning
to his original question, said, 'No further arrests
were made, I take it, in connection with the two
deaths?'

'Three deaths,' she corrected him.

'Aye, three.' He had temporarily forgotten
about Tobias, and about poor Petronilla in her
new widowhood.

'No, no more arrests. Sheriff Pelham was content to conclude that the Forest People murdered Hamm Robinson, and Esyllt told him that Tobias killed Ewen Asher. Since the former are probably hundreds of miles away by now and the latter is even further from the Sheriff's reach, there is, I suppose, little else he can do.'

'Just as well,' Josse murmured. A sudden image entered his mind, of a handsome young man, falcon on his wrist, riding out of the forest on a sunny summer's morning. Tobias, he reflected, had given not the slightest sign that he was anything other than he claimed to be, a carefree fellow enjoying a morning's hawking.

Whereas, but a few hours before, he had made love to his woman and stuck a dagger into the poor wretch who happened to disturb him.

A thought struck him. 'Of course!' he muttered.

'Sir Josse?'

'I was just thinking about Tobias, that morning I met him after we had discovered Ewen Asher's body.'

'Indeed?'

'Aye. I'd always wondered what he was doing there, and I concluded that he was putting up a smoke screen. That, by being right there, so close to the murder scene, he was trying to persuade us that he'd had absolutely nothing to do with it.'

'Quite a good idea,' commented the Abbess. 'Considering that it worked.'

'Aye.' He ignored her mild irony. 'But, Abbess, that wasn't the reason!'

'No?'

'No! Remember how Esyllt was dressed? Or, rather, not dressed? Mother-naked, from the waist down.'

'I remember.'

He read in her slightly cool tone a faint reproof: must we speak of such things?

But he had his reasons. 'Abbess, did you not wonder what had become of Esyllt's under-garments? He—'

'Tobias went back to fetch them!' she finished for him, her voice excited, all coolness vanished. 'Yes. Of course. How very incriminating, to find a woman's clothing so close to poor Ewen's body! And, once the connections had been made – the clothes belonged to Esyllt, and Tobias was her lover – then the trail would have led straight to him.'

'Aye, aye,' Josse said thoughtfully. Glancing at the Abbess, he said tentatively, 'I can't help thinking, Abbess, that maybe it's for the best that events turned out as they did.'

She returned his gaze for a long moment. Then she said, 'Neither can I.'

'Hm. But I sometimes ache to tell someone what we saw, out there in the glade. Purely, I suppose, because I know I can't.'

'Do you, indeed?' She looked amused. 'I don't.' She paused. 'But then,' she went on softly, 'I've already told someone.'

'You have?' Oh, dear God, he thought, has she really? Must the space between my shoulder blades itch for ever more in anticipation of a well-thrown flint-headed spear finding its mark?

'Don't look so worried, Sir Josse,' she said, smiling. 'I told a friend, an ever-present and steadfast friend, who loves me as he loves us all, and will not betray my confidence.'

'Ah. Oh, I see.' Yes. Of course. She had told the Lord, and He, no doubt, already knew.

She was watching him. 'You should try it,' she suggested.

He met her eyes. 'Perhaps I will.'

*

He did not stay late at Hawkenlye. Darkness would fall early, and he was eager to be by his own fireside.

The Abbess came out to see him on his way.

Putting a detaining hand on Horace's rein, she said, 'I never thanked you, Josse, for what you did. In the summer.'

'I did little,' he replied. 'The solution to the killings was hardly my work.'

'Perhaps not,' she said. Unusually for her, she appeared slightly awkward. 'What I was thanking you for, actually, was saving my life.'

She did remember.

Trying to ignore the warm glow of happiness that was rapidly spreading through him, he said, 'You wouldn't have died, Helewise. Not one as strong as you.'

She shrugged. 'Who can say?'

Then she let go of the rein and turned to go.

He called after her, 'You know where I am, should you need me.'

But her only answer was a wave of her hand.

ALYS CLARE

FORTUNE LIKE THE MOON

When a young nun from Hawkenlye Abbey is discovered in a nearby vale with her throat cut, the people of Tonbridge are quick to jump to conclusions. This brutal murder must be the work of some felon released by King Richard Plantagenet in an attempt to impress his new subjects with his charity. Richard sends his emissary, Josse d'Acquin, to investigate the gruesome death, with the unspoken order to absolve the king from blame.

Josse, a brave and loyal ex-soldier, discovers an intelligent ally in Abbess Helewise of Hawkenlye: level-headed and pragmatic, she rarely misses a trick. Combining their talents, Josse and the Abbess peel back the orderly facade of life in rural Kent, to discover the menace lurking beneath.

Fortune Like The Moon introduces a formidable new pair of detectives, and an enthralling mystery series which vividly recreates the violence and beauty of mediaeval times.

HODDER AND STOUGHTON PAPERBACKS